Allegiance *and* Betrayal

For Sofia,

Fellow line scratcher and

fine editor.

I hope you find something

here to like.

All best wishes,

Peter

3 June 2013

Allegiance *and* Betrayal

stories

PETER MAKUCK

Peter Makuck

SYRACUSE UNIVERSITY PRESS

Syracuse, New York 13244-5290

First Edition 2013
13 14 15 16 17 18 6 5 4 3 2 1

This is a work of fiction. Names, characters, places, dialogues, and incidents either are the product of the author's imagination or are used fictitiously. Any resemblance to actual persons living or dead, business establishments, events, or locales is entirely coincidental.

∞ The paper used in this publication meets the minimum requirements of the American National Standard for Information Sciences—Permanence of Paper for Printed Library Materials, ANSI Z39.48-1992.

For a listing of books published and distributed by Syracuse University Press, visit our website at SyracuseUniversityPress.syr.edu.

ISBN: 978-0-8156-1015-1

Library of Congress Cataloging-in-Publication Data

Makuck, Peter, 1940–
[Short stories. Selections]
Allegiance and betrayal : stories / Peter Makuck. — First edition.
pages cm
ISBN 978-0-8156-1015-1 (paper : alk. paper)
I. Title.
PS3563.A396A79 2013
813'.54—dc23 2013001076

Manufactured in the United States of America

With love and deep gratitude to Phyllis,
my first reader and much more

PETER MAKUCK grew up in New England and graduated from St. Francis College in Maine, where he studied French and English. After teaching French for several years, he returned to graduate school for a doctorate in American literature at Kent State University and was later a Fulbright lecturer in France at l'Université de Savoie. His *Long Lens: New & Selected Poems* was released in 2010 and was nominated for a Pulitzer Prize. He has published two collections of short stories, *Breaking and Entering* (1981) and *Costly Habits* (2002); the latter was nominated for the PEN/Faulkner Award and listed by *The Dictionary of Literary Biography* in the "Top Ten Story Collections of 2002." Founder and editor of *Tar River Poetry* from 1978 to 2006, he is distinguished professor emeritus at East Carolina University. His poems and stories, essays, and reviews have appeared in the *Georgia Review*, the *Hudson Review*, *Poetry*, the *Sewanee Review*, the *Nation*, the *Gettysburg Review*, and other literary journals.

Contents

Acknowledgments

I WOULD LIKE TO THANK the editors of the journals in which some of these stories or earlier versions of them originally appeared:

Cimarron Review: "Ghost of Thanksgiving"

Dos Passos Review: "Diving the Wreck" and "Distance"

Hudson Review: "Family," "My '49 Ford," "Visitation," and "Booger's Gift"

Laurel Review: "Allegiances"

NEO: "Lights at Skipper's Cove"

Pennsylvania Review: "Against Losing"

Superstition Review: "Friends"

Virginia Quarterly Review: "A Perfect Time"

"My '49 Ford" was reprinted in *Writes of Passage*, edited by Paula Deitz (Chicago: Ivan R. Dee, 2008).

"Visitation" was reprinted as "Piecework" in *This Is Where We Live*, edited by Michael McFee (Chapel Hill: University of North Carolina Press, 2000).

With much gratitude to George Core and Paula Deitz, and in memory of Frederick Morgan and Leslie Norris for their years of fine editorial advice, encouragement, and friendship.

Allegiance *and* Betrayal

My '49 Ford

THOUGH MY MOTHER kept telling me I was lucky, that these years would be the best of my life, I didn't feel lucky at all, only glad to be driving. After three hours on the road, rain had sheeted down and left the pavement silver and black. Beads of water stood up nicely on new wax of the louvered hood, but my rocker panels and flared fender skirts would be filthy by the time we arrived. My father, clean-shaven, in a white shirt and tie, nodded sleepily in the backseat. My mother sat in front. She was crocheting as we sped past a wall of spruce on both sides of the road. Her long fingers and crooking wrists used a single strand of black yarn to enlarge a pattern that rested in her lap. Suddenly she let out a bark of a laugh that tapered to a soft chuckle. I knew why: the restaurant where we just had lunch.

"Now don't look at me that way," she said. "You'll have an accident. I can't help it if I get a kick out of people." She tilted her head back, closed her eyes, and laughed again, the last part slurping like water down a drain. My expression must have made her laugh again. "Oh, you're just a sourpuss like your father."

"Ma, I didn't say nothin'."

"You didn't say *anything*. You're not with that stupid Road Devil gang of yours."

"Come on, Ma."

"You didn't say *anything*."

"Fine." I took a deep breath. "I didn't say *anything*."

"Very good! Speech describes the mind. Keep talking like that, and they'll think you're a nitwit before you even sit in a class!"

She was in a good mood. I wasn't. I was nervous about the general and immediate future. Out of the corner of my eye, I watched her lean forward for her purse and begin to search it.

"Ma?"

"What?"

"Don't take it wrong, but—"

"Enough preface."

"I'd appreciate it, Ma, if you didn't smoke."

Her eyes got black as hornets; the mouth became a straight seam.

"Ma, everybody knows what those things do. Look at Uncle—"

"You look! You say you worry about my health—"

"I do."

"And I don't seem to listen, do I?"

"No, you don't."

"Now, do you ever listen to me? Do what I want you to do?"

"Ma . . . you always pull this."

"Answer me."

"I try."

She laughed in contempt, the laugh becoming a long string of phlegmy coughs.

"See, see," I said. "We both know what causes that cough."

"Oh, do we?"

In the backseat, my father cleared his throat, a signal that we were getting on his nerves. God, why had I started this? But I hated smoke; I always had. At home, to some extent, I could at least escape by going into another room, yet even there the stink always found me.

"Oh, you're an expert on causes. What caused those ten stitches in your head last Christmas? What caused the cops to bring you home at four o'clock in the morning that night last summer?"

"Ma, that's a smoke screen."

"Ha! I've raised a punster."

"Ma, we're not talking about the same thing, and you know it."

"Hey, knock it off," my father said. "All you two ever do is go around in circles. Lay off!" His voice was loud.

She glowered, turned, and shot a black look at my father, but nothing more was said. We rode in silence. She lit up—she had to now. I knew that. And I knew the little perfumed pine tree dangling under the dash was no match for the volume of smoke she would produce. I cracked the vent window.

Smoke—it infuriated me. Once, I had made Peggy walk home from our parking place by the ocean because she thought she had me under her thumb and lit up when I told her not to, at least not in the car. What she was giving me wasn't worth the eye-burning smoke, and the lousy taste when we made out. And to top it off, she put her feet up on the dash, on the twenty coats of lacquer and custom pin-striping. She thought I was joking, but the look on her face changed when I began to drive away. It was dark and started to rain, and I should have gone back for her, but I couldn't. Maybe it had something to do with "Cathy's Clown," a maudlin tune often on the radio then, because a few days earlier I had let her borrow my car, and she left me stranded in town while she parked in front of the A&W with a few of her girlfriends. She was seen. I was seen. She needed straightening out. I wasn't going to be anybody's clown.

Next time I saw her I was in wood shop, and classes were passing down the aisle between the open metals and woodworking areas. Dray said, "Here comes Peggy," but she paused only long enough to kill me with a look, and say with deep conviction, very deliberately, "You lousy shit!" A great chorus of "oohs" and "aahs" went off with laughs and hoots from the guys.

All over a cigarette. And here I was in my own car, my mother puffing up a storm. Most often she smoked only when she read. She loved reading more than almost anything. When I wanted something, I always waited until she was reading. Interrupted, she would lift her gaze, the eyes clear and a bit dreamy, and her answer was most often yes. But when she was angry, her eyes seemed to blacken. Like the sky before a storm, like the sky we watched an hour ago at the knotty-pine restaurant with its elk-antlered walls.

While my mother was being chatty and outgoing with the waitress and with the couple in an adjacent booth, I stared out the window at the inky sky and the shiny black asphalt, at my car—aquamarine, lowered, dechromed, frenched lights, electric doors, customized floating bar grill, '49 Plymouth bumpers, pleated and rolled leatherette interior. Last week, Donna had her hand on my thigh. Bouncing rain seemed to cover the ground with smoke; it tattooed the roof of my Ford as we talked of my leaving town, talked and kissed, kissed and stroked, our heads descending and coming up again in the faint light. It got hot; the windows steamed. Our clothes came off. Time, as in a film, took a leap. Sweating, I rolled down the window and felt the cool night air on my bare skin, confident that I had pulled out in plenty of time. But the last quarter turn of the window crank seemed to trigger a bright light that blasted me in the face. I lurched in the seat, bumping my head on the roof. Somehow, even in this scary moment, I realized that the perforated, white, leatherette headliner was probably stained from the stuff I used on my hair. Donna cried out and clutched loose clothing to her so that I had to yank my trousers away. There was a silver badge; it hovered in the dark above the light, a patch of skin and a pair of eyes.

"Okay, Romeo," said the gravelly voice. "Get dressed and get out your driver's license." Mercifully, the light went out. I wiped the glass with the back of my hand and saw a black-and-white squad car blocking the tree-tunneled alley I had backed into. Donna giggled, but I didn't find it very funny. We were almost dressed when the cop came back. He held my license under the beam of a long silver flashlight with a red plastic collar. Above the light beam floated a thick face with a bulldog mouth and bushy eyebrows that ran together above a flat knuckle of a nose. His name, I knew, was Hearn. I had seen him around, once or twice at the YMCA, grunting in the handball pit or hitting the heavy bag. And once I had seen him on Main Street with Cowboy Sheen.

The Cowboy was a drunk in his fifties, a local character, harmless, who got into arguments with parking meters. I saw Hearn punch him in the face one April afternoon, drag him bloody to the squad car, and heave him onto the floor of the backseat. Hearn was tight with another cop who lived only two houses away from us.

"I know your father," Hearn said.

I said nothing.

"Hey, Romeo, you hear me?"

I said yes.

"Owns the Flying A station over on Tenth, doesn't he?"

"Yes, he does."

"What would he say to this?"

I didn't answer.

Hearn shined his light in my eyes. "Anh?"

"He wouldn't like it," I said.

"You damn straight he wouldn't like it." He shined the light on Donna's breasts. "What's your name, ah, young lady?" The light beam slowly descended to her crotch, lingered, then swung away.

"Donna Rodina." She folded her arms against the light.

"Rodino, anh?"

"R-o-d—"

"Don't worry, I can spell it. You want me to write it on the blottah, want to spell it for me down at the station?"

"No, I don't. I only—"

"I don't care what you *only.*" He stood up for a moment so that only his belly hung in the window, yellow undershirt showing where a button had popped. "I know your fathah pretty well," he said, leaning down again and resting a ham fist on the window. I caught an odor of beer on his breath. "Your father, Angelo, and me went through hell together. You didn't know that, did you?"

Donna said she didn't. I thought of the war, of foxhole buddies.

"We was suspended between floors down in New Haven. In a elevatah. Twenty of us. One of the guys goes bananas, like he's got costophobia. But not really. He was a priest, planted there to test our mettle, see if we deserved to be Knights of Columbus. Your fathah's got mettle, young lady, you know that?"

Donna nodded.

That was a hot one, but I was glad she played along. Metal—that's what he had all right, a metal appendage to his right hand, a constant, patriotic can of Budweiser red-white-and-blue. The proof of his metal was a huge underslung belly like Hearn's. And those fuzzy Friday night K of C eyes. Yeah, a man of metal.

"What do you think Angelo, your fathah, would say about this business?"

Donna said nothing.

"I know what he'd say. He'd wring fuckin' Romeo's neck."

My face felt like the color of stock pulled from a forge in the metal shop. Hearn. I imagined applying a piece of red-hot stock to his belly button. Hearn played the light over my pleated and rolled interior, the high pile carpets, the white headliner. "Nineteen forty-nine Ford. Hah! What color is this, green?"

"Aquamarine."

"Ooooh, aqua-marine," he said in a mocking tone. "You think you're something with this nigger-mobile, don't you?"

I gritted my teeth. With the big Corvette engine, Isky cam, and Edelbrock manifold with twin four barrels hidden under the hood, I knew I could blow that squad car out my tailpipes. I'd have loved to get him out on Cemetery Road and run him into the wall at the turn. Suddenly I thought about my Road Devils jacket and hoped it wasn't on the backseat. Hearn spoke again. "Some cops," he said, "would take you home in your birthday suit for Mama and Papa to see. But I don't work like that. First time, I like to give a guy an even break. But I might just have a talk with ya parents." He waited for a reaction, then jerked his head forward into the window space to give us a final glare and blast of beer breath. "Get ta hell outtah heah, and don't evah let me catch you in one of these Lovers' Lanes again. You hear me?"

I said yes but would be damned if I'd say, *Gee whiz, thanks, Officer*, or something like that. Donna and I watched him waddle back to the squad car. I was grinding my teeth. Donna deepened her voice: "Hey, Romeo, am I an asshole or what?" Then we began laughing.

As I thought about it now, back in the car with my parents, the episode was less funny than ever. Donna told me she would write to me when her "friend" arrived at the end of the month. The sex part of it would turn my mother's mouth into a down-hooked didactic scar. And my father would be more furious if Hearn showed up at the station, swaggered into the office, hitched up his holster, and leaned against the cigarette machine, squad car idling outside, antenna still twitching. My father had little use for the police and what they did, the way they loved to loom in your path. What they did, my father once said in disgust, was take: free this, free that. And during the war when tires were rationed, our neighbor, a cop, sold them out of his cellar. And where did they come from? My mother protested: "He'll have no respect for the law if you go on like this."

My father shook his head no. "*They* have no respect for the law. Anyway, they're just people," he said, softening things. "Some good, some bad. Just like the nuns and priests."

I watched my mother's face stiffen, then redden, her jaw drop. "You leave the church out of this!" But if at home, and she were to continue, my father would always retreat to his basement workshop. That was his sanctuary. She never followed. The workshop with its fragrance of freshly cut wood ended most arguments, my father conceding the last word to my mother. His tools hung neatly from brass hooks. My mother's tools were of a different order.

Again, as we rolled past a lake with a distant skyline dark-pointed with spruce and fir, my mother closed her eyes and laughed, breaking a long silence. I knew she was still thinking about the knotty-pine restaurant. "Boy oh boy! Those people were real doozies." She snickered quietly. "Weren't they, Fred?"

I saw my father straighten in the rearview, adjust the starched white collar tight around his neck. My father's name was Leo, but years ago, as a joke, my mother began calling him Fred, and it stuck—with almost everyone but my maiden aunts. My father looked uncomfortable, not from the joking, but from the clothes he was wearing. I rarely saw him dressed up, except for mass, but most often he went to church early, alone, in work clothes, for Sunday also saw him at the gas station.

"Timmy, your father has no sense of humor." Turning in her seat to see his unsmiling face, she laughed again, seeming to find something more deeply humorous. I could scarcely believe what humor my mother found in such minor incidents, but humor, of course, is very subjective, my father and I often laughing ourselves silly at TV comedians that had Mom shake her head and leave the room to read a book. In this case, I knew my mother would be on the phone as soon as she and Dad returned home. She was probably already rehearsing for her friends the story about the man and woman with the dog in the knotty-pine restaurant. "Is that a poodle?" my mother had asked.

"No, a snoodle."

"A what?"

"A snoodle. It's a cross between a poodle and a schnauzer."

I saw her bite the corner of her lip to keep from laughing. Then she said: "Dogs are wonderful companions."

"Ain't dat da troof."

"They're nicer than a lot of people I know."

The man and his wife beamed in agreement.

"They're grateful, and they won't argue with you."

"You can say that again." The woman wore a red turtleneck sweater like the one on the dog; she was warming to a favorite subject and said they had another dog, a Lakeland terrier, that was registered, had fine bloodlines, and was very expensive. I knew my mother was delighted because she thought anyone who spent a lot of money for a nervous, unfriendly thoroughbred was a damn fool. The woman held the dog in her lap, and there was something oddly similar about their faces: the moist, sad eyes, a pom-pom of gray hair. The woman leaned forward and in a high voice not her own began to ventriloquize: "You just say, My name is Mimi. You say, I'm four years old. You say, I'm just the sweetest little snoodle in the world. Say—" The dog didn't, of course, say anything, but it began barking and jumped on the table, upsetting a bowl of New

England clam chowder, dumping it into the man's lap, making the couple argue, the husband saying they should have left the damned dog in the car.

"Fred?"

"What?"

"Didn't you like that little snoodle?"

"Loved it. We ought to get two or three just like it."

She began gasping with laughter. My father wasn't sentimental about animals. In fact, every time my dog, Sergeant, puked in the house or left hairs on one of the good chairs, Dad swatted him with a newspaper. Then he'd declare that my mother and I were crazy. Each time, Mom and I would share hushed, conspiratorial laughter because we knew my father's annoyance was no joke.

"You know, Fred, I think you don't like it because that man said 'troof' for 'truth' and 'dat' for 'that.' They probably say 'stoonz' for 'students' too, you know, like your relatives from New Britain."

"Lay off my relatives, will ya!"

My mother, getting the rise she was after, covered her mouth with her hand and gasped with laughter that turned to violent coughing.

At a smooth, plenty-in-reserve 60 mph, I took the Ford over a high bridge of greenish ironwork with a lot of X-ed girders. At the far side was a sign: WELCOME TO MAINE: VACATIONLAND. But this was no vacation. I had never been this far from home, and a sense of distance and unfriendly space began to haunt me. The color of the bridge was like the copper-green stain on the porcelain of our bathroom sink. And the same color on the license attached to Sergeant's collar. The dog was old; it might die while I was gone. I downshifted at the traffic circle, noticing a state trooper parked on the median, and kept up the rpm's so that the dual glasspacks wouldn't back off and get me stopped.

"Don't take the turnpike," my father said, and I smoothly swung to the right, dropping it into third long before the engine peaked to keep my father happy. And quiet.

"Maine," said Mom. She sighed, her eyes misted. "'Beginnings are always delightful,' the poet says."

My father made a chuff sound through his nose. "Years ago," he said, "when I left the farm, my mother and father, brothers and sisters, to go to work in Rhode Island, the beginning wasn't delightful. It was the Depression, and I didn't know what the hell I was in for."

My mother went on as if nobody had spoken. "Yes, delightful," she said. I felt her eyes on me. "Timmy, this is a beginning for you." She sniffed. "And for us."

Suddenly my mood felt fragile. "Come on, Ma. Knock it off. You said you wouldn't start."

"Timmy, there is nothing wrong with having emotions."

"Ma."

"Okay, okay, but it's going to be awfully hard for me. Your father goes to work. He'll have things to do but—"

"Ma—"

"All right, that's it, no more." She blew her nose. "The poet says, 'Le vent se lève, il faut tenter de vivre.'" She blew again. "Right, Fred?"

"Of course."

My mother asked me if I knew what those words meant. I said I didn't, and she explained the line. "You better be ready to hear some French up here," she said. "Most of the students speak it." Her eyes were gleaming again.

"Yeah, I know."

She said she'd control herself from now on, but I knew better. She always gave in to the relief of sentimentality. I considered my parents and sensed their absence would be a great relief. I was supposed to miss Donna, but didn't. Not yet at least. With her, in the car, I was charmed by her every movement. But if I loved her, why did I feel so good when she got out of the car at midnight? Why so excited, her scent still on my fingers when I pulled from her house, a good tune on the radio? Alone, how good it was to stop on a back road, look up at the stars, the air fresh, pressure easing on my bladder, silence amplifying the hiss and sizzle of the asphalt. Moments like this wore a great halo. Moments of true feeling. But then, in the parking lot behind the A&W, with the guys, a beer in hand, could it really be me, the same person, who told the anecdote about Hearn surprising Donna and me? And wasn't there a slimy sense of betrayal?

I looked at my father's serious face in the rearview. My father rarely told stories, and if he did, they were very short. One thing I knew was that I would definitely miss the Ford. At State U a car would have been permitted. But my parents decided, me being me, not to send me to State, where I would be with guys I'd gotten in trouble with, where I would be too close to home and Donna—everything just an extension of high school, especially with the car on which I lavished so much time and attention. "We are not," they said, "going to flush our money down the toilet." So the aquamarine Ford that I had customized in auto-mechanics class and at my father's station, the Ford I had powered with a Corvette engine, would be returning home. I didn't want to think about it. I was becoming, the farther I drove, detached from my normal self.

"Tim, honey, what's the matter?"

"Nothing." *Timmy, honey, dear, sweetheart*—those words set me off for some reason.

"Nothing? You're scowling; your forehead's all wrinkled."

I looked at her, then back at the road.

"You haven't said a word in ten minutes."

"Ma, change the record, huh?"

"Listen, Mister Mouth, you're not talking to Reagan or Dray. Or,"—she changed her tone—"Donna, for that matter."

"What are you dragging Donna into this for?"

"Don't tell me you're not thinking about her?"

"What if I am?" God, I hated having somebody, especially my mother, tell me what I was thinking about, hated having to surrender my car, wished I could have traveled up here by myself, arrived on a Greyhound, emerging in the strange little town with a suitcase in one hand, jacket slung over my shoulder. Like the movies. But this wasn't the movies, and once I agreed to the plan, I had to play by their rules because they were paying the bills. For now at least.

"Donna's not"—she stared at the pattern of yarn in her lap—"she's just not the right girl for you, and I hope I don't ever have to say I told you so."

I began to object.

"That girl's mother, Timmy, went to school with me and—"

"And what?" I couldn't believe I was having this conversation; I had a panicky feeling of being trapped in an endless car trip with my parents, doomed forever to be told of mistakes I had made, mistakes I would make, pride preventing me from admitting certain things about Donna and her mother.

"That girl just wants to get married."

I asked if there was something wrong with that.

"Not at the right time, not after you've got a decent education. Let that girl get her hooks into you, and you'll be working at the shipyard like everyone else. Day after boring day. Your father worked there, but he had the courage to quit. He can tell you what it's like over there. Can't you, Fred?"

"Your mother's right."

"Money isn't everything."

"Ma, I've heard this record before."

There was a moment of silence. I thought she might let it pass. Then: "That's the second time you've used that cliché."

"What?"

"About changing the record."

"I'm sorry."

"You ought to be. It shows lack of imagination." She looked at the slow back-sweeping salt marsh already touched with seasonal brown. "You do what you want. I won't mention it again."

I looked at my father in the rearview. His eyes were gray and soft and had crow's-feet at the corners. Very infrequently he smoked a pipe in his workshop, and somehow I didn't mind the smoke, which was richer, and the pipe gave him a meditative look. Sometimes, as now, I felt the full weight of his silence, was troubled by it, admired it, and sometimes tried, when with my friends, to affect it. My father seemed to be enjoying the shore route that was punctuated with small towns, antique barns, clam and lobster stands. On a bridge, my mother noticed another bridge off to the left and the faster flow of turnpike cars. She was annoyed and said scenery was just the kind of thing my father would want when they had no time for it. She shook her head and sighed heavily, filling the car with tense miles of silence.

The curving shore road gave me something to do, allowed me to downshift and feel the car, enjoy it one last time. But soon the rocky coast I had never seen, the wave crash, and high-flung spray took my attention as well. I wished Donna could see it. The ocean and coast were much more dramatic than the coast at home, protected as it was by that long, low smudge on the horizon: Long Island, visible on clear days. The road was winding past natural coves and harbors where lobster boats with squarish cuddies and twin booms swayed on their reflections next to dockside fish shacks the color of driftwood. There were hanging nets and stacks of traps, and the late-summer air screamed with gulls. The twisting road pushed a different seascape before us at every turn; it would be a village and salt-stunted trees, and suddenly an endless spread of whitecaps. Along one stretch of beach, the houses seemed lonely, widely spaced, and set apart by their white picket fences; they were like the shells of quahogs randomly arranged by children on a treeless hillside. Out on the tidal flats was a high-sided truck where a family of kelpers was forking up seaweed to a figure standing on top.

"Harvesting the sea," said my mother.

"They must sell it," my father said.

"Looks like a painting," my mother said.

"Reminds me of haying as a kid," my father said. "Break your back."

After another mile or two was an arrow and a sign that said: ST. ANTHONY'S COLLEGE. My mother was satisfied. "It's as pretty as the pictures in the catalog, don't you think so, Timmy?"

I said yes, though I had barely looked at the catalog. My father and I lugged my footlocker up to the third floor of Padua Hall and met the prefect, a young Franciscan robed in brown with a white-knotted cord for a belt. His name was Father André, and he spoke English with an accent. He introduced me to my two roommates, Bernard and Jacques. Bernard pointed to the ceiling, an empty socket. All three of them spoke French until Father André turned to me with a big smile and asked if I understood. I said no; I had studied Spanish. He laughed and teasingly said Spanish wouldn't help much around here. I vaguely knew about the ethnic character of the college but was now overwhelmed with a sense of the foreign.

I walked with my parents out to a point that curved into the river and made a small harbor. I looked back at the green water tower about a quarter of a mile from the entrance to campus. There was a gazebo and a boathouse at the point, and to the east, at the mouth of the river, the dark fluting of the Atlantic visible beyond a long stone jetty.

Back in the parking lot, I noticed two students appraising my Ford. "Hey, I bet dat car she really go." It was the same accent Father André had when he spoke English.

My mother said, "Your father's right. We shouldn't argue. God forbid we should have an accident on the way home."

I told her not to talk like that.

"I can't help it. These thoughts just come."

I took a deep breath. The sky, still flocked with clouds, seemed suddenly sullen again. There was little left to say, yet no one seemed ready to say good-bye. My father finally said, "Well, we better be getting back. Long ride. I gotta work tomorrow."

I looked at my mother. For the first time I noticed faint lines of crow's-feet, a thread or two of gray in her hair. Behind her glasses, the eyes swam into focus, then went distant. She gathered me in a strong hug and kissed me. When she spoke, her mouth, from a breath mint, was an alarming green. "Timmy, be a"—tears slid down her rouged cheeks—"a good boy. Stay out of trouble. Your father and I love you very much."

I said I'd be good, but, what with my track record, I wondered how they could believe me, let alone tell me they loved me. It surprised me that my voice came out strangely, sounded wrong, as it had when first changing. My breath came hard. I tried to smile, but my face wouldn't obey. My nose felt sneezy and began to run. "Just do your best," said my father, extending a big shovel of a hand. I could not look him in the face. My heart knocked in my ears as it did when I knew a fistfight was close. I tried hard to concentrate on what my father said. "Your best is all we ask. Nothing else matters."

The electric doors popped, and my father got behind the wheel. Nervous phrases flew back and forth. My mother's green mouth opened and closed. Tears ran. The big Corvette engine vroomed. I watched the aquamarine Ford rumble out of the lot; it was eclipsed by the white administration building on the knoll and reappeared on the long, straight high road into town, flashing before a wall of huge green firs. As I watched that bright piece of color growing small, all that horsepower elsewhere, I felt myself shrinking, weak. I watched until it was totally gone and after a time discovered myself looking at the sky and a flotilla of clouds moving seaward on a high, blue journey. Like them, I felt blown along, felt myself caught in a wild gust of unknown feeling.

Allegiances

"HEY, MAN, DON'T BE A CHICKIE," said J. C.

We were standing at the edge of the woods, looking back across the soccer field toward the dorm. J. C. puffed on a cigar and blew two perfect hoops of smoke, the wheels of some crazy bicycle that wobbled slowly toward the woods. Magic, like the mesmerizing card tricks he did in the dorm. Mocking me with hen clucks, he disappeared among the tree trunks on a path that ran away from campus and emerged on rocky bluffs above the crash and high-flung spray of the Atlantic. One look toward the dorm director's window and I ducked into shadows.

After he arrived at St. Anthony's—during a blizzard in the middle of our second year—guys began calling him J. C. because of the blasphemous Christ jokes he put into circulation. A few years older than us, he was a dash of color against the everlasting snows of Maine and the leaden atmosphere of St. Anthony's College, a small school run by French Canadian Franciscans. We were among the first dozen nonspeakers of French to be admitted a few years after the prep school had converted itself into a liberal arts college. But liberal it wasn't—daily mass attendance, lights out at midnight, room inspection, no drinking (immediate expulsion), no cursing, no smoking in rooms, no cars allowed. Demerits restricted you to campus or expelled you for good, and they could be had for as little as a word of disagreement with Father Odorik, our dorm director. J. C. constantly grumbled, often within earshot of Odorik, whom the guys called Père le Nez because of his potato nose. Père le Nez's English was just poor enough to keep from him the gist of what we said. He was sensitive enough, however, to know that we made fun of his halting speech, the hum, and the interrogative *eh* that was a stand-in for *n'est-ce pas?* And he was vengeful enough to make us pay for not being like the tractable French Canadians.

On this spring day, the entire dorm was restricted to campus, but here I was sneaking off, following J. C. along the path toward the water, the air scented with brine and newly thawed earth. Mimicking Odorik, he said, "Père le Nez cannot, hmmmm, prove a ting, eh?"

He was referring to the incinerator, really just a cage of cyclone fencing behind the friary kitchen, next to Siena Hall, where the staff burned trash and billows of nasty smoke rode the onshore winds right into our open windows. At a special student government meeting, Odorik in attendance, we protested, complained the smoke was unhealthy. The incinerator, Odorik said in an angry voice, was none of our business. End of meeting. J. C. was furious. That night six of us ripped the thing out of its cement moorings, wrestled it to the bluffs, and toppled it into the ocean. Next morning when we arose for early mass, a notice was already affixed to our bulletin board:

> THOSE RESPONSIBLE FOR THE REMOVAL OF THE INCINERATOR WILL, AND MUST, REPORT TO ME IMMEDIATELY. EVERY STUDENT IN SIENA HALL IS RESTRICTED TO CAMPUS UNTIL FURTHER NOTICE
>
> —MARCEL ODORIK, OFM

J. C. asked me if I knew what OFM stood for. Order of Fat Monks, he said. Then, looking both ways to make sure nobody observed, he scrawled under Odorik's signature, "Eat a rubber, Fatso!"

J. C. was cunning but not absolutely reckless. He flirted with trouble, not out of fearlessness, he said, but to create a situation, a game that would keep him awake, force him to sharpen his wits. You either burn or rot, he said. His reasoning, though, didn't ease the fear that squashed my lungs. I saw my father at our kitchen table with a math book, doing problems so he could pass the civil service exam and find an easier job in the post office. He was getting too old to be crawling around under cars, burning himself on hot engines, breathing exhaust. He had put a lot of hard-earned money into me, yet here I was following J. C. along the bluffs, Odorik longing to send the new insubordinates back to southern New England where they belonged. The incinerator was a direct challenge to his authority and meant immediate and permanent expulsion.

The path became a gully of white sand that climbed steeply and topped out in dune grass. We scrambled up. Beyond the dune was a crescent of beach with a line of tide wrack that buzzed with flies. "Man," said J. C., "great day for a safari." Like the terrible Christ jokes, he put words like *safari* into circulation too—it was code for a beer run, and in no time everyone used it.

"This is living dangerously," I said.

"Don't be a candy ass, Budney. We're breaking arbitrary, pointless rules."

I said I hoped he would explain that to my parents when we got kicked out.

"We won't get kicked out. I prawmise you," he said with that great Boston accent of his.

I asked how he could possibly say that. Even if nobody confessed to Père le Nez, he could still expel us for any old thing, insubordination, say, one of his favorite cognate words.

J. C. simply touched a forefinger to his temple, gave it a twirl, and said, "Trust me."

The infractions I was guilty of now were laughable compared to what I had been found guilty of in high school—breaking and entering, breach of peace, back-road drag racing . . . St. Anthony's College was the only college to give me a chance. I felt guilty and lucky by turns. I now had good grades, something to lose, and Odorik scared the hell out of me.

In order to keep from being seen by a strolling friar who might report to Père le Nez, we kept to the beach, close to the steep embankment of riprap, until we were opposite the store, then scrambled to the road over huge rocks that had been hopelessly dumped to prevent the ocean from gaining on the shore.

The store—also a house—sat on an empty stretch of beach road with a few surrounding pines. The dark shingled roof was painted with birdlime, and two perched seagulls seemed wooden and nailed to its peak. On the porch roof, flanked by red Coke emblems was the sign: JUSQU'À MINUIT. But most of the collegians knew that *minuit* meant nothing, and a knock on the back bedroom window at any hour of the night would put a light on in the kitchen, and a six-pack in your hand. *Merci beaucoup.*

At the side of the store, under one of the pines, was a junk Ford where a huge retarded boy usually sat in pajamas, drooling and shouting unrelated words to himself and to customers. He lurched from the car and, in bare feet, limped over the sharp gravel toward J. C and me. "Dubby, dubby, dubby," he mumbled, then blurted, "Fuck!"

I laughed, but J. C. fixed me with an unforgettable look.

"Hey, I know it's awful the guys taught him that stuff, but still it's funny."

"Is it?" he said.

The boy gibbered in great excitement. His mouth broke open, a redness, a row of pointed brown teeth. He had beautiful gold hair, a freckly face that was flat, almost caved, and turquoise eyes deep set in dark sockets. The eye color made me think of my car, a souped-up '49 Ford with many coats of turquoise lacquer—the thing I was most passionate about after Donna, the girl who dumped me at Christmas. He tugged J. C.'s sleeve. "Okay, Phil, okay. You want to see the lighter?" And then J. C. struck the lighter, gave him a bright new penny, and put his arm around the huge body. Phil calmed down, but made small bird cries, and still pulled J. C. by the sleeve toward the store.

I followed them to the door, upset that I didn't have it in me to touch him the way J. C. did, the way he bent close to him talking, arm around the broad shoulders. I could barely stand the sight of Phil. In our moral theology class, when Father Dubriel discussed abortion and euthanasia, I thought of Phil. You weren't supposed to feel that way, but I did. Other guys called him Mutta Tutta and conducted mock interviews. They would stand around the car shell and extend a pretend mike into the smelly interior: "Tutta, what is your view of the governor's chances of reelection?" There would be excited yelping. "What about the church's position on premarital sex?" More questions produced more noises and lip farts from Phil, more beer-boosted laughter from the guys. Phil would bounce on the seat and scream fuck fuck fuck over and over until the wits stopped laughing, or tired of the game, or until Madame Gauthier opened the door and yelled, "C'est assez, alors!"

Most of the time, Phil stayed in the car, but he liked J. C., the lighter and penny ritual, and would always come into the store to carry what was brought to the counter. This time Madame Gauthier waved her milk-white arms. "No, he jus' been in." She reopened the door, set off the little bell again, and steered Phil outside. "Mot dit, vas jouer dans le char," she said, pointing to the junk car. "Vas-y!" But he simply stood on the steps and bellowed. "Oh, Barnac!" she sighed, then said to J. C., "Good thing we got no neighbors." With a thick forefinger, she pushed her glasses back to the bridge of a nose peppered with blackheads. The bellowing continued. J. C. said, "Is it okay if I let him come in and carry? That will quiet him down."

"Sure, sure," she said. "Sometimes he makes me a headache, that kid."

Phil lumbered in, walked to the freezer with J. C., and carried a six-pack to the counter. Calm now, he allowed himself to be led to the door. As Phil went out, the bell again tinkled, oddly the same pitch as the one that announced the Eucharist at mass. I watched Phil make his way to the car shell.

Madame Gauthier had her hair parted in the middle with rhinestone barrettes on each bang. She wore black sneakers, bright lipstick. Just as she began to punch the register, the phone rang. Bells. They made me nervous—underage and buying beer, trouble with the police, trouble with Père le Nez.

A fly preened on the white metal of the meat display case. Down the aisle that led to the blue flicker in the living room, I could see her husband, Maurice, with his white-casted foot on a hassock, tweed cap on his head.

"Way, way," she said into the phone, "'y a des clients icitte . . . laisse-mway te caller back plus tard. Okay. Bye." After cradling the phone, she said, "I tell you it don' stop. I just get the five kids out the house, and Maurice he come home with a broke foot." She rolled her eyes again. "Sometimes I want to pull out my hairs."

J. C. laughed.

"I don't ask for nothing, me. We make out. Those priest, though. They call up and say don't sell no beer to nobody from the college, eh? Ain't that something? I say, 'I don't tell you how to say the mass.' Me and Maurice, we could tell you some stories. We go to mass still, but I know some of those priest ain't no saint. One woman down the beach—her husband got paralyze at work, but she keep on havin' kids. That priest that visit all the time—he done more than bless the house, eh?" She punched the register. J. C. put in a pack of cigarettes. "Bon, quarante," she whispered, "et ça fait . . . un quatre-vingt-wit. One eight-eight all together. You want a sack to put that into?"

J. C. said, "No, but is it okay if we go out the back door?"

She winked. "Sure, help yourselfs."

At the back door was a tidal marsh and a meandering canal. I stopped for a minute to watch the Gauthier kids, five little ragamuffins throwing rocks into the canal. I couldn't see what they were trying to sink, but it seemed the target was the cruel sun itself that broke apart and reassembled on the water top. The look of liquid flames put me in mind of the incinerator. I yelled ahead to J. C. to ask where we were going. He pointed west of the marsh to a light-green water tower that was a silhouette at this time of day. Catching up, I said, "Forget it." He smiled wickedly. Relighting his cigar, he blew a smoke ring and watched it dissolve. "Breaking two rules is no real fun. We've got to go whole hog, man. Besides, I've got something to show you."

"What?"

"Oh ye of little faith," he said, handing me a beer. "Enjoy yourself. Life is short."

And enjoy himself, no matter what, is something J. C. always managed to do. My mouth was dry, so the beer tasted awfully good, especially the first few gulps. But I was all nerves. The incinerator caper had also begun with a ritual beer.

We walked past the carcass of an old boat in the tall grass, a bleached-out crab, the carapace with its look of empty menace. The afternoon was touched with its first amber, and low tide scented the air. At the foot of the tower, J. C. threaded his belt through the plastic handle of the six-pack holder, buckled up again, and the four remaining cans rode on his hip. "You want to go first?"

I let my eye climb the ladder until the rungs blurred. Moving clouds made the green bulb seem to sway. It was too high to see, but I had been told the last twenty-five feet leaned slightly backward and away from the tower, which forced you to hang-climb. "Go first?" I said. "I don't want to go at all."

"C'mon, shadows are right—no one will see us from the college."

"What the hell is up there?"

"Introibo ad altare Dei," he chanted, taking two or three rungs, then looked down at me, laughing.

I knew the server's response, but was still observant enough to be spooked by blasphemy, half believing that a silver dagger could reach my heart from one of those fleecy white clouds. I watched his figure shorten, then concentrated on my own climbing. Step by step, I lifted myself above the crowns of oak and spruce. A heartbeat banged in my ears. The cables in my legs tightened as a long stretch of brilliant green salt marsh spread below me. I stopped to rest. I imagined the ladder shearing away from the tower leg, plummeting with me still clinging to it. Muscles rigid, I let the moment register, tell me about how my life was accumulating in freakish moments like this, going backward beyond the incinerator to my decision—if it actually was one—to come to this college. Did I really fill out an application and write letters? I couldn't remember. But that was beside the point. I should have insisted J. C. do his talking back at the dorm, without beer. I should climb back down right now; instead, I studied my hand, curled around the rung, then told it to reach up. Alarming tremors shook my arms, but they came, I finally realized, from vibration transmitted down the ladder—J. C.'s vigorous, carefree climbing. Far above, his body vanished, then a small face reappeared over the rim of the catwalk, shouting phrases of obscene encouragement.

At last I reached him sitting on the sun side of the catwalk. "You horse's oss," he said, his face painted orange by the low sun, the eyes narrowed. He cracked two cans and handed one to me. We clinked, then slurped. A breeze came in soft scented gusts and pleasured the skin. After the arctic Maine winter, such weather seemed an impossible gift. He said, "This reminds me of a poem we read in Halliday's class."

"Which one?" I thought he was joking.

"'I, at this time, / saw blessings spread around me like the sea.' That one."

Was he mocking my newfound love of poems? I didn't know, but the scene suggested the lines—that was certain. You could see the beach stretching southward all the way to Fortune's Rocks, and the small lobstering village beyond. The ocean, in patches, was a blue close to the turquoise of my fast Ford. All the way down the coast there were undulating stripes of white surf. The sky was dramatic with cloud shapes, lavish with pink and purple light. Blessings indeed. I told him all this made our problem with Odorik seem trivial.

"That's because it *is* trivial," J. C. said. "*He's* trivial."

We stood and walked to the shady side of the tank for a different view, the catwalk vibrating under foot.

"From another point of view," I argued, "not trivial, not when my father's been working two jobs to put me here."

"You can't live your life for your parents," he said.

I could have said that his parents had money and could afford the loss; mine couldn't. Instead, looking at the cluster of college buildings in the distance, I said, "Père le Nez might have us in his binoculars right now."

"I hope so," he said, and cranked up an Italian salute.

We turned farther around the tank. I could see the "JUSQU'À MINUIT" on the strand, the jetty—all gold in this light—running parallel to the sandy road. The Gauthier kids still played on the bank, around the beached rowboat, pirates perhaps. J. C. took a sip of his beer, smiled, and waved his arms in an inclusive sweep. "All that you see shalt be thine, if thou but kneel and worship me."

"Cut the shit," I said. "What were you going to show me? Nothing, I bet."

"Nothing!" He squatted. "Take a look at this."

I looked at a jumble of graffiti that, over the years, climbers of the tower had scored upon the side of the tank all around the catwalk. "At what?"

"This." He pointed. The name was carved into layers of paint: Marcel Odorik.

"Son of a bitch."

"Sure. Years ago, as a student, he was up here too."

"Now," I said, "he forbids us from doing the same."

Imitating Odorik, he said, "Lex, mmmmm, est quid notamus, eh?"

I asked for a translation.

"Laws, rules—they're what we say they are."

I told him he was very clever and wondered if he was planning to be a lawyer.

"Man, my big sweat is not getting kicked out. I've been bounced from too many schools. It's gotten to the point my father will be disappointed if I don't fuck up again." He threw his can; it took a long time to reach the ground, the clank of its impact delayed. We watched mine follow the same arc, then we sat down and dangled our feet off the catwalk. J. C.'s gaze got angry. He asked me if I believed in God. Surprised, I said that was a pretty hefty question. "How about you? Do you believe in God?"

"More in Christ than in the church," he said.

I asked why.

"Them," he said, pointing with his chin toward the strand. "The Gauthiers. Six kids—they're victims of the church. And Phil, poor Phil. Then the priests telling them not to sell beer, or they'll make trouble." He laughed bitterly. "As if they didn't already have trouble." He drank again, the sun making the can flash as he tilted it back. "I'll tell you one thing," he said, wiping his mouth. "That boy doesn't have to be like that."

I asked what he meant, my own thoughts still somehow stuck on abortion and euthanasia.

"That boy can be taught things."

"You're kidding," I said. "How do you know?"

"How do I know? I've got a brother like that. He's toilet trained, knows how to dress himself, tie his shoes, how to talk. But that takes the kind of time and money the Gauthiers don't have."

I was stunned, but suddenly I knew why he didn't shrink from Phil's touch, why he acted so naturally with him, but what was his point? The damned church was the point, he explained. A child like Phil, or like his brother, for want of reason, could not participate in the so-called life of the church, the sacraments, confession, and communion. For a few moments he was quiet, then he said sarcastically that the church, though, would probably change as attitudes changed. "I have this uncle who's a priest," he said. "He doesn't exactly say it, but someday divorce'll probably be a sacrament."

I laughed.

"Why not? The church is just a messed-up government. Corrupt politicians, corrupt priests—no difference." He smiled, but there was no mirth.

I said, "I can't believe I climbed up here to have this conversation. I thought you had a way to keep us from getting bounced?"

He relit the cigar, took a few deep puffs, and blew rings through perfect rings. "Okay," he said, "here it is. Père le Nez thinks he knows who did it, right? Very unlikely you would be on his list."

"Wait—"

"Let me finish. Even if you are, it doesn't matter."

I was uneasy, ashamed to be favored by Father André and Father Odorik because I was learning French, using it falteringly with them and a few of the Canadians, and had just won a summer scholarship to study in France.

J. C. winged his can off the tower. We watched it arch, then disappear in the rising ground shadows; no sound came up. "There's a way," he continued, "of telling Odorik that somebody else did it and making him believe it, a way that will leave him no alternative but to drop the whole matter, with no reprisals."

"Well, well. And you want me to do it?"

"My reputation sort of excludes me, wouldn't you say?"

Nothing more needed to be said. Now I understood the long prelude about the church. J. C. could have pushed me into most anything, but deception was deadly, and this might have an eternal echo. We watched the light turn and work the cloud crests: violet, orange, then red. The channel looped through the salt marsh, looking like the gold curl of a bishop's crosier. I felt like a novice of some sort, understood how the Incas could have been sun worshipers because the sun and the air full of color made me feel less mortal, but the ground was already a rising tide of darkness.

The dorm was quiet. Father André's rosary beads clicked down the hall. He was nosing around to make sure the campus restriction was being observed. Most of the campused guys were probably downstairs in the game room, shooting pool, J. C. taking side bets and playing perfect position. Father André knocked at my door. His friendliness was gone. I tried to change that by saying, "Bonsoir, mon père. Qu'est-ce qu'il y a de nouveau?"

Coldly, he replied in English, "Show yourself at my room at nine, ten, and eleven o'clock. I'll come by at midnight to make sure you're in bed."

I stood at my window. The moon made silver scales on the water. It was a warm night, but my hands were cold. And I felt even colder when Father André, distant as the moon, opened the door at midnight and shined his flashlight in my face. He gave the air a good sniff, and I realized I had gotten into bed without taking a shower or brushing my teeth. The lighthouse at the shoals painted my wall white and black, white and black. I tried not to think. Thinking: J. C.'s probably right. A messed-up government. Poor Phil. My parents ashamed. Hard to know what you really think. The outer dark just a quaint idea. Just words. As I lay there sleepless, I could see my father at our kitchen table, this Christmas past. It was late, and he was studying for the civil service exam, brushing up on math. My mother was reading in the living room. On the mantel was a grade school photo of me as an altar boy in cassock and surplice, wet-combed hair, a peach face shadowed by a lighted candle piously held. "Go help your father with that math," she whispered.

"I think I've got it," he said. "Tim, see if I'm right?" He was leaning over the book, algebra, a cup of steaming black coffee beside it. His eyes were red, tired. "I let *X* equal the speed of the current, right? Then . . ."

I barely slept. A bell buoy clanged in the distance beyond my open window. All night long, the lighthouse painted my wall white and black, black and white.

Early for eight o'clock mass, I stood outside the chapel door. A faint scent of cigar smoke laced the air, but perhaps I imagined it, for only a few devout seminarians knelt inside. Over the door of the confessional hung a nameplate: Father Odorik. My arms were sore, the cables in my legs as tight as if I was climbing the tower again. I saw the photo of myself that sat on my mother's mantel. I saw my father hunched at the table. I saw J. C. with his arm around Phil. One of the stained-glass angels above the altar seemed to stare at me with a moronic grin. My heart thumped in my ears. I would name myself and a few of the rebellious Canadians: St. Tours, Michaud, Duchemin.

Pulling back the curtain, I kneel. Father Odorik looks up from his missal, and our eyes lock. The light goes out. A silhouette makes the sign of the cross. My skin feels the hot breath of the incinerator. I have blown out forever the candle I once carried. I see nothing on the face of darkness into which I am falling. Face on fire, I cross myself and I begin to whisper, "Bless me, Father, for I have sinned . . ."

Against Losing

"KNOW WHY YOU LOST?"

I said, "Yeah, you're a better shooter."

Uncle Jarek, leaning his brass-jointed cue stick against the bar, laughed and hit me with one of his patented expressions: "Don't lose you!" He tightened the turquoise bola at his throat, then reached for the VO and milk he claimed was easier on his ulcer. I said, "Try me again."

He looked at the inside of his wrist, the black watch face with gold roman numerals. "I've got to close up." He winked. "Can't keep a lady waiting."

We were in the basement of the Falcon Club, a white clapboard barn of a building with an upstairs hall for the occasional Grange dance or wedding reception. Uncle Jarek held the liquor license for this cellar tavern with its beery odors, low ceiling, and shadowy booths. Years ago, after his heart attack, he moved in with us, and my mother took care of him, saw that the doctor's instructions were followed to the letter. I was still in grammar school. Uncle Jarek continued to live with us after his recovery but finally left when drinking and gambling came back into the picture. Dad didn't get angry and didn't give him the boot; he simply said more than once that he couldn't understand why an otherwise intelligent adult would want to drink and throw away hard-earned money on pool and poker, especially after Nature had delivered a final warning.

Twice my father had gotten him jobs with benefits and security, and twice Uncle Jarek had blown it.

Something about the Falcon Club attracted me, maybe its radical difference, or just a fascination with my black-sheep uncle. I had always enjoyed the twenty-five-mile drive into farm country where my father and uncle were born and raised. Every visit to the club was something new. When I was eight or nine, in some other tavern, Uncle stood me on a soda crate so that I could reach the table rails and taught me how to hold and stroke a cue stick. In high school, I shot a pretty good game and felt important in front of club members, many of them farmers in jeans, coveralls, baseball caps. Uncle also taught me fundamentals of the hustle that put a few bucks in my pocket at the college dorm, and a few carefully selected pool halls. "Fred's boy," Uncle Jarek would say to Vlasik, Bizewski, Woodchuck, or anyone who knew my father from the old days. "Smart kid—he's going to college, studies philosophy." This praise was genuine, but the word *philosophy* in the Falcon Club was a kiss of death and probably made me redden. It also made me feel guilty about emerging tastes in clothes and food my mother had noticed and teased me about. But club members didn't notice, or let on that they did. They would buy me beers—even though I wasn't legal—and ask how my father was doing.

"You lost," said Uncle Jarek, "because you don't plan. You make shots hard as Chinese arithmetic, but the idea is not to have to make bank shots or combinations. Simple is best. You gotta see the whole picture and think ahead. You don't—that's the problem. It's all about seein', not just lookin'." He walked to the table, took two balls from the return tray—the red 5 and the blue 2—placed them kissing at midtable, and aimed toward the left-hand pocket, though clearly off center. "Think you can make the deuce?"

"Sure," I said, cutting it at a wicked angle to compensate. To my surprise, the 2 went farther from the pocket than I could have imagined.

Uncle Jarek laughed. "Whatta they teach you in college?"

"Good question."

"Physics," he said, resetting the same off-center combination that had cost me the game. "The trick is to hit the first ball like you wanted the shot to go in the opposite direction. You put reverse english on the ball. Watch."

I watched. Uncle talked. I listened and took in everything: the constant white Stetson, wire glasses ("cheaters," he called them), a purple vein in the wing of his nose, the pencil mustache, pearl buttons, black boots, and a blue cue-chalk smudge on his khaki pants. Long fluorescent tubes above the table hummed. Uncle Jarek unbuttoned his checkered sports jacket and leaned forward, his long, rough fingers making a beautiful bridge, thumb-and-forefinger circle, supporting fingers fanned like the wing of a bird, the cue making three smooth strokes before contact, english paradoxically pulling the 2 slightly to the left. I watched the ball roll smoothly, knock into the pocket's leather back, and rumble down the subway tunnel to the tray. "See?"

I jokingly thumped my cue. "Cham-peeeen!"

Uncle Jarek flashed a smile that had a bit of gold in it.

"Don't lose *you*," I said.

"Hah, don't lose *you*." He unscrewed the cue and put the halves into a leather case under the bar. "No time for another game, but draw yourself a beer. I've gotta clean up."

"Thanks." I went behind the bar, stood on springy duckboards at the tap while Uncle collected empty glasses from the booths. I filled a dimey glass, chugged it, and drew another.

On the wall to the side of the urinal where somebody had put a fist through the drywall last August, Uncle Jarek had covered the hole with a cardboard picture of "Custer's Last Stand," tavern decor advertising Anheuser-Busch under all the captured busyness of final combat. I wondered what connection Custer had with beer. Maybe the sight of all those Plains Indians made him and his men wish it was all a beery daydream. As pressure on my bladder eased, I studied the picture the way our art history prof had taught us. Internal frames, invisible triangles. Where was Custer? He had to be controlling the whole. There he was, at the center of all the buckskin and blue uniformed conflict, golden locks, saber held high above the scattered cloudlets of exploding gunpowder. Then I noticed something that made me snort with laughter, almost piss on the cement floor. "Oh Christ," I said, laughing harder because "Oh Christ" was exactly what somebody had written in a cartoon bubble that rose from the mouth of a soldier, eyes popping with astonishment. Then I noticed another bubble: "Where did all these fuckin indians come from?" I wondered what Professor Poulin would have to say about the painting. That thought had the smirky mouth and the amused eyes of a stranger watching me from the mirror as I dried my hands.

"How's that girl you brought with you last time?"

I must have gone blank.

"The one with long black hair?"

"Oh, Carol."

"That's the one. Nice girl."

Not as nice as you think, I almost said. After we had left the club, my date, an art history major, wrinkled her nose and laughed at the club's customers. "Breughel, les gens vulgaires," she had said, but the sting didn't keep me from driving down the usual rutted dirt road by the salt marsh to park, an odor of low tide especially strong. That same night, still damp with perspiration, buttoning her blouse, she told me she liked the way I didn't pronounce my *R*s—it was really cute.

"It's not working out," I said.

"No?"

"Nah, she's kind of snooty. She's one of these Mommy-this, Daddy-that kind of girls. Father's a big shot with IBM." I could never tell him, or anybody, that she had written to me only once this past semester. She was also seeing somebody else and vague about her Christmas holiday plans. Before coming out to the club, I thought I saw her near the college hangout and was surprised when my breath got short. I was thinking about quitting college.

"Play the field," said Uncle Jarek. "Get your education before you get serious with a girl." He took a swallow of his milky VO. "Better off not getting married at all. Your freedom goes out the bedroom window. And it's in people's nature to get sick of each other after a time." He paused. "Your mother and father are exceptions."

The outside door banged, and Uncle said, "Hell, I should have locked it and shut off the light."

A tall, thin, red-faced man named Jan Klemma took a seat at the other end of the bar. A smell—something mealy and fecal—made its way to my nose on a draft of incoming air. Klemma said something in Polish. Uncle Jarek said he was about to close up and was going to serve him only one drink. Klemma nodded. Uncle Jarek drew a beer and poured a double shot of vodka. When Uncle took his seat again, I asked quietly, "Doesn't he speak English?"

"A little. Don't you know about him?"

I said, "I know he drives an old hearse and sleeps in it. Didn't he shoot his wife, or his wife shoot him?"

"His wife caught the bullet. The papers said they were drunk, fighting over a gun, and it went off. She comes in here too. Hah, don't lose *them*."

"They still together?"

Uncle nodded. "Sure, they deserve each other."

Klemma raised his double and waited for Uncle and me to lift glasses.

We all said, "Nazdrowie."

I asked what it meant.

"'Down the hatch.'"

"No, I mean, literally."

Uncle laughed. "*Literally?* Hey, Timmy, the only English I know is on billiard balls. Don't lose you." He looked down the bar at Klemma, then said, "Jan always smells like the cows or pigs he's been treating, so I tell him if he hasn't taken a bath to sit at the other end of the bar."

"Come on!"

Uncle Jarek, without malice, was refreshingly direct; even my father gave him that. "Sure. My good customers don't like it."

I laughed again and asked if Klemma was really a vet.

"Not legally, but he's cheap, and they say he's got the touch when it comes to doctoring animals."

"Why hasn't he learned English?"

"Who knows? Probably lazy."

"Maybe there are too many people he can speak Polish to."

Uncle Jarek shook his head. "My mother—your grandmother—was born in the Old Country too, but she could talk English as good as you."

This was true.

Klemma held up his glass and said something.

Uncle waved him off, pointed to the door, then turned a key in the air to indicate closing. He also included a few Polish words.

Klemma, when he reached the door, turned and said something that sounded like "Potsalameyev moy dupa." Then the door boomed against its frame.

"*Dupa* means 'rump,' doesn't it?"

Uncle laughed. "In this case, his."

I said, "I know what that one meant."

We laughed. Uncle picked up the two glasses, dunked them in the soap sink, twisted them on the brush prongs, ran them through the rinse, and put them upside down on a white towel.

"So how's the big words these days?"

"Pretty good," I said.

"Tell me one."

"Let me think. Okay, here's one. *Sesquipedalian.*" The word wobbled into the air like an iridescent soap bubble and hung there until Uncle's good laugh popped it.

"What does it mean?"

I laughed. "Means 'long.' Just a big word for a big word."

"Remember when you won twenty-five dollars for first place in that spelling contest?"

I nodded and stared at a tiny chain of bubbles in my beer.

"Your mom and dad were proud as peacocks."

"Problem is that Dad sees everything in terms of winning and losing."

"I might be dead now, if it wasn't for them."

"Don't worry, they got a kick out of it."

"Don't talk like that."

"It's true. My father always needs somebody to forgive. You give him plenty of practice. Me too, I guess."

Uncle raised a mock backhand, then walked to the kitchen, limped a bit, and had to use the counter once. I thought about the times he had taken me to Lincoln Downs up in Rhode Island, how cool it was to stand by the rail when the horses came thundering down the stretch, the jocks as brightly colored as billiard balls, the flat slap of the crop as they went for the wire and the photo flash went off. I still had the binoculars Uncle Jarek brought back from the war and loved to move magnified things in and out of their bright, sharp circles. Uncle said fillies weren't only on the track—they were in the stands too, like that winner over there in the green dress. He winked, then laughed. But my father didn't think Uncle Jarek was any laughing matter. Mom always said it was the war—he came back not caring too much about anything. He was always, said Dad, a skirt chaser. Not so, said Mom; Aunt Virginia did the leaving.

"You want me to make you a kielbasa sandwich before I shut down here?" Uncle Jarek's head and shoulders were in the kitchen window behind the bar.

"No, thanks."

"You sure? It's no problem. Take a Slim Jim then, or an egg from the jar."

I puffed my cheeks: bloated. Uncle moved away from the window frame. I heard him close the big refrigerator and snap the hasp of the lock. After I was home from college for a day or two, Mom suggested it might be nice if I took a ride out to see my uncle. This was a first. Usually the thought of my drinking and driving precluded any such suggestion. In fact, here I was breaking my promise to her about not drinking.

"So, ah, tell me about school before you go."

"What about it?"

"You like it up there?"

"Not especially." I put down my glass. "I think I'm going to quit."

"Why, afraid you learning too much?"

I shrugged. "Too many phonies. Philosophy teacher goes like this: 'I'm not sure that in this paradoxical construct, you haven't erected an erroneous paradigm.'" I exaggerated the accent.

"That supposed to be a reason to quit?"

I hadn't thought too much about quitting, but now the possibility was interesting. I couldn't admit I was afraid of the math requirement. In high school I'd flunked algebra the first time through, and was lucky to get a C the second time. "The truth is I'm not doing so hot. Bored, I guess. The college is in the woods, not easy to get anywhere."

"Let me tell you something. You've got to work hard to get good at something. Work. Study hard, get good, and it will pay off. Too bad I never did that."

"I don't know."

"Your mother and father'll be hurt. My brother's not working two jobs for his health, ya know?"

"That's why I should quit."

"What are you talking about?"

"I'm goofing off, wasting their money."

"Then don't goof off. Work toward being the best at something. Or is this whole thing, ah, really about what's-her-name?" Uncle changed his voice to a crying girl's. "Carol, oh Carol, I miss you so much."

I waved him off.

"You in love, Timmy? You lonely up there in them cold woods?"

"Yeah, sure."

In his own voice again, he asked, "You quit, what are you going to do?"

I hadn't thought about it. "I don't know. Get a job. Paint some houses like you. Gamble. You've done okay."

The fine lines around Uncle's eyes hardened. "Don't talk stupid. Money games"—he snorted and shook his head—"man, they make you pay in more ways than one. Remember last Christmas I had the shiner and cuts on my face?"

I said I did.

"Well, I didn't trip on no curb like I told your father. Some punks saw me winning at a high-stakes game up in Hartford and waited for me behind a car in the parking lot." Listening, I remembered a sunny day, a big family picnic at the state park, rounded fruit trees foaming with blossoms, wooden tables with platters of salad and cold cuts, hot dogs and hamburgers spitting on a fire. A couple of guys, uninvited, wandered in and helped themselves to beer from the keg and, cussing, began to pitch horseshoes as well. Uncle Jarek approached them. I couldn't make out what was yelled back and forth, but Uncle, in a sleeveless undershirt, ducked a punch and, bing-bang, the guy who threw it was down, cupping his bloody mouth, gesturing he had had enough, his buddy helping him stagger away. "Or you have a place like this, they come in through the back window—"

I said, "When did this happen?"

"Couple weeks ago. They took whiskey, change from the jukebox, some other stuff."

"You call the cops?"

"No."

"Why?"

Uncle wouldn't answer; he shook his head. "I'm just telling you—stay in school, hear me?"

The phone rang, and he went into the little alcove at the end of the bar. The conversation was one-sided, my uncle occasionally saying, "Yeah," "Okay," "I know."

"Lady friend?"

He winked, asked me a few more questions about college, but his mood had darkened. He seemed distracted as he moved from bar to kitchen. Just as well. What could I say about the little French Canadian enclave, about my kissy, frustrating dates with Paulette

St. Tours, a townie girl, about learning French from her and my roommates, about how I loved the sound of the language, and liked to recite from memory a Verlaine poem and the Lord's Prayer in French when alone? Or how could I say I wanted to see Carol again, snooty or not? I realized that when Uncle Jarek and I weren't shooting pool, our talk was pretty much limited to family matters.

"So hang in there with them books, hunh?"

I said I would and took my leather jacket down from the peg in the pay-phone nook.

"Where you going?"

I winked. "I guess I'll hurry home and hit the books."

Uncle lifted a backhand. "Don't lose *you*!"

With new truck shocks, the old Ford felt good and hugged the curves. A husky female voice pleaded from the radio speaker to come back again, even if only to say good-bye. The night was a clear blue stunner, the moon like a cue ball on a great empty table, ready for a new game. I loved driving back roads at night. The dark was always magical. A row of windbreak cedars writhed up into starlight in a way that made me think of Van Gogh and Father Jean's enthusiastic talk about art. Quit school? There had to be a way of smuggling my car up to Maine. I could lie, tell my parents the priests had changed the rule, and sophomore students could now have a car. I loved the rumble of that Corvette engine as it came through twin glasspacks; this wasn't your ordinary Ford. The engine swap had taken a lot of after-hours time at my father's gas station. A specially modified radiator, transmission adapter, and torchwork—a real shoehorn operation. What did Marc and Gaston, my roommates, know about working on cars? About shooting pool? But they knew plenty about French and philosophy.

Coming off the stringer ramp, I downshifted, booted it up to eighty, then let the speed fall back to fifty. Entertaining myself, I laughed and lifted a beer can from between my legs. "Father Norman, I'd like you to meet Jan Klemma. He says he's not sure that a paradoxical and erroneous construct exists to the proposition that moonlight makes a scream as it falls, even if there is no one there to imagine it." I introduced various characters from the Falcon Club to professors at the college, allowing them to swap various kinds of knowledge. Father Gerard watched Uncle Jarek cut the coat hanger with wire cutters. "See, you bend it at right angles, like this. Two inches, then four. Now you just worm it up the coin return—you'll never have to give the telephone company another dime." Astonished, Father Gerard turned it in his hands. With crafty pride, Uncle Jarek said, "That's right—a gen-u-ine phone fucker!"

A single cloud, long and sharp, daggerlike, drifted toward the moon. I took my foot off the gas pedal. Suddenly I felt quite sober. Something was wrong, but I couldn't say what, something about Uncle Jarek, that odd phone call. Or was it my overactive imagination? The road was empty, and I took the hill of the bridge at the posted speed of 35 mph. At the crest was a black cutout figure of a man looking down at the silver moonpath on the river. I couldn't explain it to myself, but I saw Uncle dangerously alone. I saw him doing the polka with a lively redhead at my cousin's wedding last summer; now I saw him sitting alone, pale, with that milky drink. The man on the bridge made me think of Uncle's story about a guy in New Haven, a guy with heavy gambling debts that Mafia leg breakers were looking for.

On the other side of the bridge, I made a U-turn, peeled rubber, and flew past the dark figure at the crest. "I can't find my wallet," I'd say. Maybe my uncle had already left, and I wouldn't have to say anything. Come on, I thought, too many B movies, but it was an excuse to speed, and speed gave voltage to my awareness of the farmland flowing under the moonlight with fences and barns.

Uncle's Buick still had its nose to the front entrance. I idled past and coasted, engine off, down the alley in back of the building. I killed the lights, eased the door shut, and made my way to the evergreen bushes where, unseen, I could peer down through a small dusty window that framed a narrow section of the barroom: jukebox, pool table, four red-topped chrome stools at the end of the bar.

Uncle had just moved beyond my range of vision when there was a screech of tires at the bottom of the short street that dead-ended into the club parking lot. An engine gunned, and headlights raked the white clapboards. An old Chevy pickup with a rotted-out rear fender pulled in next to the Buick. Two guys got out. One wore a brown jacket with a sheepskin collar and a red hunting hat with earflaps. I thought he had a black cigar in his mouth until a quack came out. Then another and another.

"Jesus," said the other guy. "You got us kicked out of the fuckin' Wigwam—put that fuckin duck-call thing in your pocket!" He was tall and skinny and wore a cowboy hat with a feather band.

More quacks.

"Place is closed, Ray." The tall guy staggered up to the door. "Closed."

"Shit!"

"Jarek closes early weekdays when there's no business."

"Okay, let's go find Zippy," said the red hunting hat. "He gonna think he been ambushed."

"Awriiight!"

"I'll be all over him like stink on a hog."

There was a cough, gagging, a splattering sound.

"You awright?"

"Yeah, fuck Zippy!"

"Whattya want to do then?"

"Go to the firehouse, shoot some eight ball."

I had no trouble seeing them at the firehouse table, wrists frozen, choking the stick to death, slamming, balls bouncing, jumping the rails. My uncle said most guys never learn the fine points of anything, lovemaking included. After the heart attack, he told people he planned go out with his boots on. To annoy my father, he'd say, *By that I mean, I plan to die either makin' love or shootin' pool.* Mom would cover her mouth and laugh. Dad would look at the floor and shake his head. Later Mom would remind my father that it was all an act; Uncle wouldn't finalize his divorce from Virginia because he was still in love with her and hoped she'd take him back. Uncle's talk about women, she said, was simply pride doing a silly dance.

Finally the guy with the red hat got behind the wheel, gunned the engine, and sent cinders flying until the tires squealed on tar. The noise dwindled to a whisper. The outside light over the Falcon Club sign went out. There was really no need, but as long as I was here, I wanted to wait until Uncle was safely behind the wheel of his Buick. Minutes went by. He didn't come out. I went back to the window, kept seeing my face reflected in the pane until I got the right angle on the violet streetlamp behind me. Everything was dark except the pool table—a compelling green rectangle in the dark. Green like the bills I used to find on the dresser of Uncle Jarek's room when sent by my mother to wake him for breakfast. I'd gently knock. Opening the door, I'd catch a whiff of sour-mash breath. Uncle would sometimes be lying there almost fully dressed. On the floor the one boot he managed to remove before passing out. My eyes always skipped to the dresser where bills that had been hurriedly stuffed into pockets in the heat of winning now grew like brussels sprouts on the snowy bureau scarf. Uncle would awake with a groan, wink, and encourage me to take a bill. "Go ahead. Our secret, okay?"

Nothing moved in the dark fringing the table, and then I noticed Uncle sitting at the bar. Finally he turned to the table and racked the balls. Breaking for a game of Straight, he made two of the object balls touch the rail and return to the pack, cue ball rolling back to the head of the table near the corner pocket, on the rail: a tough leave, but planned. Alone, I would have moved it away from the rail for an easier shot. But even alone, Uncle didn't cheat; he circled the table, leaned over the pack, found something, then pointed with the cue stick to the corner pocket. The stick, held with three fingers, lightly as a violin bow, made rhythmic strokes, and the pack exploded, the 6 ball dead, a green streak to the corner pocket. Uncle smiled, making shot after shot, the cue ball rolling into perfect position. No Chinese arithmetic. But what was he doing? Waiting for his girlfriend? Just killing time? I had no idea, except that I was seeing something unforgettable. After the first rack, he removed his jacket and played in his white shirt, the silver-tipped bola strings tucked into his chest pocket, Stetson low and hiding his face. I realized I had never seen my uncle shoot like this. He always seemed to barely beat me. Never had I seen him run so many racks. Almost four now, nearly sixty balls, and it seemed he could go on forever. *You've got to work hard to get good at something.* Though the scene couldn't last, I knew that, for me, this curtain would never come down. Uncle called each shot to the spectator dark: deuce in the side, tray in the corner . . . and each ball, as if charmed, rolled slowly and dropped from sight. The field of the table grew greener, bright combinations and possibilities disappearing until a new rack exploded in all directions.

Visitation

WHERE DEREK LIVED NOW, the only real snow was remembered, so it wasn't until the patterns of farmland below the jet pod began to turn white that the purpose of his trip came back. At LaGuardia he had switched planes and was almost glad for the heavy weather that buffeted this small twin-engine DeHavilland. Thoughts of his mother disappeared as the plane bounced and made sickening turns. The cockpit curtain was open; he could see a red flashing light, hear the kind of beep a smoke alarm makes. The engines suddenly changed pitch. Outside the window, nothing but blackness. The sailor beside him hadn't spoken once since boarding, but now groaned, "Oh, Mama," then laughed. Beads of sweat had collected like tiny pearls along his dark hairline. Suddenly a torrent of personal history poured out of him: the Sixth Fleet, Beirut, Libya, long watches, alerts, shore leave, the lure of Italian quiff—the last not for him: disease. Besides, he was a Christian. He couldn't wait to see his wife and parents. His mother-in-law, though, was a Martian, but after almost a year, he'd be happy to see even her—well, for the first few minutes anyway. The nose of the plane finally dipped, and a runway lined with white lights appeared between the pilot and copilot's shoulders. As they taxied, the pilot cautioned continuing passengers not to deplane: "Our stay on the ground will be brief."

Through a tattered curtain of snow, and the morbid smell of jet fuel, Derek walked a few paces behind the sailor. In the terminal, Bill

Dumfy was waiting. "You look a wreck," he said. "Rough flight?" His handshake was clean and hard. Bill was good-looking, had clear blue eyes that were always on guard, and a jaw shaped like a trowel.

"Bags?"

"This is it," Derek said, holding up his carry-on. "I've got to be back in the office two days from now."

"Your father's got some plumbing problem at the house," he said, turning from the parking lot. "He asked me to pick you up."

Derek and Bill hung around together in high school and were in college together until Bill flunked out. After that, he worked for Derek's father at the auto parts store until he could find something better. If you were friends in high school, you were supposed to be friends forever—that was Derek's mother's idea, to a lesser extent his father's. People gravitated to her openness and easy humor and told her their problems and stories, like Herb, the furnace man who, when Derek was very small, bet his mother a shot and a beer that he could put three golf balls into his mouth at the same time. To head off the attempt, she quickly put a shot and beer on the oak table in the kitchen and told him to forget the bet, but he wedged them anyway into his mouth until his eyes goggled and cheeks became stubbly balloons. All, no doubt, to entertain a small boy kept home with a bad cold.

"Hey, how about my new wheels?"

"Very nice," Derek said, not able to sound enthusiastic.

"Look, why don't you call your old man, tell him you got in okay."

Derek said there was no point in stopping—he'd be home in twenty minutes.

"Hey, we don't have to stop." And he held up a cellular phone. "Neat, huh? Saves me lots of time and mileage."

"You must be knocking down the bucks."

"Not bad for a kid who didn't finish college."

What Dumfy did for a living was a mystery to Derek. He worked for a jeweler named Fenster who not only had three stores but was a silent partner in the cable TV company, owned two new condos, and was a heavy gambler. Though Dumfy would neither confirm nor deny, Fenster was into other things as well, things that required a black-belt tough like Dumfy for a driver. A teenage destroyer of bricks, boards, and faces, he had been lethal, way ahead of his time.

"You still working for Fenster?"

"I might be," he said with a cagey smile.

On the radio, too loud, was an oldie by the Byrds, "Turn, Turn, Turn."

"Bill, lower it, huh?"

The phone rang and rang. Derek began to worry, but his father finally answered. His voice was a husk. When Derek said he'd gotten in okay, his father said there was no sense talking now. They'd see each other in a few minutes.

Dumfy tucked the phone into his jacket pocket. "Killer, huh?"

"Not bad." Then, for something to say, he asked about their buddy Fagan.

"You'll see him later. You coming to Ziggy's tonight, right?"

Derek said he didn't know: this trip wasn't business as usual.

"Well, bring your father down. A few drinks. Take his mind off things. Your old man's a great piece of work. Remember the time . . ."

Time and memory—a heaven and a hell, Derek thought, but this was not something he could say to Dumfy, who played his cards close. The personal or reflective was best kept private. On the radio, the Byrds were singing about seasons.

From the crest of the new bridge he could see the amber lights of the hospital where his mother lay in a coma. He asked Dumfy to take him there.

"Your father told the nurse not to let anybody in."

"Why?"

"That friend of your mother's."

"What are you talking about?"

"The one who used to buy ground sirloin and feed stray dogs in front of the A&P—"

"Mrs. Penland?"

"Right. What a piece of work, huh?" He laughed, a great lover of new slang, amusing himself.

"Well, what about her?"

"She was taking Polaroid pictures. You know, of your mother, in that . . . state. Your father went ape, told the head nurse not to let anyone in."

Dumfy's taillights got small and disappeared at the curve. With no streetlights on their country lane, it was very dark and the basement windows of his father's house were warm squares of yellow. He crunched through the snow and peered in. They were laughing. Stan, as usual, needed a shave. Bulky and bearish, he held a beer in his big paw. A recent widower and one of Derek's father's old buddies, he wore only a T-shirt, tufts of Brillo-like hair escaping from the frayed collar. His father illustrated something with his hands, and they laughed again. Derek threw up the overhead door.

"Christ, it's cold," said Stan. "Get that door down."

They shook hands. The gust of cold air and Derek's presence made them solemn. He set his bag on the floor and blew on his frozen knuckles. His father asked how the flight was. Stan asked if the weather was any better out there in Arizona. They said a few things about the election and new president who, during the campaign, claimed he was a southerner. "He claimed three states as his home," said his father. "Like Satan, he's from everywhere."

They shook their heads. A reminder to mourn, Derek had shattered their good mood, but Stan finally said, "Politicians would say anything to get elected. Then they tell you to go hump a sandbag."

It was a relief to laugh. They avoided any talk about his mother, talking instead about college and pro basketball. Stan popped a propane torch, heated a joint, and his father muscled an overhead pipe with a Stillson until the joint gave and a braid of red water bled into a white plastic pail. Derek asked about the plumbing problem. Stan handed him the length of old pipe he had just hauled down, explaining there was mineral buildup. Derek held it to the light like a telescope and squinted; the inside diameter was reduced to the size of a pencil.

"Makes the water pump work twice as hard," said Stan.

"Pressure really builds up inside the system," said Dad. "Then something's got to give."

Derek thought about his mother's stroke. Every move Stan made was an effort. His breath came heavily. Derek wondered how he could stand it with just a T-shirt. Though the pipes wouldn't freeze, the basement was fairly cold. A drinking man, he reminded Derek of Herb, their old furnace fixer with golf balls in his mouth. "This PVC is great stuff, huh, Ace?" The old gang of softball players knew his dad as Ace; Stan was the only one left.

"Great stuff," said his father. "What an improvement over metal."

Stan carefully poured himself a hooker from the bottle of Seagram's on top of the furnace. "PVC," he said, looking at Derek over the rim of the jelly glass, "won't narrow down with mineral buildup." He winked, then knocked it back. "This stuff'll outlast the house."

Derek looked up at the ceiling where bright-white lengths of it ran ahead and disappeared in the dim light.

"We'll have plenty of water pressure now," his father said, almost apologetically, for the shower ran weakly, something his mother had long complained about.

"We're going to put in a new water pump too," said Stan.

"No sense taking any chances," his father said. "Might as well do it all. Won't take too much longer."

Derek thought, *Fine, but why now, especially given the circumstances?* He wanted to talk, but couldn't, not in front of Stan.

"How's Dumfy doing?"

Derek told them about his cellular phone.

Stan finished sawing a pipe and grunted himself up from a kneeling position. His face was red and shiny with sweat. When he finally caught his breath, he said, "Car phones! What'll they think of next, huh, Ace?"

Derek asked them if he could help.

"We're knocking off," said Dad.

Derek headed for the stairs.

"Oh, by the way," said Dad, "we don't have water. If you have to, you know, take a leak, go out back. Otherwise, drive down to Mr. Donut on the Post Road."

He couldn't believe it. Climbing the basement stairs, he heard Stan telling his father how easy life was now, what with indoor plumbing and conveniences they never had as kids.

Restless, Derek walked from room to room. His trips home were usually in the summertime, so he never realized how cold his parents kept the living room. Conservation. Oil's expensive, his father was fond of saying. Your father's a riot, his mother would say, and joke about his Depression mentality. His mother grew up in the city, and at first she resented living in the country, in "the sticks" as she put it. But she grew to love birds and could name every one that came to the three or four feeders she put up near the living room and kitchen windows. She was proud of her self-reliance, the way she managed while his father was off working two jobs. Foxes, pheasants, raccoons, deer, and even ducks from the pond across the street would make their way into yard for handouts. His mother described them and talked about them to her telephone friends. "What else have I got to do out here in the sticks?" she used to ask. Once upon a time, they also had a dog, two cats, two parakeets. His father was indifferent to animals. His refrain was: "You and your mother wouldn't be so sentimental about animals if you had to take care of them like I did as a kid, get out of a warm bed at four in the morning to milk the cows."

Then he remembered Molly, the black and white cat, wondered where she was, and opened the door to his mother's room, a private sanctum he was almost afraid to enter. The bureau mirror framed an empty wall. Suddenly it hit him that this would be the first night he had ever spent in the house with his mother not there. Looking at the empty mirror, he imagined what she saw years ago when he finally left home, for he had been her only career.

The hollow strokes of a hammer boomed from below.

TV greased the walls with its narcotic blue flicker and made it easier somehow for them to talk while watching the screen. His father said he hadn't been able to go to the hospital for the past two days.

"Do you want to go tonight?" Derek asked.

His father shook his head. He had been there for ten straight days, staying all day. He could do nothing but hold her hand, and that didn't help either of them. He couldn't take it—he needed to skip a few days. Besides, he wanted to be here to help Stan, who was saving him the arm and leg that a real plumber would take. Derek told him he'd pay for a real plumber, but his father laughed. "Big spender."

"Really, I mean it."

"If I pissed away money like you and your mother, you'd never have gone to U Conn."

"Lighten up," he said. "We can afford it now."

"What about when the hospital gets finished with us? Now don't get upset with me, but somebody's got to think about these things."

"I'm not upset with you," Derek said, catching his reflection in the window and appearing like a stranger. Then he told his father that a few days before her stroke, they had argued on the phone. "Mom got angry and hung up on me."

He shook his head. "She never said anything, so it must not have amounted to anything. Forget about it."

"I was trying to get her to exercise, cut down on the booze."

"But why?" he asked. "You know how she is."

"Why?" Derek said. "That shit is behind her stroke."

His father shook his head and looked away, then suddenly assumed his mother's role, fixing Derek with a disgusted look for *that kind of language.* Derek expected his father to side with him, but there was no such betrayal. Finally he said, "You don't know what it was like for your mother."

"I just wanted her to *live*," Derek said, probably implying that his father didn't and should have long ago taken measures to put a stop to what she was doing to herself.

"She really worked at it a couple of times, you know?"

He knew, and didn't want to know. Vodka was merely a symptom, one term of the complicated equation of which he was a part. After a while, he said, "I'm going to the hospital."

"There's no point," his father said.

Derek explained that he needed to say a few things. There was an outside chance she could still hear.

"Suit yourself," he said, eyes glazing, "but Dr. Farrington told me there's too much brain damage for her to hear anything."

The refrigerator was frighteningly empty. Shelves that were usually laden with nicely wrapped leftovers, cheeses, crackers, juices, fruits, and fresh vegetables were now almost bare. There was a jar with one pickle afloat, a few black bananas, cold cuts, and two six-packs of beer. Derek made sandwiches, and they sat at the kitchen table where he had eaten thousands of his mother's good meals, the grainy oak table where old Herb had long ago performed for a shot and a beer.

After they had eaten, his father told him that there were things that had to be done in the morning. "We've got to be ready," he said.

"Sure, I'll help you." Derek vaguely knew what he meant, but didn't want to think about it.

"I've already done a few things," he said. "Made some arrangements myself." *Myself* meant alone, utterly alone. Derek should have come sooner, but his father said no, there was nothing he could do. She might stay in this coma for months. "Tomorrow I want you to help me with something else."

"Sure."

They cleaned up and went back to the TV room. On the screen, Mickey Rooney, in a comical green top hat, was flying a helicopter to rescue a downed jet pilot played by William Holden, who was in a muddy ditch and being shot at by North Korean soldiers. The sound was down low as it usually was after his mother went to bed because the house was small. Radiators pinged and sighed to each other from different rooms. Derek hadn't been tired but suddenly found himself exhausted. He drained the last of his beer and went out the back door to take a leak before turning in. A nostalgic scent of wood smoke hung in the still air. The sound of snow underfoot worked a cruel magic, and he had the feeling he had never left home. Snowflakes were softly falling, touching his cheek and melting. Overhead a plane made its blind way toward the northeast. *Our stay on the ground will be brief.*

Stan's first poundings in the basement woke him. Then it was quiet. Stan and his father were talking. Derek's old room, small, with the faded fleurs-de-lis wallpaper, college pennant, the same crack in the ceiling plaster that suggested the outlines of Italy, the bedside table and doily—nothing had changed except for the presence of a big cobweb on the bedside lampshade.

A few more inches of snow had accumulated during the night, and the sun made everything dazzle. The radiators sighed in their sad, familiar way. The kitchen smelled of coffee, and for a little while, home seemed more than just a word. Warm cup in hand, he wandered from room to room, looking at objects he knew so well, wedding pictures, pictures of grandparents, his mother's collection of books. He stood by the front window. His mother, at this hour, would be enjoying the birds, except that the feeders were all empty, and there were few birds in sight. He put his coffee on the kitchen counter. On the back porch he found plastic bags of millet and sunflower seed and filled the feeders. Scarcely had he finished when juncos, chickadees, titmice, and a few jays arrived. Not to mention squirrels. The pines gave a moaning sound to the wind and made the cold seem colder. He was glad for the movement, something to do. He noticed cat tracks at the back door, but Molly, the big black-and-white, was nowhere to be seen. Then his father came upstairs.

"I don't know," he said. "I haven't seen her since the rescue squad took your mother."

"I see her dish on the back porch."

He looked puzzled, as if the cat were something from another life. He scratched his head. "Look, could you go to the hardware store for us?"

"Sure."

"We've run out of U brackets to hold up the pipe."

"Tell me about Mrs. Penland."

He bit his lip and shook his head. "Since Sam died, she's not all there. Never was, but she's worse now. Did Dumfy tell you? She was taking Polaroid pictures of your mother, right there in the hospital. Can you imagine!"

Pieces of family history that had somehow escaped Derek's attention now seemed very important. "How did you and Mom ever get to know the Penlands anyway?"

"Derek, we need those brackets, okay? I'll tell you later."

His father's Chevy, always garaged, was spotless, perfectly tuned, and had, as he put it, a lot of "pep." You had to have power, had to be ready for difficult situations. After his first teenage accident, and the few other accidents he'd had over the years, he'd always get the lecture about defensive driving and hear about his father's perfect record, but the lecture was never cruel and, in fact, became a joke, his mother bowing an invisible violin. Nonetheless, he was quite serious when he said you had to be alert, ready to react—it was a personal philosophy more than just a way to drive. Derek's mother was too preoccupied to drive, he said. Too much of a dreamer behind the wheel. Of one of Derek's old college friends, a guy who was stupendously absentminded, and about whose impracticality his mother loved to hear stories, his father would always shake his head in genuine dismay: "When's that guy going to snap out of it?"

Derek drove to the Tru Value by way of Immaculate Heart and the hospital. He stopped for a minute next to the parochial school and watched an old nun in her black habit gingerly pick her way over a patch of ice on the sidewalk. He thought of going into the church to say a prayer. At the hospital, he looked up at the windows, trying to accomplish . . . he didn't know what. There too he thought of going in, but didn't. Instead, he just stared at a huge wall of windows, as if his mother might suddenly appear and bless him with a wave of her hand.

At a light on Boston Post Road, a Jaguar pulled up beside them in the next lane. The guy had a phone to his ear. His father said it must be the kind Dumfy had.

"Cellular," Derek said.

"Right," his father said. "I read they have fake ones people can impress each other with. TV ads for the real ones say you need 'em to beat the competition."

The guy had a grave look on his face. He exhaled deeply, shook his head solemnly. Derek hoped he wasn't simply beating the competition, hoped he was saying just the right thing to the right person, hoped the expensive phone, in this case, was a matter of personal salvation.

They pulled under the portico. The building was of brown brick, new, with cloister walks joining both wings, two white birch trees in the atrium where that generic music of all funeral homes meets you either before or just after the unctuous man in a formal dark suit. Derek's father gave his name and said, "The director, Mr. Sullivan, is expecting me."

"Oh, yes, right this way, Mr. Blaney."

The high-pile carpet silenced footfalls and gave Derek an unreal sense of floating. And there was that grim flowery odor, always too strong, as if to conceal.

But Mr. Sullivan was a good man; they had known him for years. He was a classmate of Derek's mom from Immaculate Heart. "A terrible thing," he said softly, coming from behind his walnut desk. "Louise was too young for this." He shook his head. "I'll never forget her wonderful humor." Tall and stoop shouldered, he ushered them into a room with row upon row of coffins on display:

Metal and wood. Bronze, silver, and gold; oak, pine, and mahogany. Glossy. Hidden hinges. Brass and stainless-steel handles. Sectioned lids, the top half of each open for inspection, printed cards on the pillows, each describing the materials. A wall phone discreetly chimed three times. "Excuse me," said Mr. Sullivan.

The coffins had supports curtained off so that each seemed to be fixed in permanent levitation, the magician gone. Unwanted, an image from a sci-fi movie came to Derek: brain-dead humans in a special environment, vitally tethered, were suspended from ceilings, warehoused for their organs. Suddenly he felt the shame of what the nuns at Immaculate, in a different context, used to call "impure thoughts." He felt even less pure when Mr. Sullivan returned and they had to ask prices, decide how much his mother was worth. Finally they chose plain oak with a subtle rivering grain much like their kitchen table.

Outside they were bitten by an icy wind. The broomlike tops of trees rocked back and forth. Streamers of slate cloud were moving quickly across the sky. His father shivered as he got into the car. "Now we're ready," he said.

Derek wasn't so sure, but knew what he meant.

"I've got to get back to help Stan, but there's just one more thing I want you to see."

He stood in the curtained-off, cold front room and looked out at the snowfield and swamp across the street. The late light was pale and cold. Night seemed to lurk in two or three of the big swamp cedars, ready to spread. An owl, chased by three or four other birds, swooped and swerved out of sight around the corner of the house. Stan was gone when they returned, and without him, his father seemed lost. "I wonder where in hell he's gotten to?"

"He'll be along," Derek said. "He probably needed something else at the hardware store."

"Or the liquor store. He's a good soul though."

Soul—his mother used the word exactly that way too, a word from another time. Derek wondered about the soul, the spirit, where it went, if anywhere. Was it like smoke that curled from a bottle and dissolved once the cork was pulled? Was it an outmoded poetic idea?

His father looked out the window at the woods beyond the swamp. "They're going to build a new mall over there," he said from a distance, from some gray place in the future. Old people, you saw them often in malls. Derek was angry that his mother would be leaving his father alone. Why couldn't she have taken better care of herself?

"Ah, here he comes," said his father, hustling off.

Derek watched the red Ford pickup plunge up the drive and Stan, carrying a large bag in one hand, a toolbox in the other, lumber toward the house. His father met him halfway and took the toolbox.

A doer, his father wasted no time. After the funeral home, he took Derek to the cemetery. They stood at the southernmost end of the stones under the extended left hand of a bronze Blessed Mother twenty feet high. Steady wind had blown away the snow and exposed the earth. At their feet was a new marker stone, flush with the ground. At first, Derek was confused; it said:

LEWIS J. BLANEY
AUGUST 20, 1915–

"I bought two plots," he said. "Your mother's marker will go right beside mine. The Benetti Monument people have it ready and are just waiting . . ." His breath caught. He sighed and turned quickly away. Derek followed him. He wanted to put his arm around him, but his father wouldn't want it.

Heavy clouds scudded out of the northeast. The sunshine was spotty. His father was looking east, out toward the bay below them and several miles away. "Beautiful, isn't it?"

Derek said it was. The cemetery was on a narrow strip of high ground confined on three sides; over the years since his grandparents died, gravestones had migrated almost a quarter mile eastward. He could see the end—a stone wall some hundred yards down the snowy slope, then the twiggy crowns of winter maples, then the distant water. "Your grandparents are way up the other end," said his father, as if reading his thoughts. Derek watched the cloud of his breath dissolve. Skin was tight on his father's face; it was ruddy, weathered from years of outside work, and now all the little lines were showing deep and sharp, like cuts, as if made by a sculptor's knife. His eyes watered.

Derek said, "Every year Mom and I pulled weeds, trimmed around their headstone."

After a while, his father said, "Cemetery's come a long way. That's progress, huh?"

Derek tried to smile.

"You know why they have these high walls?" His father pointed.

Derek said no.

"People are dying to get in."

Just when Derek got the joke, his father sobbed. It was like a soft retch. "Oh Christ, let's go."

Far out on the wrinkled silver plain of the bay, a tiny black boat was pushing out to sea.

He walked around the house, looking at his mother's objects of affection (knickknacks that belonged to her mother), then her books, finding the Hardy Boys, *Treasure Island*, *Robinson Crusoe*—things she started him off with in grammar school. He stood by the rocker where she liked to read and watch birds at the feeder, the one where she once sat and wanted to talk. A teenager just home from school, he was in a rush to get somewhere. She talked about a blue parrot she had as a little girl; the bird was given to her by her adoptive parents and was killed when a drunken friend of her father staggered into the cage. The parrot fluttered to the floor, and the heavy cage fell on top of it, breaking its back. That blue Brazilian with a gold breast had brightened her girlhood. The loss was terrible, like the early loss of her parents. Her nostalgic mood would have produced other pieces of the same story had he not said, in an unthinking adolescent way, that he had heard the story before. Her look was stricken. Saying nothing further, she simply picked up her book and continued to read. He apologized immediately, but it did no good, and over the years she reminded him how deeply she had been cut.

Once, on a rare visit to their home, Mrs. Penland said, "The more I realize how cruel human beings are, the more I love animals." His mother, newly angered by some empty argument he'd had with her, looked at him and said, "Amen," driving Derek toward the door with her black eyes.

The phone rang. It was Mary Dryer. He didn't recognize the name. School. She had gone to Immaculate Heart with his mother and was a friend in high school too. It was a real shame; his mother was so young, such a good soul. Becky Penland had run into this Mary Dryer and given her the news. Had his mother's condition changed? Was there any hope? How was his father taking it? She felt bad that she had lost touch with his mother; as a matter of fact, she had just recently been thinking of calling Louise, renewing their friendship. Derek felt like saying she was a bit late but knew she needed to talk, needed to tell him that life was sometimes hard but God was good, that after a certain point people start to fall like autumn leaves. Then she began to list the fallen leaves, describe for him how hard it was for her after Jake, Tillie, and Arthur went. Finally, though, having no idea who she was or who any of these people were, he interrupted, describing things he needed to help his father with. Of course, of course, she knew how much he must have on his mind. God bless him, Louise was so lucky to have such a fine son. And how was Derek doing? In his life? Where was he now? He told her where he was living, but her voice was full of doubt; she was positive he was living in Nebraska. That was what Becky Penland told her, and she was always right about things like that. Derek said that he was fairly certain he was living in Arizona. In fact, he'd never even been to Nebraska. Well, she said, your mother would have wanted it that way.

All the new one-way streets and downtown redevelopment made the once-familiar somewhat strange, but the steeple of Immaculate

Heart, Star of the Sea, always told you where you were, and Ziggy's Bar was in sight of it. Though he wasn't any longer a kid, a bedside visit to his mother was nonetheless daunting, as difficult in its own way as remaining home above the whine of Stan's power tools and pounding. He stood in the icy street of this working-class neighborhood and looked up at the steeple, remembering the door behind the organ in the choir loft, the climb up to the forbidden bell tower with Fagan one recess, and paying bitterly at the hands of Sister Paulita for that shining view of the town that threw itself together at their feet, a vivid geography.

Peering through the sweaty plate glass of Ziggy's, he could see Fagan at the bar sitting under the sign that read "Blarney Spoken Here." It was crowded, hazed with smoke. Dumfy, in shirt and tie, circled the pool table, cue in hand. Fagan's eyes were already at half-mast. Eddie, the bartender, brought Derek a beer. Fagan told Eddie that Derek was bad news; there would definitely be trouble.

Derek thanked Eddie for asking about his mother. Bald down the center of the skull, with bushy eyebrows and thin lips, Eddie reminded him of the actor Peter Boyle. Younger than Derek's father, he looked older. In between customers, prompted perhaps by the situation, Eddie told them about his mother's final illness, how he was still paying bills. She wanted to die at home, and he saw to it. She wanted visits from the priest, and he tried to see to that too. "But those priests," he said, "are like doctors nowadays—they don't like to make house calls. I phone the rectory at Immaculate and get Father O'Brien. Ya 'member him?"

Keat, hunched next to Fagan, laughed. "He must have beaten the shit out of all of us."

"At least once," said Fagan.

"Whatta piece of work," said Dumfy.

"So he asks all these questions," said Eddie. "How bad is she? What parish do we belong to, Immaculate or Saint Joe's? Did she make her Easter Duty? What color's an orange? All this shit. Finally he says he'll come, right? 'Meet me at the door with a lighted candle,' he says. Fine. So he comes with the holy water, oil, and all that shit, and hears my mother's confession. What can she tell him? She's an old lady, a saint, right? Anyway, he gives *her* the last rites. And I give *him* a contribution. Nothing for nothing, right? But guess what? My mother perks up, fools everybody. Seeing the priest made her feel good. A week or so goes by, and she wants the priest again. I call, beg him to come. Another priest, this time a young guy, different generation. I get all these excuses. He's going on a retreat, needs to get in touch with himself, he's got a cold, can't get his ass in gear, what have you. Not lazy, right? Just resting before he gets tired. So a week goes by, and I call again. This time they're shorthanded, et cetera. The bottom line is: We *gave* your mother last rites. One per customer. As far as we're concerned, she's already dead! Fuck you. End of story."

Everyone laughed. When Eddie was off on refills, Fagan said, "He's in heaven, loves to entertain."

Dumfy said, "He should have more respect."

Keat said, "He got kicked out of Immaculate in the eighth grade, and he's never forgiven them. End of story."

"Eddie's an act," said Fagan.

Keat shook his head. "Wrong. The church has got him bent out of shape. If you're against, he's for. If you're for, he mocks the clergy."

Eddie came back and drew beers from the tap in front of them. "Watch out," he said. "Here comes another Immaculate wacko."

It was Mike Murray, dragging in fresh cold air that reddened his large face. Snow on his black overcoat quickly lost its white and glittered. Derek enjoyed seeing these guys, but his mother was alone, unvisited.

"It's the bullshitter," said Keat.

"Look who's talking," said Murray.

Keat laughed and began taunting Murray, who was already well into his Friday-night tour of duty. Drinking, Keat could be quickly mean.

"The church," sighed Eddie. Then he wondered why the most screwed-up people he knew all graduated from Immaculate, why they had swallowed all the crap the nuns dished out. Dumfy objected—he never believed any of it. Eddie laughed. "What are you talking about? You're all contradictions. You wouldn't say *fuck* or *Jesus Hairy Christ* if your life depended on it, but if Fenster told you to put one of his bad loans in the hospital, you wouldn't think twice."

"I just don't like profanity," said Dumfy.

Everyone laughed.

"What a piece of work," said Keat.

Eddie, Keat, and Dumfy began to argue about lying, what was wrong with it, why it was sinful, wondered why Murray was such a bullshit artist.

"Great theologians," said Fagan. He said that Derek brought out the worst in people. Normally these guys talked about sports.

Derek asked Fagan how his parents were. "Christ, I haven't seen my parents since—well, I didn't even see them at Christmas. You know, I've been reading this essay in *Psychology Today* about how you're never free until your parents are dead." He dragged on his cigarette. "I believe it." He looked at Derek and laughed. "You're too sentimental, man. I mix cement all day. I'm a realist."

Man. He used that word all the time, as if he had been born on the black side of town and his father wasn't president of Valley Tool and Die. But tonight that didn't bother Derek. He liked Fagan, his openness, and didn't want to think about his mother. Tall, Fagan often stood one-footed, if there was something to lean against, and put you in mind of a heron with a salt-and-pepper cowlick. He had left college only a few credits shy of graduation, probably to spite his parents and dramatically say no to what he called "all the brie-and-Chablis people of Turner's Cove." He read a fair amount and saw himself as a kind of working-class intellectual.

Eddie delivered two more beers. "So how long you home for?"

Home—that word again. Derek explained he had to leave tomorrow afternoon. How did he like it out there in Arizona? Derek coughed up the usual sound bites about mild winters, a slightly different lifestyle, and how nice it was not to have to scrape ice from his windshield.

"Lotus land," sneered Fagan.

Derek said nothing.

"Hey, just kidding," he said. "Maybe your mother'll pull through. Doctors might be wrong—it wouldn't be a first."

Keat and Murray were heating up. "You wouldn't know truth," said Keat, "if it pissed in your eye."

"The fuck I wouldn't."

"The fuck you would."

Fagan informed Derek that this was a continuation of an argument about Murray now claiming he was a college graduate. Over the years, Murray had claimed a lot of things, like being in a bar in Tijuana when the margarita was invented, sometimes saying that salt around the rim was his contribution. Sometimes he claimed to have met and talked with famous athletes and celebrities, had caddied for Arnold Palmer. Keat had warned him about insulting other people's intelligence. For some, Murray's stories were a harmless, if not pathetic, way of keeping the hounds of insignificance at bay, but Keat was pathological about truth telling. And now this story about the college degree.

Derek looked into the mirror just at the moment Keat hit Murray square in the face. Murray dropped below the bar. Fagan, jumping back, clipped Derek's ear with his elbow. He saw things as if the sound were suddenly turned down. The fighting was far away for a moment. Murray came up with blood on his face, his mouth a black *O*. Dumfy intervened. Somebody held Murray. Dumfy cocked a warning finger, but Keat swung. Dumfy blocked with one hand and did a quick karate thrust with the other. Keat doubled over and sank to his knees on the floor.

Then the sound was back, far too loud, and the air seemed thicker than ever with cigarette smoke. Leaving, Derek heard Eddie asking what the hell was the matter with them. "You known each other for years, you supposed to be friends, for Christ's sake!"

Derek drove around in the lightly falling snow, rolling slowly through familiar streets, but the closer to the hospital he came, the more detours he made. He felt like a criminal rehearsing some horrible deed, worse for having stopped at Ziggy's. Nothing had the right feel.

The hospital was an old rupture that popped out here and there, all annex and bulge. As instructed at the desk, he went left and right, up and down ramps, through tunnels, past glassy labs and supply rooms. The place was a labyrinth of secretive twists that led him past green-garbed workers and a woman shuffling along with a walker. Finally he took an elevator to the indicated floor and asked further directions at the nurses' station. The nurse at the desk had reddish hair and freckly skin, large green eyes that seemed to brim. Because of his father's orders, Derek had to identify himself. Then she told him she was sorry and pointed to a door a few feet away.

His mother lay peacefully on her side. Freshly washed by someone who had taken pains, her hair was fluffy and had more luster than he had seen in years, had very little gray. Not knowing what to expect, he was surprised. She breathed heavily and made slight snoring noises, the kind he always heard at home when passing her room, sneaking in late at night. There were not, as in movies, a lot of wires or hoses. Just an oxygen clip under her nose and a wire to monitor her vital signs. And a mouthpiece, taped in place, to keep her from swallowing or biting her tongue.

He sat down and took her hand; it was warm and dry. He said his name and told her he had flown home to see her. He sat close enough to see the pores of her nose. Her fingers, astonishingly, were not yellow from years of cigarettes (he wondered if they had been cleaned with some kind of solvent). And the nails were nicely manicured, not bitten. Her hand, though warm and alive in his, did not clasp, did not respond to the pressure of his grip. These were the hands that had held him, cooked and washed, played the piano, and wrote to him—when he was in college and in Europe—hundreds of mentorlike letters full of the titles of books he should read, the names of museums and places he should see. Was it simply this body he needed to be free of, or was it this kind of sentimental thought, the kind that had his breath coming hard? He cleared his throat, hoping he'd find the right thing to say, but before he could speak, one of her eyes opened. Her breath altered, paused, then the eye that burned a hole through him finally closed. Was this simply reflex, or was she giving him a sign she could hear?

She had lost weight, and her face was dreamy, almost smiling, as he'd often seen it when she was especially enthralled by a good book. Instead of saying he was sorry about anything, about what was unchangeable and beyond them in the past, he told her things he thought would amuse her. He told her about his blurting seatmate on the commuter flight, he told her about Stan, about his father's bathroom arrangements, and about Mrs. Penland taking photos. Once started, like his seatmate on the plane, he couldn't stop, and remembered aloud their one dinner at the Penlands' years ago when their high-strung terrier growled under the table. "He won't bite, he won't bite," Mr. Penland kept saying, but the dog finally latched onto his father's trousers and tore them up. His mother thought the incident was wildly funny; she enjoyed the Penlands' eccentricities, their house filthy but full of artwork. "Sure," his father had said, "laugh, but pet that dog, and you'll be wearing a three-fingered glove next winter." When the red-haired nurse looked in, she found Derek, to her astonishment, laughing and talking excitedly. Her look said he was unhinged, as bad as the nutty woman with the Polaroid, and when she left, he laughed again, but quickly sobered. What if his mother died just then? Would they accuse him of mercy killing? What was wrong with him?

But he had little time for thought, for her eyes snapped open, her throat rattled, and her body stiffened under the sheet. Maybe she was not hearing what she wanted to hear and was telling him so. Maybe she wanted apologies. He felt pinned by her stare until the eyes again closed. He had only one more thing to say, but after he whispered his apologies with tears on his cheeks, he still could not leave. Her rattling breath measured the minutes. Several times he was vaguely aware of a figure in the doorway, and then the rustle of clothing faded away. There was no telling how long he finally sat without words. He knew he was seeing his mother alive for the last time; to let go of her hand and rise from her bedside was to take leave forever. There was nothing further to be said or done, yet he needed permission. Then it came to him that this was a body and not his mother; his mother had been absolved by her body, quickly, and was likely already gone; the way of his own absolution would be longer and less certain. Permission would have to come from within. He put her left hand back on the right where it rested on her chest. Then, to avoid being turned to stone once again by that terrible look, he kissed the cheek and hurried from the room.

Under a cold starry sky, he took a deep breath and felt the sharp air slide in and bite; it hurt, and that's what he needed.

At home, he and his father were watching a Celtics game. Derek asked him how friendship with the Penlands got started.

"I answered a newspaper ad," he said. "She wanted a driver to take her and a few of her friends to operas in Boston."

"You did that often?"

"Maybe once a month. They paid me good money, bought me dinner, then a ticket so's I wouldn't have to wait in the cold."

Derek didn't realize his father had ever been to operas and asked if he liked them.

"Sure. I didn't much follow the stories, but the music was nice. To tell the truth, though, I sometimes nodded off. I was landscaping part-time and part-time at the store, don't forget."

"Did Mom ever go?"

"Once. That's how she met Mrs. Penland, Becky."

"Were they really good friends?"

"I guess. Your mother got a kick out of her."

"Why?"

"She was different. Listen, she was way ahead of her time with this, ah, animal-rights business. She carried a protest sign against vivisection right at the university where her husband taught. She didn't care what people thought. And that was back in the '50s."

"So Mom just saw her as an amusing crank?"

"I wouldn't say that. They talked to each other on the phone two or three times a week. Women things, you know. Remember the time you and me poured concrete and made them a new driveway?"

Derek said he did.

"Becky Penland is more eccentric now than ever. Maybe even crazy. Taking pictures of your mother!" He sipped his beer and shook his head. "But generous people. Dr. Penland wrote you that recommendation for U Conn. On the other hand, your mother listened to Becky Penland's troubles by the hour. Mostly neurotic, imaginary stuff."

Derek had to say that the imaginary was real too, but his father wasn't really listening; he was going on about his wife's virtues in a way that made Derek worry. What he said was true, but Derek had never heard him talk this way. It was a question of control. "Your mother," he said, "is a very generous and sympathetic person. Another thing I've never denied—she's a lot smarter than me. She did the books for the business, taxes and all, and, I'll tell you, she didn't need a calculator to do it either."

A fight had broken out between Kevin McHale and one of the Lakers. Benches emptied and things escalated. It was ugly, and Derek again saw Murray's face like a bloody moon rising above the bar. He stood up, said he was going to bed, but his father asked him to wait, have another beer. Derek said he had to go to the bathroom first. "Wait. We still don't have water," he said.

"I thought—"

"Stan miscalculated a little bit," he said. Then he explained that two lengths of PVC had been cut too short.

"Dad, the guy drinks too much. You ought to hire a real plumber."

"Yeah, well," he said. "I've got my reasons."

Derek went out the back door. Everything was powdery, the snow squeaky underfoot. A thin crust of a moon was embedded in the sky with a filigree overlay of winter branches. A lot of stars. Urinating in the backyard—it was absurd. He could imagine his mother, ever tolerant of his father's foolish economies, finding the situation amusing, telling his aunt the story.

When he sat down again, his father said, "Your mother thinks Stan's life is almost funny, but it's not. He got arrested down on Bank Street, the gin-mill section Dumfy calls Dodge City."

"Drunken driving?"

"Solicitation, I think they call it. He was caught in a parking lot with some prostitute in his car. Well, I laughed too, but it's sad. It was in the newspaper, a bigger story than usual because the new police chief is cracking down on pimps, drug dealers, and hookers. Johns too. But imagine how Stan's kids must have felt. You know? How would you feel if that happened to me?"

"It wouldn't."

"Listen, like your mother always says, 'You never know.'"

His use of the present tense was beginning to bother Derek because he knew a widow who still could not bring herself to use the past when speaking of a husband long dead, and her life was a fragile dream.

"Since his case is coming up next week," his father continued, "I asked him this afternoon if he had a good lawyer. I said I knew the cops probably set him up. But he says, 'Hell, what good's a lawyer going to do? Christ, I didn't have any pants on. Like the saying, you know, 'caught with my pants down'!"

"Why didn't he take her to a motel?"

"He was probably drunk, not thinking." He laughed, then his eyes misted. Finally he said, "I feel sorry for him."

After a story like that, or when someone in the family died, his mother would sigh deeply and say, "What can anybody do?"

Sometime during the night he was awakened. A choking sound or the muffled sound of a child crying. Maybe the cat, he thought. He rushed into the hallway. The sound seemed to be coming from his father's room. At the door, ajar as always, he could hear nothing but the old house creaking in its bones, the radiators plinking and sighing in their familiar way. He eased open the door. His father was turned to the wall. He always slept with the shades up. Moonlight blazed on the snowfield beyond his window. Derek stood there staring at the snowy yard until the room came back.

In bed again, he had trouble sleeping and lay awake thinking about home. Maybe it was just where you were visited by memories, or the place that triggered your dreams. Stan sometimes passed out and slept in his truck. Stan was a piece of work. His father too. Everyone was a piece of work. There were a lot of things he could say to his mother. She could laugh and smile, but her eyes could just as easily blacken and accuse. Fagan's essay was wrong. The death of parents didn't leave you free; they left you haunted by memories. Derek listened to the radiator next to his bed release a long sigh, then nothing.

Ghost of Thanksgiving

THE WIND rubbed a moaning sound from a loose pane in the kitchen window. Lester tapped the pane to stop it, then looked at the snowy yard. The rusted Coke thermometer read 34 degrees. He factored a number of things into his decisions these days, and temperature was one. A decision to leave the house was a yes-no proposition. A no could be expected from his back, a lifetime of lifting: cement bags, beer kegs, hod, mail sacks. And two grandchildren. Lately he had been seeing a chiropractor who talked about subluxations, wanted him to drink distilled water, eat sunflower seeds, apples, not use any salt. Lester ate as he pleased and told a few workmates at the post office that the guy must have had him confused with a bird or a raccoon.

However, you did have to take care of yourself. His hair, curled up at the back of his neck, needed cutting, but at least he had plenty. The yard was sunny, oak limbs crooked against a cold blue sky, mocking crows nowhere in sight. Good sign. This trip to the mall might turn out well. You had to trust your luck, but days also required planning because time had a way of losing its shape, and for a long time after Jane died, it did. When not at work, he often found himself staring into space, forgetting things. He picked up the notepad from the counter:

1) wash bath & kitchen floor
2) haircut

3) Di-gel
4) pay utilities
5) coffee & frozen dinners
6) fix roof TV antenna

Next to the phone he found a pencil and added:

7) putty for loose window pane

The next item on the list might be to take out a classified ad for a live-in companion: his sister-in-law's suggestion. But her suggestion was more helpful than what his brother had to offer. His brother was locked into stories about lunatics they knew as kids, like Bugbee, who used to chew the caps off of beer bottles and talk through his nose. Serious talk with his brother was close to impossible, and Lester had no close friends.

He turned up the volume on the TV and adjusted the vertical roll before sitting down at the table with Jane's sewing kit. The picture on the screen was terrible. The rabbit ears were useless. And the rotor on the roof antenna wasn't working; the red light came on, but no rotation. He wanted to see the Giants game tomorrow, but not in some smoky bar. Once upon a time, he'd have already gotten the ladder, climbed on the roof, and muscled the antenna to face the right direction. One more thing to be done, like this button on his coat that had popped a few minutes ago when he was heading out. Jane's sewing basket had a red satin interior glinting with needles that wouldn't quite focus. He patted himself down. "Where the hell are my specs?"

Wind gusted and the house joints creaked. The door to the big front room was closed; it was too expensive to heat in the winter. He spent most of his time in the kitchen, where he had moved the TV. It was time for *Search for Tomorrow*, which he sometimes watched with Jane, but *The Kennedy White House: Twenty Years After* was preempting the soap. The screen flickered with black-and-white footage of John Kennedy, his wife and children. Then the Dallas motorcade, Ruby breaking and rushing at Oswald, the shrouded caisson and riderless horse, little John saluting, the voice of Cardinal Cushing (now dead), white rows of tombstones in Arlington, De Gaulle (another dead), Jackie veiled in black.

"Jesus, twenty years! Aristotle Onassis—he's dead too. You wonder why she—"

Lester whistled, put on his glasses, unspooled some thread. Jane thought what Jackie did was awful. Like a queen marrying a mobster. If Lester remarried, a few people might whisper, but the real question was how would his children, Sara and Henry, react to another woman? If any woman married him, it wouldn't be for money. Half of the little he had was willed to Sara, for her kids' education. "That husband of hers—what a useless bonehead! Couldn't empty a piss pot with instructions written on the bottom."

The commentator said, "Had Kennedy lived, he would now be sixty-six."

"I'd still be six years younger," said Lester, "but never as handsome. 1963. Same year Y. A. Tittle threw thirty-six touchdown passes for the Giants, a new record. Some brutal sacks toward the end, but he kept getting up." Lester spoke to the red satin innards of the sewing basket. Jane once flared when he made a crack about Kennedy, calling him Jack the Zipper. "Man, those Irish Catholics stick together." Pushing the glasses back up his nose, he threaded the needle. Black stitches. Quick loops and pull-throughs. He tied off a knot, tossed the scissors and spool back into the sewing kit. "There, goddammit!"

On the country road that made an easy curve between snow-patched fields, siren whooping, a blue Ford police cruiser swerved past him, red light throbbing away. He lifted his arm from the wheel. "Kids—goddamn cowboys!" Lester's house was on a shortcut road to police headquarters, and sirens often jerked him from midnight sleep or an afternoon nap. He slapped the wheel. It was a goddamn joke! The cop was probably on his way to Mr. Donut for coffee. Lester once followed a cruiser to a minor fender bender in the Safeway parking lot. Nobody hurt. A little broken glass, a headlight ring on the asphalt. Why the siren? He took it up with the town selectman and got no satisfaction. But the pharmacist at Walgreens complimented him for his letter in the local newspaper, said it was well written, long overdue. And so was the one about woodstoves and air pollution.

A lot of good letters did. Look at all this hazy air. Even his brother had one of these woodstoves. What a joke! Oh, the joy of splitting logs! His brother. The good old days. He could keep the good old days, the outhouse, the cows, chickens, the woodstove, and the rest of it. But Lester had to control himself. Sara and her brother, Henry, teased him: "Dad, you're becoming a grump." For his birthday, Henry sent him a device called White Sound (like a small cake with a softly humming motor inside) that would help him sleep through sirens. The thing worked! Lester stopped at a red light, and while he waited, an old guy with a shopping cart piled high with returnable beer and soda cans in a huge plastic bag crossed the road. "Christ, how'd I like to wake up in that guy's shoes?"

He parked away from the entrance so that nobody would squeeze next to him and bang open a door into the side of his dentless Maverick. People were stupid, all trying to get as close to the entrance as possible, going around and around, wasting gas. Too lazy to walk a few extra steps, like that waddling fat woman. What a joke! Cold air felt good in his lungs as he walked past a white van that said Electrical Supply, its side door open, a guy in the rear.

A woman and her son were a few yards behind him. The bubble canopy entrance made him think of the sunglasses he needed. It was windless, quiet, and he heard the two barking dogs before he saw them. One was black with a shepherd's face and ears; the other was smaller, cereal colored, some kind of mongrel. They came at him barking, circling. The black one snarled and bared its teeth. Lester stamped the ground, deepened his voice, and yelled. The dogs were now circling the woman and boy. They backed toward the van. The cereal dog took the boy's trouser leg. Lester ran toward them. The woman screamed. The guy inside the van reached Lester a thick length of 220 house cable knotted at the end. The dog held tight to the trouser leg, the boy kicking, off balance, the black dog moving in, when Lester caught the cereal dog square on the head with the knot; it yelped loudly, fell, found its feet, and scuttled off in a series of diminishing squeals. The black dog he tagged on the haunch, and it vanished between cars with a yip.

The boy's face was red. "Look, it tore my good pants."

Lester got to one knee. "Let's see there, son. Did you get bitten?"

The boy didn't know. The woman lifted the material. "Thank God you were there," she said, looking at Lester. "I don't think the skin's broken." She was trim and had a nice face, a saddle of freckles at the nose, full lips. She wore jeans and a silver conch belt.

Somebody was yelling. Lester looked up. A guy in a maroon Nike running suit. Lester got to his feet, stretched to loosen his back. A woman in identical sweats was there too, probably his wife, baby-talking to the cereal dog, now on a leash: "Beany, Beany, what did he do to you?"

Both dogs were leashed. The black one had a dirty rag doll in its mouth, was shaking it and growling.

"Hey, man, what's the idea?" He was a head taller than Lester and was letting the black dog get too close.

"Keep that dog back, or I'll let him have it again," Lester said. "First I'll get the dog, then you!"

Things happened fast. The electrical supply guy jumped down from the truck and pointed at the Nike guy. "The idea is that your dogs attacked these people. I saw the whole thing."

"Now wait just a minute!" shouted the Nike guy.

There was blood on the cereal dog's head. The woman was stooping, dabbing at it with a Kleenex, saying, "Beany, Beany."

"You wait!" yelled the handsome woman and pointed to a policeman who sauntered toward them from the entrance. "He'll handle this," she said.

"So what's going on here?" The cop was big and heavy, his voice like sandpaper. Everyone spoke at once. "Okay, okay," he said, raising his voice. "One at a time."

The van driver said he saw it all. "The gentleman here"—he turned to Lester—"and the woman and her son were minding their own business when these dogs attacked."

The policeman adjusted his belt and holster. "Were the dogs leashed?"

The Nike man looked at the pavement.

The policeman repeated the question, adding to the Nike man, "You deaf? Yeah, I'm talking to *you*, pal." The man shook his head no. The policeman snuffed and said, "I didn't think so." He looked up at the sky, then wagged his head thoughtfully. "A loose dog can mean big trouble." He made it sound wise, as if it were a proverb. He looked at Lester, at the length of white plastic-coated cable dangling at his side, the knot touched with blood. "Then the dogs, on their own, just commenced to be provocatative?"

Provocatative? Lester said yes, suddenly amused, for there was something else about the policeman: instead of black shoes to go with the blue-black uniform, his were brown, as if he had been standing in dog shit.

"Yeah, but he had no right to hit my dog."

"Yeah," his wife chimed in. "He must have done something to antagonize Beany."

"This is true," said Lester. "I was trying to get into the mall."

"Beany don't usually—"

"*Usually*. So the dog has gone after other people," said the woman in jeans, holding the boy's hand.

"Listen, I don't have all day," said the policeman.

Right, thought Lester. You probably have to turn on the cruiser lights and siren and head for Mr. Donut.

From his inside coat pocket, the policeman fished a spiral pad with a cartoon duck on its cover. "I got to have some names and addresses here." Then he explained what was what. The town leash law meant that dog owners could be arrested, if the lady wanted to press charges, but his advice was to settle it among themselves. The Nike man softened: he would be willing to pay for the boy's new trousers. Lester studied the policeman. There had been three or four of them at the station when he went to complain about the unnecessary sirens. They moved behind the desk, trying to seem busy, traces of amusement in their eyes. He was sure. But this guy took his name, registered it with large childish letters in his pad, without any sign of recognition. Lester couldn't decide whom he disliked more—the cop or the Nike guy. People like that lifted his shingles.

Inside the mall entrance, by the door, a guy wearing a cowboy hat banded with pheasant feathers said, "Man, don't you know you supposed to let them dogs eat you all up?"

"Right," said Lester, laughed, and continued down the echoing concourse, his back tighter with every step. The attractive woman in jeans caught up to him. She wanted his name, seemed in no hurry, asked where he lived, this and that. Lester's irritation quickly changed to spreading warmth, like a gulp of brandy, which seemed to have its source in the woman's face. She said her name was Vicki. They shook hands. "This is Mike," she said, looking down at the boy. "Can you say 'Thank you'?"

"Thank you, sir," said the boy.

"You're very welcome."

Vicki asked him, didn't he have a son named Henry who recently won a big research grant? Lester said yes.

"I read that in the newspaper a few weeks ago."

And Lester would have to add that to the list: *Xerox the piece about Henry, send it to the cousins.* "I have a daughter too," said Lester. "She lives down in Georgia. Married. I've got two grandchildren." He coughed and willed himself not to talk too much.

Her smile was lovely. "You work at the post office, don't you?"

"I'm a sub—I work when they call me. But I've been out with a bum back for a few weeks."

"I thought I recognized you. You work the window."

"I do," said Lester. "How old is your son?"

"Not my son, my nephew. He's going into fifth grade next year."

"Nice-looking boy."

"My two girls are in college. They'll be coming home soon. One vacation they spend with their father, one with me." She rolled her eyes. "Between times it's a big house. You know how it is."

Lester did, was tempted to elaborate, but didn't.

She thanked him again. "We're going to get Mike here a new pair of corduroys. That guy told me to send him the bill."

Vicki. He watched her weave through the crowd, holding the boy's hand, a fine swing to her hips, a rolling walk that had a bounce to it. She was a bit older than Mandy, his workmate friend at the post office, but easily as pretty.

Friendly Hair Design. There was that unpleasant smell of perm fluid, wet hair, and cigarettes. The walls were hot orange, the floor and ceiling bright white. Murmurs drifted from behind the curtained-off section. A woman sat under a whining egg-shaped dryer. The men's barbershop felt more comfortable, but Jane said that Alex, the barber, chopped up his hair, simply chopped it up.

His daughter too was always giving him advice. Two years, she said, was a crucial grieving period, the hardest. Then it was supposed to be easier. She had read that in some journal. But his son—he rarely heard from Henry. That was the difference, Jane would say, between men and women.

From a table covered with women's magazines he picked up a lone *National Geographic* with a cover photo of a bald eagle, beak open, flapping upward from the polished surface of a lake, a huge fish in its talons. Putting on his glasses, Lester lost himself in the photos and read captions about endangered birds.

"Do you have an appointment?"

Startled, he looked up from the photos. "Well, I was supposed to see Roxy."

"You're mine then. I'm taking her appointments."

Lester hesitated. "Fine."

Her voice was husky, dry. She wore a black velvet pantsuit, a blouse with a white ruffle front, and had dark silky hair that fell to her shoulders. "I'm Dawn," she said.

"I'm Lester." He climbed into the chair and looked at himself in the mirror. She gathered his hair and pulled it out into wings, ran her fingers through it appraisingly, and, tilting her head with a half smile, let her hands follow the curve of his skull, studying his features in the mirror, all the while cupping the back of his head and molding it. "You have good hair, and your head is nicely shaped."

He laughed. "Well, at least I've got something going for me." With her hand resting on his shoulder, his neck felt limber for the first time in weeks.

"Are you interested in rinsing out some of that gray?"

Lester laughed. "I never thought about it. It's kind of—"

"Well, look at it this way. Our president does it."

"Ronald Reagan?"

"And he's older than you are by—well, a lot, I'd say."

"But he's Hollywood. People like that can get away with it."

Again, she held up hair from sections of his head again. "You know," she said, "how you feel is often a matter of how you look. Look good, feel good."

Lester nodded.

She laughed that catchy laugh of hers. "I guess you didn't vote for Ronnie."

"I guess you're right."

She leaned close and took another fistful of hair. She lowered her voice, spoke in confidential tones into his ear almost, but casually. "Who was it cut your hair the last time?" He could feel the heat of her breath on his neck.

Roxy was on vacation then. One of the other three. He couldn't remember which.

"Did they layer you?"

But before he could even redden, she said they probably didn't, and wouldn't know how to razor if their lives depended on it. "They wet your hair?"

Lester said no.

"Well, I'm going to shampoo and style you up a bit and not charge you for it, just charge you for a trim. I'd like you to see how good you can look. Is that okay with you?"

"It's awfully nice of you, but—"

"No buts. Come on."

He didn't want this extra fuss but found himself getting out of the chair, following her, and catching a mirror glimpse of the beauticians in smirky whispers as he stepped through the curtain. *Did they layer you?* Once, on a hot summer day, he was working part-time at a Shell station, and some bikers gunned in on big Harleys. When he fumbled the hot gas cap, the brassy biker chick in skimpy shorts said, "You'd be hot too if you were between my legs for two hundred miles." Bikers, station hangers-on—everyone howled. But Lester was too embarrassed, couldn't laugh until later. Jane, though, had a saltier sense of humor.

There were two other curtained roomettes; each had a deep sink with a notch for the neck. Dawn eased him back in the adjustable chair, and the ceiling slid into view. The Muzak speaker with hundreds of tiny holes was directly overhead, and out of it came—he forgot the title, but it was a Willie Nelson tune he heard on the Barbara Mandrell show. He and Jane never missed the Mandrell show. Dawn said, "I'll be right back."

The sink was cold on his neck, and, turned slightly, he could see through a gap in the curtain where a woman, horizontal, was draped in a white sheet, only her face exposed, completely still, eyes pinched shut, sharp chin and the blade of a nose in pasty profile. People he hadn't seen in months and years took his hand and squeezed it and asked if she had been sick long. They said quick was good. Jane was the lucky one. Best way to go. She looked beautiful, better than she had in years. Almost alive, like any minute her eyes might pop open and she'd sit right up in that coffin and crack a joke, like always. Flowers were beautiful—she'd have loved them. What were they? Mums? Did a great job on her. We can always be thankful for something.

"I'm sorry," Dawn said. "I forgot something."

"That's okay."

She adjusted the water temperature of the hand nozzle and applied the warm, high-pressure stream to his head, massaging his scalp for a long time, smiling down, her face shaped by the fall of her hair, before she applied the chilly shampoo. "Relax," she said. And he did, her hands moving rhythmically, stroking firmly all the way down to the muscles of his neck. "Feels good, don't it?"

"The barbershop was never like this," he laughed.

She said, "I'm going to rinse you cold. It's good for your scalp, for circulation, the roots of your hair."

Scalp tingling, head towel-turbaned, he followed her back to the other section of the salon.

"Can I tell you something?"

"Sure."

She looked at him for a long moment as if deciding. Her cheekbones were flat, eyes folded at the corners, curved up like wingtips—a hint of the Asian. "Let me put it this way. How old am I?"

Lester guessed twenty-seven, deliberately low.

"You're sweet." She put her back to the other beauticians and lowered her voice. "I'm thirty-nine. But you can't tell it in my face. Know why?"

Lester didn't.

"Facial exercises."

Lester nodded. "I'm too—"

"You're not *too* anything. Look."

He looked at her carefully, allowing, even liking, her bossy overtones. She stretched open her mouth. "This is 'The Scream,'" she said. Then she thrust out her chin so that the cables stood out in her neck. They laughed. She demonstrated several others and said you had to do certain things to keep a bulldog face at bay. Lester was tempted to tell how he had just kept two dogs at bay, but she might be a dog lover and he might get carried away on the subject, ruin things. Even his farm-kid brother had gone fuzzy about cats and dogs, talked to them now like a fool.

Clipping, lifting his hair in clumps, she talked about her contact lenses, how neat they were, how there were a lot of things people could do to improve their appearance, how you couldn't even feel the lenses because they were practically water. Imagine that. Almost made out of water. And his brother with the good old days. Pretty soon there might be a cure for his bum back and the start of arthritic fingers. If he lasted that long. She told him a cute one about a senior citizen on a standing-room-only bus who invites an attractive woman to sit on his lap. The joke, she said, was told by a woman 102 years old on *The Tonight Show*. She laughed and repeated the punch line: "'You better stand up, lady. I'm not as old as I thought!' Isn't that something? God, that lady had more life in her than most people half her age."

"You don't sound like you're from here."

"Nope. I was born in California. My mother was Korean. My full name is Dawn Lee Madden."

The eyes—that explained the eyes. "Do you, ah, miss the West Coast?"

"Not really. I married a sailor, but now I'm on my own. I'm my own person, say what I think." She rolled her eyes toward the other beauticians. "They don't know how to take me." She explained how these women got customers, sweet-talked them, then laughed behind their backs. That wasn't her style. She wanted commission too, but there were some things she just wouldn't do.

"There," she said, turning him around to face the mirror. "How's that?"

It was a good job, the hair full, blow fluffed, and he liked the way it shaped his face. For a while he had been afraid she was redesigning him to look like one of those old clowns with an open shirt and a gold choker. But she was right—he did look better, even felt better, but knew it had little to do with his hair. He was grateful to her. She shaved the back of his neck with hot foam, then tickled and fluffed his hair again, her touch unbelievably good. "I think it flatters your face this way. You're a good-looking man."

At the register, she said softly, "Please ask for me next time, okay?"

"I wouldn't have anyone else." He tipped her a dollar and found himself asking if she would be interested in having lunch with him sometime. "On me. Just lunch—no funny business."

"Sure." She gave him her card. "But what if I want some funny business?"

He felt his face begin to pink. "I—" He laughed. "Let me think about that," he said, and touched her arm good-bye.

It had gotten colder. The sun was still above the horizon. He felt light, his back flexible, and he fought back an urge to jog to the car. The snarling dogs, the Nike jerk, the cop. It was unreal, seemed to have happened ages ago. Like the Kennedy funeral. But Dawn's touch lingered still, and what was the other woman's name? Vicki. She was lovely too; such a lively expression she had.

At home he parked the car and sat looking at a huge barnacled moon already up in the East, the sun not quite gone. It was quiet, peaceful. The pizza he bought was getting cold, but he felt good for the first time in weeks and was enjoying the moment. A shadow moved on the far edge of the field next to his house. Delivering newspapers years ago, he taught Henry not to show fear or turn from a snarling dog. The pines made little noises, sudden but soft, as if they were trying to be still. The place heaved with ghosts, but they were his own, a family in the blood.

"Well, well," he said. "What's this?"

Standing by the front door was a slim, bright-colored gift bag, but his hands were full. Putting the pizza on the kitchen table, he turned on the TV, then retrieved the bag from the porch. French wine, Château Something, with a card taped to the dark glass. Slipping on his glasses, he read the card: "Thanks for helping us out this afternoon." It was signed, "A friend in need, Vicki Delos," and included her address and telephone number.

A siren wailed past the house unnoticed. He took off his glasses and put them on the table, staring absently at a snowy TV image of Marlon Brando, a cowboy bank robber about to break out of jail. Lester clapped his hands, stood up, and turned on the oven to reheat the pizza. He hunted for a corkscrew in the drawer. It seemed wrong to drink wine alone, but he didn't feel alone. There was his image in the kitchen window. He watched himself straighten his collar, then do "The Scream." Closer to the glass, his image disappeared and was replaced by the yard, the sky with clouds on the move.

He laughed. "Goddammit, now's the time to fix that TV antenna." Turning off the oven, he put on his coat and went outside to the shed to retrieve the extension ladder and an adjustable wrench. He thought about that Giants quarterback and how nicely he moved in the pocket, knew exactly where his connections were. Grunting the ladder upright, Lester leaned it against the rain gutter by the strut for support. He'd let a day or so go by before he called Vicki and invited her out to dinner. This wouldn't be easy, but he had to do something to improve that picture. He lifted and dropped the ladder to break the icy turf and anchor it. Loosen the two bolts on the pole and hope it wasn't frozen. Feeling lighter and surer than ever, he started up slowly, one rung after another, amazed by the whiteness of his own breath.

Lights at Skipper's Cove

Meditation and water are forever wedded.
—Herman Melville

THE WATER was a light turquoise, and clear to sixty feet down. Looking like iridescent parachutes, jellyfish drifted below us, a visual echo of the small puffy clouds overhead. The motor quietly hummed. My wife, Erin, was at the helm, watching the sonar and occasionally glancing sternward to keep our four lines straight. My friend Nick sat in one of the deck chairs, his eleven-year-old son, Billy, in the other. It was hot. The western seascape glittered—hypnotic, unreal. We were at the Gulf Stream, fifty miles out. It was one of those lulls between strikes. Nick and Billy sat facing the stern as if they had deliberately turned their backs on me. Maybe I had tried too hard to prove something.

I was of two minds about Rainy's absence from the boat. Despite their differences, she and Erin enjoyed each other's company. Early on, we often had Nick and Rainy to our house for dinner, but Rainy never returned the favor, claiming she couldn't compete with Erin as a cook. Erin was unfazed. People considered Rainy a knockout, but she had a pouty mouth and a voice to go with it. She couldn't or wouldn't adjust to the South. Once in front of Erin, oblivious of the insult, she claimed she could barely understand North Carolinians when they spoke to her. She missed Connecticut, especially Bridgeport, her hometown, and spoke about it in tones that suggested a fabulous lost civilization. At one of our parties, alone with her in the kitchen, I was trying to make a point about something when she grabbed my crotch and squeezed, but not as a come-on. "Things aren't what you think." Her voice was a whispery hiss. "Wake up!" Then she stumbled toward the crowd in the living room. What, I had always wondered, was that all about? Since both of us were half blitzed, I wrote it off to booze.

Blood was bright on the white pebble decking from the wahoo I just gaffed aboard. He was now fluttering and making a racket in the fish box. Nick's catch. A nice thirty-pounder. I told Erin to hit the toggle switch for the water pump. I started to hose blood toward the stern scuppers, watching it turn pink. Small red bits stretched and clung to the edges on the pebble flooring. I had to put the nozzle down close for the pressure to work. Finally, water that backed up at the scuppers turned faint red. Then, like a bad thought, it was gone.

Nick was a good-looking guy with deep-set eyes, wide shoulders, and a bad-boy grin. He kept his hair in a short ponytail and had a silver stud in his ear. He could crack me up with his laugh, a high-pitched whinny oddly out of sync with the rest of his rugged self. We were walking toward the faculty lounge at Stokes Academy where we taught. Students in my French class had just groaned at their last translation assignment of the year. It was warm and sunny, and we were laughing about something. Along the sidewalks azaleas were in bloom. It would have been a great day to be out at the Gulf Stream. In the distance I saw Dr. Tuck, our headmaster, and told Nick about the Ed Psych course he was insisting I take.

"Our noble leader," said Nick, and let out that great whinny.

"I'd rather hump a goat than take an education course," I said.

"Relax, relax," Nick said. He showed me the cover of his new book on Zen, a foggy mountain with a few brush-stroked Chinese characters. Some time ago I had put him on to Alan Watts, and he couldn't quit—meditation and sport, Zen and golf. But now he said, "Forget Dr. Tuck, man. You've got to take out the trash, yank them mind weeds."

"Look who's talking. Have you come across Shantideva yet?"

He shook his head.

"'Conquer your angry mind, and rivals become friends.'"

"Discipline," he said, "like training camp. I love it."

I was coaching tennis when Nick was hired to coach football and teach history. That we became friends on the tennis court is hard to believe because he could never beat me. I recall his joking, "I don't like to lose, even at a fag sport like this. In fact, I'm not sure it's even a sport."

Nick had been a star running back in college, but tackles blew out his knees and surgery left them looking like jigsaw puzzles, his NFL dreams down the tube. So as not to be typecast, he was often in conspicuous possession of a worthy book, ready for competitive discussion.

Ahead of us on the sidewalk, two tenth-grade boys were laughing and shoving each other until they caught sight of Ginny. "Whoa, check it out," said one, and they stopped to watch those lovely legs climb the stairs into Haddon Hall. Ginny Shepherd had long blonde hair and taught Spanish.

Nick laughed. "Well, at least they've got good taste."

The wood-paneled faculty lounge was lit by tasseled-shaded floor lamps and had deep leather armchairs and a sofa. Nick went to the fridge for his usual Coke. Ginny was looking at *USA Today* and entertained us with a wry reading of the headline about steroid abuse. Colin was smoking his pipe, and a few other teachers were reading memos from their mailboxes.

Julian said, "Barry Bonds and Roger Clemens—man, these guys are *ballplayers, role models.* They would *never* lie." His ironic inflection was perfect. Everyone laughed. English teacher and drama coach, Julian was a beanpole with thinning hair, hunched shoulders, and almost no neck. He loved an audience. Sports was the new religion, he said. He didn't understand how people could so deeply identify with certain teams that they were idiotically happy or suicidally depressed when the team won or lost. "It's just a bunch of spoiled multimillionaires," he said, "who behave badly. They carry guns, organize dogfights, rape women, do whatever they want because they've been spoiled from the get-go and feel entitled. Pathological brats."

Nick got next to Julian, tilted his head to the side, squinted, and said, "Do you, ah, think you could come up with a few more empty generalizations?"

With a teasing grin and perky tone, Ginny said, "If football were banned tomorrow, I'd do what cheerleaders do best—I'd get drunk and jump up and down with my pompoms." She winked. "Or huff some of that evil weed."

Everyone laughed, though Nick let out only a half whinny's worth. He pointed at Ginny and said, "Watch it, lady, or I'll tell some blonde jokes."

Julian said he knew a very bright ballplayer, somebody who could become irrationally violent about sports. "My friend Mark—"

"Riiiight," said Nick. "I was waiting for you to say that some of your very best friends are jocks. Whoever would have guessed? Man, if bullshit were music, you'd be a brass band."

Smiles disappeared.

"I wouldn't believe a thing you told me," Nick said. "How about the time you told us your wife was on an extended concert tour when, in fact, she had dumped you."

Julian's face reddened. "You don't expect me to level with you about my personal life, do you?"

Ginny jumped in. "Now, now! Is there anyone here who hasn't told a few fibs for reasons of self-protection?"

In a veil of pipe smoke, Colin said, "Of course. But somehow we get surprised by the little fibs that athletes tell, especially outstanding role models like O. J. Simpson and Pete Rose."

Nick shook his head and put up his hands in surrender. "Hey, I give up. I just want you all to know I haven't got anything against sports-hating wimps." He looked at me. "And you, I don't know how you could still teach that frog talk, not after those snail-eating surrender monkeys wouldn't back us in Iraq."

I reminded him about the mocking opposites of Zen he always talked about.

For a few seconds he just smiled, then he said: "Frog lover!"

Everyone laughed, so he said it again.

"I thought you were a wine lover," I said. "And what country makes the best wine?"

"Yeah, and you people remind me of a certain kind of white—light and enticingly fruity."

The bell rang, and the lounge slowly emptied. I had a free period, so I picked up the *USA Today* and poured myself some coffee. Nick was still smiling when he said, "Fucking intellectuals."

"Hey, as the French poet says, 'Ta mère, elle pète à l'église.'"

"Which means?"

"'The sea is inexpressibly beautiful,'" I lied. "Hard to translate. *La mer* means *the sea.* Speaking of the sea, we're still going offshore on Sunday, right?"

"Right."

"My brother-in-law tells me yellowfin tuna are running."

"Great. I've been hearing these fish stories of yours forever."

I told him I hoped Rainy was coming along.

His smile faded. "Nah, Rainy wouldn't go for that. But Billy might come. What about Ted? Is he coming?"

My son, Ted, was in tenth grade and didn't like to fish. On the swim team, he loved the water, but not the rock and roll of deep sea. I told Nick he was studying for finals. "By the way," I said, "to play it safe, you might want to take a Dramamine when you wake up, or put a patch behind your ear."

"Hey, you're the one who's always on the patch."

"Suit yourself," I said. "Seasickness isn't fun."

He grinned. "You're looking at a ballplayer."

"Has nothing to do with it."

"Do you realize how tough training camp is?"

"Fine, see you at the marina."

"At?"

"Five thirty. That's the one before sunrise."

"Aye, aye, Captain."

I had studied the maritime satellite reports and knew what kind of weather we were getting into. Nobody else did. But I also knew we could do it. Casting off from the marina, we had three or four miles of smooth running behind the barrier island. Then we hit the inlet, and waves rose up to six feet. Erin told me to take the helm, went into the cuddy cabin, and yelled we should return to the marina. I timed the breakers, and we got over the worst. Nick had never been offshore, and his face was slightly green. I shouted that the ocean would flatten as soon as we got past the Knuckle Buoy, in another thirty minutes, but Nick's stomach couldn't wait that long. Holding on with one hand, and using the other to wipe his mouth with a handkerchief, he told me to keep going; he'd be okay.

"Are you sure?" I yelled, knowing his response.

"Sure," he said, then leaned over the gunwale again. I kept hoping I was right about the seas flattening out past the Knuckle. When Nick finally straightened up and wiped his mouth, I enjoyed telling him he should have worn the Dramamine patch I recommended.

"I'm fine," he said. "I'm fine."

Nick saw himself as a winner and hated to lose, even if it was only his breakfast.

The smooth blue swells were deep but gentle, the up and down like a roller coaster in slow motion. Very little chatter on the VHF, no code talk about what was being caught and where. Most skippers had probably stayed in port. First boat we saw was a light-blue charter a quarter mile off our starboard, tuna tower pipes glinting in the sun. It was the *Nancy Lee*, and I knew the skipper, Bill Morris. His son was in my second-year French class. Bill was a nice guy who always knew where the action was, and on several occasions, he fed me some GPS coordinates that put fish in our boxes. I watched him disappear. With nothing else on the horizon, my eyes went to a stubborn brown stain on the deck that was about two feet in length. The longer I stared at it, the darker it got, and mind weeds started to sprout. One minute the stain looked like a saguaro cactus, the next a huge middle finger.

In the early evening, I drove to Skipper's Cove to put some gear onboard *The Bottomline*, this twenty-six-foot Parker I own with my brother-in-law. Next to the ship store, overlooking the docks and floating finger piers of our no-frills marina was an old weathered gazebo where guys kicked back at day's end, drank beer, and swapped lies. I hoped Vince wouldn't be there. Vince, a retired New Jersey barber, was the alpha dog of the low-rent gazebo boys. Actually, we were all low-renters, people who could barely afford boats. All the zillionaires kept their Viking, Trojan, and Hatteras sixty-footers at Paradise Harbor, a swanky yacht club across the sound. So you would think there might be a spirit of camaraderie at our place, but . . .

Vince. Unfair though it is, I've always associated the New Jersey accent with either retardation or the rackets. For me it's more than harsh, and I could never disassociate Vince from his accent, from the callous, know-it-all character it represented for me, and certainly for some southerners who summed up their feelings with a bumper sticker: *I Don't Give a Damn How You Did It Up North.* A Yankee living in North Carolina for close to twenty years and married to a native, I had always been embarrassed when I heard him tawkin' Joyzee ta da locals. After one beer-fueled argument about election politics, Vince and a few other gray-haired retirees at Skipper's Cove told me to my face that I was naive, then started calling me "Mr. Lib." No more invitations for beers and fish stories with the gazebo boys. And insult took other forms. If somebody is coming off the ocean and trying to dock his boat single-handed, you always help out. Once when I was by myself and it was blowing hard, they sat in the gazebo, feet on the railing, and watched me struggle against wind and current to back my boat into its slip.

When the hull bonked into one piling, then another, I could see their laughing faces lift toward the sky.

Now from the gazebo, I heard, "Hey, Lib, you going out tomorrow?" It was Vince. Skinny Kenny and the Chief were there too, retirees with too much time on their hands. Kenny had worked in sales, and the Chief, who had a thick face and a bulldog mouth, was retired from the navy. A few weeks earlier, I had towed in a guy whose engine broke down about five miles off the beach. Making my way down the dock, I wondered if any of the gazebo boys would do the same for me.

Low tide was in the air, and dark rings of barnacles and weeds were exposed on the pilings. When I got to our slip, there was a big dead mullet in the cockpit of *The Bottomline.* It had been there in the sun all day. From the gazebo, I heard sniggers, then a few guffaws. A brownish runnel curved from the mullet and spread toward the stern; the fish was a teeming city of maggots.

Though Erin might disagree, I don't see myself as a competitive person. Normally, I wouldn't care about filling the fish boxes. I'd be happy just to be out on the Big Blue, but today, more than anything, I wanted action. The marine weather forecast had been accurate. Another front would be coming through, but not for at least twelve hours. Cloud cover broke by noon, and the Gulf Stream went from the color of an old tin bucket to a limpid blue radiance. Trolling southwest, we hit a long line of sargasso weed, great yellow rafts that promised dorado—fish that show up as "mahi" on restaurant menus. Soon we began to get strikes. After years of watching his tough jock routine, I can't say I was too sorry to see Nick toss his breakfast. But he perked up once the reels started their high-pitched wailing. I taunted him a bit, "Wasn't it some coach who said, 'When the going gets tough, the tough get going'?"

"Okaaay! Point made!"

He and Billy both wore baseball caps and numbered jerseys that advertised Jason Kidd and Kobe Bryant. Slight, with blond hair and high slanted cheekbones, Billy looked a lot more like Rainy than his father, something Nick might not be happy about.

Because we toughed it out through steep seas while other skippers waited out the weather in the marina and got a late start, we had this seemingly endless weed line all to ourselves. Over Erin's shoulder I could see the sonar showing a four-degree temperature break and a red bloom of baitfish. Not bad.

Only one other boat, barely visible, in the silver distance.

Nick was eating a banana, bad luck among serious offshore fishermen, but I've never been superstitious. Besides, we had just put two more twenty-pounders into the portside fish box and iced them down. All of us were beginning to have reasons to feel good. Nick liked the way these leapers fought, glowed like neon tubes, and turned color at the transom before you gaffed them aboard. Little Billy had reeled in the other big dorado, his first ever, and was nothing but ramped at the prospect of more.

Erin was happy at the helm in her Stokes Academy T-shirt, baseball cap, and shades. Her hair was ginger red, and her skin was constellated with freckles, needing a lot of sunscreen. Small and thin in the shoulders, she didn't grab a rod unless she had to. For her, just being out at the Gulf Stream when cumulus billowed and added shape to the show of color and light was enough, fish or no fish. But she knew just what to do when we had a hookup. She kept her eye on the line and steered so as keep it off the stern quarter.

After hosing more blood off the deck, I rebaited the ballyhoo rigs and got them back in the water. I wanted to put Vince, Skinny Kenny, and the Chief into the shade at the cleaning table that afternoon.

Standing in the cockpit, Nick slapped Billy on the back. "You really hung tight with that big dorado, Champ."

Erin said, "He sure did."

The dying dorado did a loud flutter in the fish box as if in agreement.

Billy said, "How much do you think he weighs?"

I told him twenty pounds, maybe more.

"Think it's a record?"

"Not on forty-pound test," I said. The kid seemed disappointed, a competitor like his father.

"So, Nick, do you think this is a sport?" I asked.

"Depends on the definition. Three hours ago I'd have called it an ordeal." He looked at me and let out that patented whinny.

Beyond the motor drone, it was quiet. The four lines were running nice and clean on the surface: two yellow teasers close at ten and twenty yards, a red witch at fifty, and a blue-and-white at eighty in the shotgun position. The cockpit was clean except for the brownish mullet stain that still needed scrub work. One hand on the wheel, Erin swiveled the captain's chair, watching the lines.

"See that stain?" I asked.

"What about it?"

I told her about last night, finding the maggoty mullet, and my suspicions that the gazebo boys had put it there.

"Don't you reckon we call 'em jumping mullet for a reason?" she asked. "That fish might could of jumped right over the transom."

"It could also have been thrown there by—"

She laughed and said to Nick, "Did you know your buddy is just about *clinically* paranoid?"

Nick laughed. "That and a few other things."

"I'd call it healthy suspicion," I said.

Fifty yards off the stern quarter, dorado were breaking water and greyhounding toward our sea witches. "We're going to get strikes," I yelled and pointed. Seconds later we had a triple hookup, rods bending and bucking, the gold reels screaming. Erin backed off on the throttle, left the helm, and cleared the fourth line. All three dorado were big, leaping and tail-walking to throw the hooks. We laughed, ducked under each other's lines, and staggered, trying to avoid tangles, all on a rolling deck. After fifteen minutes, Billy grunted: "This guy don't want to come in." I had put Billy into a fighting belt, the rod handle in its cup. I told him to just lean backward, take it easy, and not force it. My fish finally came into view, glowing silver in the clear water about twenty feet down. It soon surprised us with one last leap.

"Excellent!" yelled Billy.

"God, are they beautiful, or *what*?" Nick moaned. His face was dark and shiny with sweat.

Erin left the helm and took my rod when the fish was next to the boat so I could gaff it into the fish box.

"Okaaay!" I said. "One down, two to go!"

It took almost an hour to boat all three fish. When Nick's was finally in the box, we gave each other high fives. I hosed blood from the deck, rebaited, got the lines out again. Erin said, "I don't know about y'all, but I'm hungry." I took the wheel, and she handed out chicken sandwiches and Cokes. We ate quietly, watching the lines. Two shearwaters tilted above our wake, following, barely moving their wings, dropping down to look at our bait, then swerving up again. The sun kindled the ocean surface where two distant boats were like small black cutouts. Clouds unfolded, thinned, then bunched together again like muscles. Hypnotized by the sun and the hum of the engine, I found myself staring at Nick's scarred-up knees. He startled me when he said: "So what are you reading these days?"

"A book about Émile Nelligan's poetry. French Canadian. English father, French mother, wrote his poems in French."

"Frog talk and poetry—what a double loser you are!"

"What's wrong with poetry?"

"Hey, I'm pulling your chain." Then he recited: "Alone in mountain fastness. / Dozing by the windows. / No mere talk uncovers truth. / The fragrance of those garden plums!"

"Bravo! I like it," Erin said. She's a paralegal but had been an English major in college.

"Bankei," he said. "Zen poet. Seventeenth-century Japanese."

I had never heard Nick recite a poem, but wasn't really surprised. He always took his interests to the max. In Boy Scouts, he told me he made Eagle at age fourteen. I gave up and quit after Star.

I told him I was impressed, didn't know he had committed poems to memory.

He let out a whinny. "There's a lot you don't know. Hey, why don't you say one?"

Reluctant to play the game, I said I could recite Baudelaire's "L'amour du mensonge," but I only knew it in French. He nodded, so I gave him three or four lines before he cut me off.

"Frog talk," he laughed. "Forget it. What were you saying about this Nelligan?"

"The guy wrote all his poems by the time he was nineteen, good ones, then lost his mind, spent the rest of his life in a mental hospital."

Nick said to Erin, "See what frog talk and poetry does to you? Better keep an eye on this guy."

"Jocks lose it too," I said. "Jimmy Piersall probably wasn't the first. Two defensive players, one for the Bears, the other for the Dolphins—"

"I know, Spellman and Underwood. But a lot more intellectuals get bonky and suicidal."

I laughed. "That's because they think. Jocks don't. You're the exception, of course."

"You prick."

Erin groaned. "That's enough, boys!"

"Okay," I said. "No more games."

Billy knelt down on the deck and opened the starboard fish box. Scooping away the ice, he studied one of the dorados. "These are really pretty," he said.

Dorado get their name because they turn gold when they die. The dorsal is still iridescent blue verging on green, but the flanks turn a mellow gold with tiny line squiggles and dots of red and blue. After looking at them for a while, then mounding back the ice, Billy closed the lid, got up, and went into the cabin. When he didn't come out after a while, I looked in and saw him asleep on the portside bunk.

"How sweet," said Erin.

Nick said, "He's not used to getting up at four o'clock in the morning, but he won't nap long. Trust me."

The sargasso weed line petered out, and we fell into a lull, sinking into deep swells, then coming up again as if on an elevator. Erin asked me to put more sunscreen on her neck. Nick pointed into the glitter field west of us where fins appeared and disappeared. Erin explained that it was a pod of dolphin, not sharks. The motor droned on. Our sea witches skipped on the surface, leaving momentary white flashes.

Nick got out of the deck chair and came under the canopy: "I've got something to tell you guys."

"Go for it," I said.

In a softer voice, after checking on Billy, he said, "Rainy and I have separated and will probably divorce."

"You're kidding."

"I wish. Remember I told you that someday I'd tell you what happened in Connecticut?"

I said I did.

"Well," he said, looking down into the cabin, "it's boring really, a cliché, and I'm definitely not proud of myself, but I had an affair. You can't keep something like that a secret for long, especially in *my* hometown. Her husband finds out and comes after me at the Hilton on I-95 where she and I were having a drink. We throw a few punches, and the cops arrive. It wasn't on the front page, but it might as well have been. Parents didn't think I was setting the right kind of example, and I didn't either. Rainy was hurt, but she forgave me, or seemed to, and didn't have a problem with us moving down here. The move was my idea, to help save our marriage. You know, fresh start, and all that. And we settled in fine, thanks to help from you guys. But I should have known some kind of payback was coming. Luck, I mean, fate or whatever. I don't think she deliberately planned it, but about two months ago, she tells me she's been carrying on with some guy she works with in social services."

Erin shook her head. "I'm really sorry. Is Billy aware of what's going on?"

"He just knows we've been arguing and decided to separate for a while. I got a furnished one bedroom over at Blue Moon Cabins."

I patted his shoulder. "Man, I don't know what to say."

"Not much *to* say. You probably know that I've been seeing Ginny Shepherd. She's a good listener. Very supportive. I know what you're thinking, but it's not true."

"No, this is all news to me," I said. Then that crazy moment when Rainy grabbed me in the kitchen came back.

Nick said, "That little bit of entertainment in the faculty lounge the other day. Julian's performance, I mean, that antijock shit. Since his own divorce, he's been hitting on Ginny, and the best way to eliminate what he sees as competition is to trash sports, make me look like a jerk. I almost lost my cool."

Erin said, "Any chance y'all might get back together?"

He took a deep breath. "We've got a meeting with a marriage counselor next week. Believe it or not, I'm the one who pushed for it."

The shotgun rod began to scream, apparently like an alarm clock, because Billy scrambled out of the cabin in two seconds. He quickly shoved the rod in the holder cup still belted to his waist. Pulling up while leaning back and then cranking on the rod's down swing isn't something everyone gets the hang of. But Billy did, even faster than his father. What he had hooked into was a fifty-pound yellowfin that took almost an hour to boat. Billy handled it all by himself. After that, we put two more into the fish box.

I was ready for the two-hour ride back to port, but Billy whined, "Let's get just one more. Please!" I was about to say no when I heard Vince's voice, then saw his laughing black pie hole. Skinny Kenny and the Chief with his bulldog mouth were there too, looking right at me—all of them laughing.

"Fine," I said. "Let's go for it."

Erin frowned. "Are you sure we're not pushin' it?"

"No, Captain, I believe not," I said. I looked at my watch. "No strike by four, we pack it in."

Our faces were lit by the ocean's upward glare. I could see myself reflected in Nick's sunglasses and wanted to say something about Rainy, but couldn't in front of Billy. A long purple cloud darkened the seascape for several minutes. Then the sun came back, putting color to the tops of clouds: rose, gold, and lilac. Far to our west was the silhouette of a yacht with a tuna tower. As I watched, the boat climbed onto plane and headed north to port. Our engine droned steadily. I checked the oil reservoir under the jump seat and topped it off. Just a few minutes before four o'clock, one of the starboard reels began to whine.

I cleared the other rods and stowed them in their cabin racks below deck while Nick was fighting his fish, something big that wasn't budging. Nick was shiny with sweat. He said, "Man, I never realized how you have to muscle it out, like pumping iron." He let out a whinny. "This is definitely a sport."

"Means a lot to me," I said, leaning on the sarcasm. "You know, coming from a ballplayer and all."

Erin shook her head and shot me a frown.

The horizon was empty. The few boats we had seen were just about home by now. Nick finally turned the fish, and I saw in that clear blue water the yellow fin of a huge tuna. Five more minutes and it was almost at the transom. Anxious to head for home, I lunged at him with the long gaff, a bit too soon. The gaff nicked his dorsal, and he shot under the boat, sawed the line against the prop skeg, and was gone.

"Forty-five minutes," moaned Nick, "and nothing."

"At least we saw him," said Billy. "He was a beauty! And big! Wish we had a photo."

The loss was my fault. I knew that empty feeling, though. All I could come up with was the old cliché: "Well, that's fishing."

"Zen too," said Nick.

"What's Zen?" asked Billy.

I told Erin to power up and head in.

Nick said, "Well, it's partly about the danger of wanting anything too badly."

Billy and Nick sat in deck chairs facing the stern and watching the wake fan out. I squared away the cockpit, tossed the unused ballyhoo, then sat in the pedestal chair across from Erin. There were smooth four-foot swells. I could already see myself at the cleaning table, playing it cool with questions from the gazebo boys. We had just about filled the two fish boxes. I was eyeballing the distance and bearing on the GPS. We had gone barely ten miles when the engine began to lose power, surge back, then lose power again. Erin looked at me and frowned: "What is it?"

With plenty of gas in the tank, I thought it might be a sediment problem in one of the three fuel filters. Weeks ago, I had cleaned the two on the engine, but not the one in the gas-tank pickup tube, which was overdue. I told Erin to back off on the throttle a bit, went to the stern, and pumped the primer bulb. The engine soared back to power. Nick smiled and wiped his brow. For maybe five minutes things were fine. Then the power flagged again. If the problem was what I thought, there was no fixing it at sea. I didn't want to risk raw fuel in the bilge. I motioned Nick to squeeze the bulb. The sun was getting lower, reddening the sky.

A dramatic Mayday wasn't necessary, but I needed to radio the Coast Guard. I was trying to recall how old our batteries were because, without the engine, their juice could go down fast. I turned to channel 16. "Fort Macon Coast Guard, this is *The Bottomline*, come in, over."

I released the button on the mike and waited. Nothing.

Erin said, "We've never radioed shore from this far out. I wonder if we've got enough range."

I played with the squelch to get static, then backed off. GPS said we were forty-two miles from the inlet buoy. Just as I was about to repeat the call, I heard, "*Bottomline*, this is Fort Macon Coast Guard. Switch to channel 12, channel one two, over."

I switched channels, explained that we were losing power, were making barely eight knots, and would soon be dead in the water. The radio operator asked for our coordinates, a description of the boat, and the number of people on board. Then he asked if anyone was injured. The last was an important question. Towing disabled vessels is big business, and the Coast Guard will not intervene unless there is a life-threatening situation.

"Do you have an EPIRB, a locator beacon? Over."

"That's affirmative, over."

"Captain, should we lose radio contact, deploy the EPIRB, over."

"Will do, over."

"*Bottomline*, please stand by."

Nick was sitting on the deck, shaking his head: "Un-fucking-believable."

Billy looked scared. "What's going to happen?" he asked, his voice spiking.

I told him they would send out a boat to tow us in.

"But how will they know where we are?" he said. "All you can see is water."

"Here, put this on," I said, handing him a blaze-orange life vest. I gave one to Nick and Erin too. From the cabin I retrieved the inflatable life raft and the EPIRB. I showed Billy the red beacon and explained that when you throw the switch, a signal bounces off a satellite and tells the Coast Guard exactly where you are. "But we won't have to use it. Trust me."

The radio squawked. I smiled at Billy and said, "See?"

The operator told me he had given our position to Sea Tow. A boat was on the way. He also said he would check back with us on channel 12 every fifteen minutes. Nick was sitting in the stern, working the bulb, and couldn't hear what was said, so I relayed the info.

"What are we looking at for an arrival time?"

"About an hour," I said. "Their boats have twin engines, deep V hulls. Really fast."

Billy asked, "Will we get back in time for the Spurs game?"

"Fort Macon Coast Guard to the *Bottomline*."

I keyed the mike and answered.

"Captain, a line squall just passed us and is headed your way, over."

In the distance I could see a wide wall of black pushing toward us, not an isolated storm cell we could easily skirt. "I see it, Fort Macon. NOAA predicted that front for much later tonight, over." As soon as I said it, I realized how stupid I sounded.

"Captain, weather has its own schedule, over."

I could think of nothing to say. It hit me why no other boats were around. They had been monitoring the Weather Channel and gave themselves time to get back to port. The operator told me to do what I had already done—get everyone into life jackets. He reminded me again to deploy the EPIRB if we lost power completely. I told him I would. "By the way," he said, "a phone call came in about your vessel—" Static interrupted the transmission for several seconds. "Good luck, Skipper. Fort Macon clear of the *Bottomline*, standing by on one two alpha."

I hung the mike on its bracket inside the doorway. Billy and Erin went down into the cabin. Nick stayed topside with me. I shut off the radio and took down the antenna to better the odds against a lightning strike. I checked the bearing on the GPS. We needed to steer 320 degrees north. I yelled to Nick and told him what was what.

Now there was nothing to do but watch. A massive black wall approached us from the north; it advanced on us so quickly, you had the feeling you were watching time-lapse film on the Weather Channel. The light dimmed. There was a momentary stillness. The first breeze was wonderfully fresh and only wrinkled the smooth swells. Then the waves got steeper and developed ravenous white peaks under the squall's leading edge. Fat drops of rain plopped on the deck, spattered against the windshield, and drummed loudly on the canvas top. Then stabs of lightning. In just minutes the ocean went from four to eight feet. The boat plunged into steady sets of waves that broke, rushed over the bow around the windshield, and spilled onto the deck where it choked the scuppers. I prayed the engine wouldn't quit. The sight of the cockpit awash was unnerving, but I had only a week earlier repaired the bilge pump and could see it shooting water out the side of the hull. In the shadowy cabin Erin had her arm around Billy, whose face was shiny with tears. Thunder and lightning froze us into incandescent snapshots.

Nick needed relief. I motioned him to the wheel and yelled for him to keep the compass on 320 degrees. The fuel bulb had to be squeezed. I left the canopy and was instantly soaked. I had heard that line squalls don't last long, but how long was long? Meanwhile, thunder boomed and lightning stabbed about, but less and less. Then the squall vanished, as if somebody had thrown a switch. The black wall with its intermittent silver veins retreated sternward. A new sun, the color of our life jackets, appeared low in the sky like a huge searchlight.

Nick let go of the wheel, took two quick steps to the side, leaned overboard, and blew his lunch. Erin came up from the cabin and took the wheel. Billy stood next to his father. "Dad, you okay?"

Nick spat, wiped his mouth on the Lakers jersey, and said, "Yeah, Neptune's revenge. I'll be fine."

Still squeezing the bulb, I said that somebody needed to get the antenna back up and the radio turned on to channel 12. The engine was doing little more than sputtering now. The bulb trick wasn't working anymore. Billy looked really scared and needed something to do. I told him to get the flare gun from the toolbox in the cabin. I loaded a shell and told him to fire it into the air if he saw another boat. He needed to keep his eyes open.

The motor quit. We looked at each other. For maybe five minutes, we heard nothing but wave slap and hull slosh. Then a crackly radio voice calling for *The Bottomline*. It was Sea Tow. The captain said his boat was fitted with an ADF and could pinpoint our location if I slowly counted from 5 to 0. "Okay, Skipper, I've got you," he said. "You're directly off my bow. I'll be alongside in twenty minutes or less, over."

I asked him if a flare would be helpful.

"That's a negative, over."

I took the flare gun from Billy and put it on the dash.

Erin said, "We've got a leak in the cabin roof where the GPS antenna wire comes through."

I laughed. "That's the least of our problems."

The quiet was oddly peaceful. The big orange sun was less than an hour above the horizon. Nick sat in the deck chair with his head lowered. Billy put his arm on his father's shoulder and once again asked if he was okay. Nick looked at me and tried to laugh, said I had better not spread it around that he tossed his cookies. I told him not to worry. My own humiliation was in the offing. Getting towed into port is like having to wear a scarlet *L* for Loser. I could already hear Vince talking Joyzee, see the gazebo boys, feet propped on the railing, having a good laugh: *Hey, we always thought you was a fuckup. Now we got da proof. You don't maintain your engine, man, you got no business goin' offshore. Kill yourself is one ting, but take these other people wit chew—hey!*

"There it is," said Erin.

A growing speck off our bow became a brilliant yellow hull with SEA TOW in black letters on each side of the bow. When we were hooked up and under way, the towboat radioed to ask if we were okay and if the speed was to our liking. Nervous, I said, "It's nice and quiet back here, just like sailing. I wish I had a motor this quiet, over."

There was a static-filled pause, then: "Well, Skipper, apparently you do, over."

Nick's laugh was contagious. Billy and Erin caught it too.

I tried not to think of arrival. Instead I leaned back and let the orange glitter plain to our west absorb me.

Ten minutes after the Cape Lookout Lighthouse and the white beaches of Shackleford Banks slid past on our starboard side, we slipped under the train bridge and turned into Skipper's Cove. The marina closes at six on Sunday and would normally be dark, but the boathouse doors were wide open and glowed from within. The docks, ship's store, and gazebo were also bright with light. More than a dozen people were standing on the retaining wall where Sea Tow would leave us. I recognized Vince and Kenny and their wives, and Timmy, a college kid who ran the forklift. Dave, the dockmaster, was there and other familiar faces as well. I spotted the Chief too with his bushy eyebrows and bulldog mouth. He looked happy. I half expected him to start barking. Then Dennis, my brother-in-law. When we got to within thirty feet of the pilings, everyone hoisted beer bottles and whatever else they were drinking and gave us three cheers. It seemed we were landing in the middle of a party, a surprise party for our safe return. All sorts of questions came at us. Nick climbed out of the boat and told of our ordeal. He seemed in his element, as if at a postgame interview.

"So you had a little adventure," said Dennis.

I told him it was likely a fuel-flow problem.

"Good," he said. "We'll get on it tomorrow. I'll square things with the Sea Tow guy. You better start on the fish. I'll help Erin soap down the boat."

I dragged the two biggest dorado to the cleaning table and turned on the sluice. Nick and Billy hauled two fish by their tails. Unbelievably, Vince and Kenny helped out. Each lugged a yellowfin. I took out my knife and started in. With pliers, after a primary cut by the dorsal, I ripped the skin in one sheet from each side of the biggest dorado, then made two long slab fillets. I asked Nick if he wanted to take home some dorado and tuna.

"Nothing," he said. "We're meat-and-potatoes guys."

Vince said, "Coach, you don't know what you're missing."

Kenny said, "Tuna steak. Nothing like it."

Nick indicated he had to go. He and Billy wanted to catch the Spurs game. "Thanks," he said to me. "Definitely a sport."

No whinny, though. I told him to call if he wanted to talk.

"We'll have a beer one of these nights," he said.

Billy said thanks and held out his hand. Mine was sticky with slime and blood. "You don't want to shake this," I said.

"Well, anyway, I had a real good time," he said. "I learned some good things."

I went back to making fillets. Vince actually stood there and held open the freezer bags for me. After a while, he said, "It was me called da Coast Guard."

"Thanks," I said. "I appreciate it. Didn't know you cared."

"Hey, you one of da crew."

I had no idea whether he was being ironic.

Kenny said, "Yeah, when it started to get late and you wasn't back afta the storm, we got a little worried. Anyting bad happen, we wooden have nobody's balls to bust."

They both laughed.

"We didn't know you was friends wit Coach Nick," said Vince. "He's a helluva guy. Gives our grandkids a lotta time, keeps 'em on a right track."

From behind my back the Chief said, "He's real smart, too. Nuttin' phony about him."

Their accents were starting to grow on me. After washing down the boat, Dennis and Erin arrived to help out. I steaked the fifty-pound tuna and gave it to Kenny and Vince to divide and take home. And the Chief took one of the dorados. He asked me and Erin to have a beer with them before we left.

I said, "You just want me to get drunk so I'll tell you where we caught our fish."

He laughed. "You got bigger cojones then us. It was too rough. We didn't even go out."

And things got better. Dennis said that our Sea Tow membership made the tow a freebee. Otherwise, we would have been out eight hundred and forty bucks. Before we left, Vince and Kenny asked Erin and me one more time to have a beer with them and their friends. Erin said she had to get up early for work and begged for a rain check.

After I loaded two coolers of fish, rods, and other gear into the back of our truck, we headed home, listening to an oldies rock station. Lights were on in houses we passed. Erin said, "I feel so bad for him. For Rainy and Billy too."

"I don't know about Rainy," I said.

"You never know what's going on in somebody else's marriage," she said. "Sometimes it's hard enough to know about your own."

"Meaning?"

"Nothing. I'm really tired."

I wondered if it was true what Nick said about Ginny, or if she was the trigger for Rainy's own fling. Tempted as I was to ask Erin what she thought, I couldn't. She'd say I didn't trust anyone. Years ago at an education conference in Atlanta, I had a one-night stand. I met this woman in the hotel bar, had a few drinks, etcetera. Guilt hit big time in the morning, and I'd often thought about confessing. Now I saw how risky that could be.

Erin reminded me she was looking at a busy morning in the law office, then a trip to the county courthouse for a fraud case that might last all afternoon. She needed to get to bed early. "You'll have to vacuum-pack and get those fish into the garage freezer yourself," she said. "Maybe Ted can help you."

As we turned onto our street, an oldies station was playing a classic by Three Dog Night. They sang that everybody was helpful, everybody kind, and asked how my light shined in the halls of Shambala. This wasn't a question I wanted to hear. My light was dim, and my hands smelled of dead fish.

Friends

"THAT FELT GOOD," said Lynne, coming out of the water. She toweled her blonde-streaked hair and sat down at a table with Rick and Vivian. The deck of their neighborhood pool overlooked the narrow Tar River. They were drinking premixed gin and tonics under a big blue umbrella. It was four o'clock, the sun still fiery. Owen, Lynne's husband, had just arrived from several emergency cases and was still floating in the pool, his belly above water. Lynne leaned back in her chair, took a deep breath, and watched droplets of water slide down her arms. What Rick was saying finally shifted her focus. "I don't get it," he said. "I mean, how do friends of twenty-two years sell their house, move to Florida, and not say good-bye, leave an address, phone number, anything?" She watched his features harden. He slowly shook his head and looked toward the smooth black river. College students were drifting downstream in kayaks, canoes, and clownish rafts they had thrown together—some kind of fraternity/sorority thing. Beer cans floated in their wake. There was yelling and laughter. Lynne watched two girls in a silver canoe lift T-shirts and flash their boobs. Guys on a barely floating raft yelled, "Wait, come back!"

"See that?" said Rick. "Sorority girls didn't do that when *I* was in college."

"But you wish they did," Vivian said. "Mr. Perfect. At their age, I suppose you never did anything questionable?"

Rick refilled his plastic glass from the thermos jug. "What's questionable," he said, taking a sip, "is that Scott and Angie Tapper, our friends of twenty-two years, walked out of our lives and never said good-bye. Twenty-two goddamn years!"

Lynne and Owen had moved here from other states, left friends behind, and had themselves been left behind. Lynne recalled her parents' reactions, ages ago, when she announced that she was leaving home for Chicago. She could still see the tear-boosted color of her mother's brown eyes. Her father's cheeks slowly reddened, and he rose from the kitchen table to look out the window. Her sister wouldn't answer Lynne's letters and refused to talk to her for more than a year.

Vivian said, "It hurt me too, but—"

"But *what*?" Rick's laugh was strangled. "You're hooked on forgiveness. What a masochist!"

Vivian smiled, shaking her head. "Nothing is as it seems. Judging other people is more than just risky."

Lynne sometimes found it hard to believe that Vivian had been a nun before she met Rick. Vivian rarely if ever got churchy, but what was attractive about her and Rick was their openness. They didn't play mind games. No subject was taboo. Vivian was still slim with a model's shapely legs and not a wrinkle on her face. Her auburn hair alone was enough to inspire envy. Rick had a lanky tennis build, was nicely tanned, but today his face was overly red and glossy with sweat.

Owen climbed out of the pool, walked to the table, then woofed and shook himself like a dog. Lynne always wondered at this need of his to entertain, but everyone laughed.

Vivian said, "What got you called out on a Sunday?"

"I can't answer that," he said, "until I have drink. Free at last! No longer on call!" Lynne poured him a gin and tonic and, from a Ziploc of slices, dropped in a lime. Sitting down, he took a sip. "First case was a golden retriever hit by a car. Beautiful creature. A few bad lacerations, some stitches, but the worst was a broken front leg that needed pins in two places."

"Full recovery?"

"I should think so, *if* the owners can follow instructions."

"What would you rather work on, cats or dogs?"

Owen said he had no favorites. Dogs were socialists, cats were anarchists, and human beings were probably a bit of both. Lynne watched the black water pull a red kayak out of sight under a live oak with dangling boas of Spanish moss. She wondered about the Tappers, why they would do such a thing, deliberately hurt the feelings of old friends.

"My second case was a cat," said Owen. "It was bitten by either a moccasin or a diamondback, probably the latter. Sad. A cat's too small to deal with that much toxin."

"Do you see a lot of snake bites?"

"This time of year we do."

Rick cleared his throat. "World is full of snakes, but some don't have rattles to warn you."

"The third case was owner idiocy. This woman comes in with a Yorkie that had eaten some of her Xanax, a woman so out of it she'd probably give her six-year-old a loaded handgun to play with. People like that drive me to drink," he said, finishing his glass with a big grin. Then he looked at Lynne. "My boss here says I'm too critical."

"Yeah, right. You know damned well I'm not your boss."

Rick laughed and clicked his plastic glass against Owen's. "Here's to our bosses."

"Tolerance," Vivian said, tucking a strand of auburn hair behind her ear. "This morning our pastor gave a sermon on why *in*tolerance is good. I almost walked out."

"Pastor Frank," said Rick. "Three chins, weighs a ton. Should have given a sermon on gluttony and used himself as an example."

Yelling came from the river, then a prolonged cheer.

"So what have I been missing?" asked Owen.

Vivian laughed. "Coeds just went by in a canoe and flashed their boobies."

"Man, I'm always missing the good stuff."

Rick said, "We've been talking about the Tappers."

"Ahhh, Scott Tapper. What a talent! Piano, guitar . . ."

"And don't forget that voice of his," Lynne said.

"Great tenor," said Vivian.

"A fucking Judas. I mean, how could somebody who was your best friend, somebody you played tennis with, somebody who moved you with his music—how could he and Angie just up and leave town without even saying good-bye?"

Lynne wished she could say something to lighten Rick's mood. Maybe Owen could joke him out of it. "We didn't know the Tappers," she said, "or any of their friends, except for you. Owen and I were in their house just once for a recital reception. Rachel and Justin took piano and guitar lessons from Scott out of the music store, but we didn't see him after our kids got into sports and left their instruments behind."

They watched a frat boy yell and splash his way back to the raft he had fallen from.

Owen laughed. "Ah, to be young and clueless again."

It was quiet for a minute. A dog barked in the distance.

Vivian said, "The guy who owns the Harmony Shop must miss him. Scott brought in a lot of business."

"Yeah, Mr. Charm . . . Smooth as a suppository."

Vivian shook her head. "Rick, please."

"We didn't even know their house was up for sale. One day I stopped by for a coffee, but nobody answered the doorbell. I peeked in the window, and the house was fucking empty!"

Two blonde coeds in a green kayak exchanged splashes with two guys in a blue kayak. One of the girls screamed, threw an empty beer can at the guys, then both boats slipped around the river bend.

Owen said, "Hey, maybe they're in the Witness Protection Program."

"Right!"

Owen said, "Scott might have changed his name. His real name is Tappinga. He probably knows people who know people. Heavily armed with that *pinga* of his."

Lynne shook her head at Owen, but Rick hadn't been listening anyway and said, "I don't get it. I mean, for years we were in and out of each other's houses. Parties and dinners, recitals and birthdays. We've got him and Angie and their kids in our photo albums. Now I can't stand to look at them."

Owen lifted the jug and topped off Rick's glass, then his own. "How long have they been gone?"

Vivian said it was almost a year.

"No Christmas card?"

"Nothing," said Rick. "And I kept thinking we'd hear from them, that they'd send an address or phone number."

"You could find their phone and address on the Internet," Owen said.

"Too late," said Rick. "If they walked into this pool right now, I'd get up and leave. Take that back. I'd piss on 'em, then leave. Speaking of which . . ."

Slowly getting up from his chair, Rick wobbled toward the clubhouse restroom.

A pretty girl in a green two-piece dove into the pool. It was humid and very hot. Lynne decided to get wet again. She climbed down the ladder until water was up to her neck. When she sat back down, Vivian apologized, said that Rick's anger about the Tappers sometimes gets out of control after a few drinks. Lynne asked if she had any ideas about why they left town.

Vivian said, "I've got a theory, but . . ."

Owen raised his glass, "Well, as a famous vet once put it, 'Best let sleeping dogs lie.'"

Vivian said, "I agree. What we see of other people's lives is mostly surface. Theories are only theories."

Owen said, "That's not what I mean. Quite a few people knew that ol' Scott Tapper was living up to his name—here a tap, there a tap, everywhere a tap tap. I mean, going into these homes with husbands at work, the guy was tuning more than pianos. That gay pediatrician's wife, for starters. On the other hand, maybe Angie had her own game going."

Vivian said, "I seriously doubt it."

Rick sat down again and leaned back. "What's this about Angie?"

"I said Angie could have been messing around too."

"As payback for Scott's affairs?" Lynne lifted her arms and fluffed out her drying hair.

Rick said, "I really don't think she knew."

"Wait a minute," said Owen. "If *we* knew, she *had* to."

Vivian said, "But denial can be pretty powerful." Looking up, she shielded her eyes. "Look at that." Two ospreys circled over the river, barely moving their wings, teetering, balancing on a rising thermal. "I wish I could do that."

Shadows grew toward their table from the clubhouse. With a large green bag slung over her shoulder, a young mother with two children carrying towels flip-flopped along the other side of the pool toward the high wooden door.

Rick said, "Scott told me what Angie didn't know wouldn't hurt her. I didn't agree with his messing around, but he had a lot of good qualities too. People aren't just one thing, you know."

Lynne asked Rick if he felt any obligation to tell Angie what he knew.

"No way. She'd have thought I was lying. That would have been the end of our friendship."

"What if it had been *Angie* cheating? Would you have told Scott?"

Rick sipped his drink. "I don't know. Probably not."

"Interesting," said Owen. "An old college friend of mine died and his wife, Ella, remarried. Ella's an artist. I was going up to Rochester for a conference, which is where she lives. But she was going to be in New York City for an exhibit. I knew Steve, the new husband, had met him a few times. Anyway, Ella tells me she'd like me to stay at her house, even if she's not there. Steve would love to entertain me, she says. Fine. I've got the key to their house and come in from the conference earlier than expected one night, and there's ol' Steve going at it with some blonde sweetie on the sofa." Owen paused to clear his throat. "Doggie style, as I recall."

Everyone laughed. Lynne blew out her cheeks and shook her head. After all these years she could still never predict where Owen was going with a story. Rick kept laughing, then said it reminded him of Mr. Pierce, a high school geometry teacher they called "Itchy" because he always had a hand in his pocket scratching himself, more vigorously if looking at Karen Goodwin, a real looker. One spring day two dogs were going at it on the lawn outside the classroom window, and one of the girls, pretending innocence, kept asking Itchy what those dogs were doing. Itchy was giving his pocket hand a real workout, and the guys later wondered if he was more turned on by Karen Goodwin or the doggie show outside the window. To the girl's questions, Itchy kept saying, 'Shhh, shhh, quiet now, what you do is square the hypotenuse . . . Get the angle of the dangle . . . '"

Owen was cackling.

Lynne and Vivian looked at each other: men!

"I guess you had to be there," Rick said.

Vivian said, "You and Owen are *still* there."

"Where?"

"Back in high school."

Rick said, "Fine by me. Being a kid was probably the happiest time in your life. Being an adult is overrated."

"I like that," said Owen. "Here's to arrested development." They clicked glasses again.

"So, what about the doggie-style guy in Rochester?"

"Steve."

"Right."

Owen jiggled the ice in his glass, then crunched a cube between his molars. "Well, next morning ol' Steve tells me it was a mistake, an accident, that it wasn't really what it appeared to be. Incredible, right? Fast-forward. A year or more later Steve and Ella get divorced. So I'm wishing Ella a Merry Christmas on the phone. A few drinks has me tell her about the time I caught Steve on the sofa with the blonde honey. Well, after asking me a few questions about the blonde, Ella calls me every name in the friggin' book. She seemed more pissed at *me* than Steve. But guess what? She had a right to be mad. I should have told her when it happened. We'd been friends for years. Where was my loyalty? Ella had suspected he was messing around, would have divorced him sooner, and saved herself another year of misery."

Thinking about Ella and Owen, Lynne watched three shirtless guys on a raft of two-by-six planks tied to four giant black inner tubes slide past on the current. They had a boom box throbbing out an old Jackson Browne tune that she and Owen liked right after they met, lyrics about 1969, being twenty-one, and calling the world your own. When the river had taken the students from view, Vivian said, "Though I can't prove it, my theory is that Angie became very insecure after her mastectomy."

"She had a mastectomy?" Lynne was surprised.

"She did, and that set off a bunch of things."

Rick said, "The mastectomy was ten years ago. That still doesn't explain why they left town the way they did."

Owen said, "Did they leave anyone else an address or phone number?"

Vivian said, "One of Angie's colleagues at the middle school told me where they had gone."

Rick said, "I've asked myself a dozen times if we somehow offended them. The only thing I can think of is that we got out of the habit of going to Scott's jazz gigs."

"Musicians aren't exactly without ego," Owen said. "He could have been miffed."

"What gigs?" Lynne asked.

"He played at the Amnesia Lounge. We used to go all the time—until I got put on the road and was a corporate nomad most of the week. Scott's trio played on Thursday nights, which was when I usually got home. I'd be really wrung out."

Owen said, "Best I ever heard Scott play was at the Meek girl's memorial service. She was a friend of our daughter Rachel. What a sad thing! And her drunk-ass, drug-addict boyfriend survived the wreck and never even went to jail. I'd like to have taken that kid apart."

Rick said, "Well, Scott was pretty shook up too. He told me she was one of the most talented students he ever taught and could have easily had a scholarship to Julliard."

Owen said, "She loved cats. Last time I saw her was at the office. About a week before the car wreck. I spayed her calico."

"I'll never forget that memorial," said Vivian. "It was the 'Marche funèbre' from a Chopin sonata that Scott played."

"I thought it was Liszt," said Rick.

"No," said Owen. "I'll tell you why. Right after my father died, I was in the car with our daughter Rachel. I had just bought a new Chopin CD with that sonata. When it hit the adagio, Rachel—she was barely seven—Rachel says, 'This music makes you very sad, Daddy, and I know why. It makes you think of Grandpa.'"

"Whoa!"

"I know."

For a while nobody said anything. Bank swallows swerved after insects along the river. Lynne could still hear those bass chords, dark and relentless. The gin and tonic had her drifting. Across the pool, she watched a teenage couple. They were stretched out side by side on lounge chairs holding hands. Suddenly they got up, went to the edge of the pool, and jumped in still holding hands, something she and Owen used to do.

Owen said, "Vivian, we interrupted that theory of yours."

Vivian looked at her empty glass on the table. Owen picked up the thermos jug. "No, no," she said. "I've had enough. Probably too much. My theory is that Angie was insecure. She said to me once, without being specific, that she knew Scott had his faults and she didn't care. She loved being with him. They had a lot in common besides music. But just imagine having to look at friends or colleagues, or students at the middle school. In a town this size, you had to imagine they knew your husband was cheating on you. Once Angie's daughter had established her ophthalmology practice down in Tampa, she probably gave Scott an ultimatum. This town was full of bad memories for her. I watched her get more and more bitter, heard her say outrageously mean things about people. My theory is she wanted a new start."

Silence held for a minute. Then Owen said, "Fine, but the only way for her to get a new start would be to have Scott's penis surgically removed or get a new husband. Sorry, Rick, I know he's your friend."

"*Was* my friend."

Owen said, "It's not for nothing they say a dog is man's best friend. Loyal to the end." He raised his glass and clicked with Rick. "Here's to friendship." They drained their glasses. "We've got to finish this jug," he said, and divided the rest. "Rick, I promise that if we ever leave town, we'll have a big party, say good-bye, and we'll give you an address, phone, bank account numbers, the whole nine yards."

"I have another theory," Lynne said. "Some folks just can't bear to say good-bye. Good-byes are painful, have a finality to them, especially if you love somebody."

Vivian said, "That's very true."

"Owen cried like a baby when our daughter Rachel moved to California."

"C'mon."

"You did."

Rick said, "Musical chairs." He said it with a lisp, as if he had a hair stuck on his tongue.

Vivian said, "What on earth are you talking about?"

"Remember that game we played as kids at birthday parties?"

"Yeah, a game of elimination."

"I can still hear that Chopin funeral march," said Rick, and hummed a snatch of it. "Jesus. I mean, how do you go from loving people, from being ready to do anything for them, to hating them? I don't get it. Damn it! I'm not going to talk about this shit anymore."

"We'd better get going," said Vivian. "We need to leash up Wally and take him out for a walk."

Owen said, "If Scott and Angie did it deliberately, for whatever insane reason, they win if you don't let go."

Vivian said, "I'd just add what a great theologian wrote, 'Therefore we must save ourselves with the final form of love, which is forgiveness.'"

"Amen," Lynne said.

Rick said, "I don't know about that turn-the-other-cheek stuff—I mean, Christ had to be kidding, right?"

Vivian stood up. "Wrong, and I'm *not* kidding. We need to get going."

"We'd better get going too," Lynne said. But they didn't. She and Owen watched Rick and Vivian walk through the wooden door, then just sat there looking at the river where bank swallows plunged and swerved.

Owen said, "Rick might not get it, but he needs to get over it. I mean, Christ, everything ends. He's got this ridiculous attachment to something that no longer exists."

"Rick has no brothers or sisters. And he and Vivian have no kids like us."

"So?"

"Think about it," said Lynne. "I suppose you have no trouble getting over things?"

"I don't think I do."

"Well, think again. It's been more than two years since Rachel went out to California, and you can still get into a twit and rant about it after a few drinks."

"Not true," said Owen.

"True. That she rarely calls and hasn't been home kills you."

"Not you?"

"I didn't say it didn't."

For several minutes, they looked at the river, Owen finally breaking the heavy silence. "Everybody's been talking theories," he said. "I've got my own, about Vivian's calm and balance. I never said anything about this, but early one morning a few years ago I was on my way to the office and I see ol' Tapper coming out of Rick and Vivian's house."

"They were close friends. So what?"

"Maybe better than friends. Rick's car was gone."

"Don't go there," said Lynne. "Vivian wouldn't. Impossible."

"Nothing's impossible. Just watch the evening news."

"You shouldn't have joked and made a big production about giving Rick an address if we ever moved. He might have thought you were mocking him. You clown around too much."

"It's my way of being serious," Owen said.

A car horn sounded in the distance. A man with a leashed Doberman walked along the riverbank.

"Would you stop wanting me if *I* had to have a mastectomy?"

"Come on, Lynne. That's no joke."

"What about Ella?"

"What about her?"

"Have you ever messed around?"

He waited a moment. "Not that I know of."

"What's that supposed to mean?"

"Okay. I messed around once. Just once. And it wasn't with another woman. I was trying to cheer up a despondent nanny goat."

Lynne looked at the river and shook her head. "Jesus."

"Come on," he said, jostling her shoulder. "Lighten up."

The late-afternoon quiet was overwhelming. Owen took her hand. They just sat there looking and listening. She could almost feel the current's pull. From a nearby tree came the cry of a jay, the sound sharp as a knife. There were no more kayaks, canoes, or rafts on the river, just a beer can, some leaves, and a branch drifting by on the smooth black water.

A Perfect Time

FROM THE LIVING ROOM WINDOW in the rental cottage, Hank studied the ocean. It was sunny and blue, but still too windy, white-caps all the way to a freighter that rode the horizon. On the beach, waves were tall and broke far from shore, giving long rides to the kids on boogie boards. A perfect day—except for boating, at least for launching through the surf. Part of him wished he didn't have the boat; it altered his way of looking at the ocean, where winds, tides, and currents had never much mattered. The first year they rented a house on the island, they didn't even fish. The second year, they dug for clams in the flats of the sound, discovered oyster beds in the marshes. Third year they caught sea mullet, spots, and pompano out of the surf. In following years came the crab traps, flounder gigs, pier fishing, live bait, and lures.

Now the boat, a small inflatable Zodiac with a Suzuki outboard. Not quite right for catching kingfish, blues, or Spanish mackerel. Possibly a mistake altogether. Without the kid present, Hank would be able to put the boat out of mind, but there he was, a lanky teenager, stretched on the sofa in wet red surfer trunks, staring at a TV greed show: buzzers, flashing lights, hysterical contestants. Hank wished the kid would go down for a swim with the others. Jim, his father, came up the boardwalk, shaking the stilted house, and opened the door. "Joey, c'mon, we're gonna play some ball."

"Nah, I'm gonna stay," the kid said. "In case Uncle Hank needs some help with the outboard."

Hank said the outboard was going to stay put for a while.

"Joey," Jim said, turning his voice to a growl, "take a break, take a break." The kid moaned, and Jim gave out with that hoarse barrel-chested laugh, an eruption of delight.

From the shady porch, Hank watched Jim and the kid cross the dunes and vanish behind the glisten of dune grass. Arms and heads of a few swimmers poked from the big glassy rollers. In no time, Jim would have children from other cottages playing baseball too. Forty-five now, with salt-and-pepper hair on his chest, a square cleft chin, Jim was in love with sports, Cleveland teams in particular. He had a gift for the moment, cared not a thing about politics, and lived with a steady deep level of cheer that to Hank was a disturbing mystery.

Slumped in a hammock of white cord with varnished oak spreaders, Hank rocked himself with a mop handle, pushed off the porch wall. Years ago at their lake rental, his father had strung a canvas navy hammock between two oaks. The old photos showed uncles and aunts in the hammock asleep, or posed in front of their new postwar Fords or Buicks. Arms around each other, always a beer bottle in hand, squinting, laughing, they seemed to be having a perfect time. Hank wondered if he and his cousins had pestered them much. Of course, the lake had no giant waterslide, miniature golf, or raceway. But Uncle Jake had a Harley, and Uncle Bat had an Indian, and the kids always begged for rides. And got them.

The hammock rocked slightly. The cover of *Time* showed a terrorist with a gun to the head of a pilot. Hank didn't feel like reading. His mind was held hostage by something else—that feeling just before the wave gathered and rose toward the bow of the Zodiac, when he yanked the starter cord frantically, and the kid rowed, trying to get them past the worst of the breakers. He never quite saw the wave, or the kid jump clear. Hank remembered a sudden bottom of shiny black cobbles from the top of the curl, then falling, the boat tumbling over him in the surf, the motor striking him between the shoulder blades. When he finally got free, came up for air, the boat was already in the shallows, bottom up in the foam, the prop like a glossy black pinwheel. Jim and his wife, Connie, were right there and, with the help of the boys, quickly righted the boat and retrieved the red gas tank. But one of the fishing rods was broken in half, the other gone, and the motor, full of sand, would have to be hosed off, WD-40 squirted into plugs, cylinders, air cleaner, and carburetor. The worst was being seen by people in the flanking cottages. A tall blond guy padded with inflamed baby fat rose from his sand chair, folded the *New York Times*, and laughed. "I knew you'd never get that thing launched."

"We've launched through the surf before," said Hank. "It's just that our timing was off." But his breath was coming hard. Christ, he could have broken his neck, or the kid his.

The guy laughed again. "It's easier just to go down to the fish market and plunk down a coupla bucks."

Before Hank could speak, the kid said, "Everybody knows you can *buy* fish. That's not the point, you . . ."

Hank turned his back on the neighbor and said to the kid, "C'mon, let's get that motor off the transom. It's full of sand."

"Hey," said Jim. "Take a break, take a break. What's the fuss?"

Hank felt the porch shake: somebody was coming up the boardwalk. Water from the outside shower splashed on the planks, then made a secondary patter in the sand below.

Standing over him, toweling her hair, Ellen said, "Water's great. You going in?"

"I've had my dunk, remember?"

"Aren't you going to fix the motor?"

Didn't she realize how dangerous a launch through the surf could be? All she seemed to want was that Joey have a good time. Hank did too, but . . . "Of course," he said, "but give me a five-minute break."

"Your son would like to go fishing too."

"I know, but he's too small. You saw what happened."

"Are you okay?"

Hank nodded and watched five olive Sea Stallions with twin rotors fly low toward an island firing range in the southwest.

"Funny, a year ago, Joey wouldn't have said boo to an adult."

"Did he give you some lip?"

Hank told her about the guy with the *Times.*

"That's not so bad." Her hair was slicked to her skull, droplets falling from her nose tip, chin, and ears. She looked toward the beach.

"I know."

"Then what's the problem?"

He swung himself with the mop handle. "This is the first year we've had a TV, and I hate it. We've always come here to get away from that kind of crap."

Ellen said, "Weren't you watching the French Open yesterday?"

"I was keeping Jim company. He's a tennis fan."

"Right. You're not, I suppose."

"To a degree."

A Hobie cat with a bright-orange and green sail moved quickly out of the framing posts of the porch.

Ellen smiled. "We should get a sailboat next."

Hank made a face. "Next?"

Ellen's laugh turned into a string of coughs.

Hank said, "This isn't funny. I was thinking how when we first came here there used to be empty dunes, unpaved clamshell roads. Now look."

Ellen said, "I am. The beach is still uncrowded."

"But listen and you'll hear hammers and the whine of power saws. Cottages going up everywhere. Lousy fucking developers."

Ellen rolled her eyes toward the porch ceiling.

"The shore is supposed to improve your mood. But every year there are more people, like that guy with the *Times.* Pretty soon it'll be wall-to-wall yahoos."

Ellen said, "I thought we promised each other."

Hank said, "Didn't you ask me something?"

"I asked about the *outboard*," she said.

The surf boomed. At the end of the boardwalk, a white-eyed grackle switched its stance on the railing, rose a few feet into the air, then hovered by merely adjusting its wings. "Maybe we ought to find a different place to vacation. One of the lakes in Maine maybe."

Ellen said, "What about people?"

"I'm not thinking about people so much as change, a change of scenery."

The grackle landed again on the railing.

She laughed, then shook her head. "This beach is never the same two days in a row. Sky, water, sand—it changes every day."

"Maybe we're too jaded."

"Speak for yourself."

When Hank was still a mile from the swing bridge at the east end of the island, traffic was thick by the surf shops, zip marts, bars, clam shacks, and marinas. Teenagers on motorcycles, teenagers performing for each other from jacked-up Jeeps with fat tires and from Trans Ams with surfboards strapped to the roofs. Teenagers with radios blasting beach music. All that energy. Joey too had energy to burn, but this year he didn't care to burn it at the pier catching flounder or blues. Now it had to be the hard-fighting albacore or Spanish mackerel you caught offshore, or nothing. But the boat was the problem; surf conditions had to be just right. Hank teased Joey about last year, about how they had to drag him sunburned from the pier at midnight, then teased him about how they had to *buy* fish this year because he was no longer putting it on the table, but the kid would just yawn, continue to stare at the TV, and mutter, "Hey, bottom fishin' gets old, man."

The humidity and heat were worse on the mainland side of the bridge. He should have had the work done at Island Marina, but a mechanic would have charged for every breath he took, and the plugs themselves would be double the price, say, of a discount store.

But K-Mart didn't carry marine plugs, and Hank again drove at trolling speed on glary streets past the fish market and run-down houses of blacks sitting on skewed porches, rocking and fanning themselves. Across from a tobacco warehouse already smelling of broadleaf, he pulled into a gravel lot under a NAPA sign and parked next to a pickup with a gun rack in the back window. A man with a Quaker State patch on his shirt took his feet from the counter, untilted his chair, and stood up. "That little American girl they interviewed at Hiroshima," he was saying. "You see that on the TV?"

One of the guys said, "Yeah, I seen it."

"It had to of been her mommy and daddy got her all hyped up, crying like a damned fool, saying she's ashamed a bein' American. Hail, I'da dropped a hundred A-bombs on them little Jap bastards."

The two younger guys laughed, one slapping himself in the thigh. "Stay calm, Red, stay calm!"

He turned to Hank. "Yessir, can I hep ya?" Tall with pale, thin skin, he had bloodred freckles on his cheeks, pouchy eyes, and long earlobes. His hair was still faintly rusty where it had not yet turned thin and white. A wooden match with a red tip jumped from side to side in his mouth. Hank said he needed two marine plugs and a standard-size plug wrench.

"What kind of outboard?" He stood behind a bank of greasy dog-eared catalogs, looking at Hank over half-moon reading glasses.

"Suzuki."

He glared, his mouth rigid. His long upper lip had beads of sweat like blisters. The matchstick danced. He cut his eyes to his buddies sitting on Coke crates and removed his glasses. Walking away from the counter without looking back, he said, "We don't carry no parts for that kinda product."

One of the buddies hooted. "Stay calm, Red, stay calm!"

Behind the great storage shed at Island Marina, by some rusty barrels, Hank, shirtless and sweaty, grunted the motor out of the car trunk, swung the lower unit into the test tank, and tightened the clamps to a two-by-twelve plank. When he yanked the starter cord, the motor caught for a few seconds, then sputtered and died, leaving a blue cloud of smoke. He yanked again. Nothing. And choking it didn't help.

"You got problems?" A guy wearing a Coors hat walked from the dock with a wrench and a rag in one hand, a Coors in the other. He was grinning, happy about something. Hank told him the motor had gone in the drink. No, he hadn't touched the air cleaner—tools got lost when the boat flipped.

"Lessee," the guy said, smiling, intrigued. "You got fire, because it sputtered. When you tried to start it, you might could of pulled sand into the carb and clogged the valve." He laughed. "I might be able to help you. I *like* problems. I'm just guessing. It's cheaper"—he lowered his voice—"to guess than have to put one of these part replacers what call themselves mechanics on the clock. I'll be right back," he said. "I got a toolbox onboard." Whistling, he walked away.

Hank squinted toward a jetty made of huge gray stone blocks. An air wrench went off inside the boat shed—it sounded like an automatic weapon. Hank had left his sunglasses back at the cottage. The light was brilliant. His eyes hurt. He had no trouble imagining an atomic whiteout. He watched a seagull tack, glide, and release a clam that took a long fall to the jetty below where two other gulls quickly converged on the first in a squall of screams, an explosion of white feathers. *Stay calm, Red, stay calm.*

When Hank got back to the cottage, wind was from the southwest against the outgoing tide and the ocean heaving itself into steep white crests. Ellen asked if the motor was fixed.

"Like new."

Connie asked what was happening on the mainland. "Make it good. We could have used another pair of hands to shuck these blue shells."

Connie liked Hank's humor, the exaggerations everyone had grown to accept. But the guy in the parts store couldn't be exaggerated, and there was no humor to his potent hatred. Both Hank's uncles experienced hand-to-hand combat in the Pacific, had nightmares, but never said a thing about the war. Never. Uncle Jake was the only uncle still alive, and he was in a VA ward staring at a wall.

Connie laughed, then said, "I can't believe you didn't have a comeback."

Hank felt suddenly ashamed. He should have said something, triple-teamed or not. Once upon a time, he'd throw a punch with little provocation. What had happened to him? Too many books?

Jim said, "Take a break, take a break." He was making gin and tonics, glass rod clinking against the side of the pitcher.

"Dad, wanna play Trivial Pursuit tonight?"

Hank looked at his son, blond, nose red and peeling. "We'll see."

"How come you can never say yes? It's always"—he mimicked his father's voice—"'We'll see.'"

The other boys cackled from the sofa.

"I say that," said Hank, trying to put some comic bluff into his voice, "bee-cause the few-chur is al-ways ve-ry un-cer-tain." After tickling the hell out of him, Hank went to the window, studied the ocean.

Jim said, "Whyn't you say you were going off the island to fix the motor? I could've given you a hand."

"No problem."

Framed by the porch posts, appearing and disappearing in the leaden gullies, was a white shrimp boat with its nets lowered; it seemed to be making no progress.

Jim said, "No reason Joey can't fish on the pier."

Joey groaned from his place in front of *All in the Family.* He said, "Man, bottom fishing don't make it."

Jim said, "It used to make it!"

Joey said, "Hey, you gotta try new things."

Connie arched an eyebrow and said, "Flipping the boat was quite a novelty."

Looking at the plunging shrimp boat with lowered outriggers made Hank anxious, but he heard himself say, "We *will* do it. And I'm not going out just for Joey. I want to catch some mackerel too." He laughed. "We haven't put any fish on the table yet. We've bought everything, even blue crabs."

"Well, you'd better be careful," said Ellen.

In the bay window on the other side of the room, the *Times* guy appeared on his porch to watch the shrimp boat.

After dinner, Hank avoided Trivial Pursuit and got into bed with a novel and a few inches of Dewar's White Label in a jelly glass. Wind gusted and the house swayed on its stilts. Vents whistled and the surf slammed. Hank kept seeing the white shrimper rising out of the dark sea gullies. If the wind prevailed, he wouldn't have to go out tomorrow with Joey. Only a few more days—he might get out of it completely. He wondered if his parents, uncles, and aunts had enjoyed those times at the lake that seemed perfect.

The novel was pleasantly boring: a banana plantation, the stain of a crushed cockroach that grew and diminished with the husband's jealousy and hatred . . . Had there been a murder or only the murderous thought? Hank fell asleep and was twitched about by a violent dream.

When Ellen slid into bed, he bolted up with a muffled shout, thinking it was already the next day, time for him to take the Zodiac through the surf. "It's just me," she said. He groaned, fell back, and rolled away from the light.

The next afternoon Hank watched an electrical storm with zigzag daggers that reached down to the horizon, but slowly it moved away. Wind out of the northeast lessened. Stringy storm scud was moving out to sea. The waves were still bangers, but regular, and the whitecaps beyond were faint. He wanted millpond conditions and hoped somebody would discourage him, but it wouldn't be Joey, and nobody else seemed worried.

Rain had driven bathers indoors and the sands were fairly deserted, but most likely gawkers were at the plate glass of flanking cottages tasting their first gin and tonics of the day, getting ready to guffaw. Hank's stomach was tight, his mouth metallic. For some reason, standing in the shallows, feeling the down pull of water on his ankles, he saw Red's face in close-up, the pale skin, the red-tipped match jumping on his lip. *Stay calm, Red.* The gas coupling was on, choke half, motor out of gear and ready to flop down. Jim and Connie were on opposite sides of the boat, holding onto the gunwale ropes. Hank was timing the waves: every fourth was a giant. "Now," he yelled. "Go." The boat gave a long sandy scrape, then floated. Hank jumped in. Connie and Jim pushed until they were chest deep. Joey pulled himself up, flopped over the side, and quickly hauled on the oars.

"Come on, Suzuki!" One pull on the cord and it started with a cough and a blue cloud. Joey swung in the oars and hung all his weight over the bow, as Hank popped the motor into gear. The bow lifted, hiding the view, but the giant fourth wave swelled harmlessly astern. Another, though, began to break thirty feet ahead and slightly to the starboard, but the boat was now on plane, skimming fast, and Hank, moving parallel to the wave, easily outran the curl, up and over the hump, his fear becoming small, like the figures shrinking and waving from the beach.

A few hundred yards out, he cut speed and eased into the wind, moving away from the beach. Joey said, "Man, that was the easiest one yet." Hank breathed deeply and made himself comfortable at the motor's tiller arm.

They bucked the wind and ran parallel to the shore, three hundred yards off the beach. Low chop slapped the bow, and, with little freeboard, water sloshed in and inched up the transom. To keep up with it, Hank sponged with his free hand.

"All the conditions are right."

"And Spanish are afternoon fish," said Joey, playing out line.

Hank said, "We ought to get something."

"Man, we deserve some luck."

"Well, *deserve* is a little strong."

Clouds were on the move, but none were dark. The sun came out and scattered a path of orange chips on the water. In places the shore was all dunes, surprisingly empty of houses—perhaps defiant owners saying no to greed. Probably not.

Distance had a softening effect, the shore a white ribbon of sand with a whiter fringe of waves, the turquoise bulb of a water tower, toothpick utility poles, house fronts of various colors and shapes: a buff rectangle, a white square, a yellow triangle. Tiny figures walked the sand. Another cluster seemed to be playing baseball.

"Is your father always so calm?"

Joey said, "Yeah, mostly. I get him hot once in a while."

"How?"

"Got sent home for fightin' a few months ago."

"What did he say?"

"Said I should ignore jerks, walk away."

"You like to fight?"

Joey shrugged. "Not really."

Hank breathed deeply, the air was so clean. He could stay out here forever. The sun had become the same red color that spelled out Suzuki on the cowl. He liked being with his nephew, the boy's skin dark and smooth as it was on Ellen's side of the family. A good kid, not a whiner. A long teenage jaw that showed a few skips of the razor. He was a senior in high school. Next summer he might not be back here with his parents. "I might go in the navy."

Hank asked why.

"Learn navigation, be a charter boat captain."

Hank thought about serious talk but decided against it. "You better learn about fish. I don't see you getting anything."

He laughed. "They could be deep. We need rod planers."

"Tackle's too light for planers. You'd need a thicker rod, heavier line."

They were quiet again. The cottages were more elegant on this end of the island and built high on the dunes, wooden stairs to the beach looking like ladders the cliff dwellers used to haul up against their enemies. He pulled the tiller toward his belly and headed farther out.

Hank was almost mesmerized by the water and motor but noticed the gulls, a cloud of them, circling and diving. "Joey, look." But before the boy could answer, his rod tip plunged and the reel sang out.

"All riiight!"

Hank said, "Look at 'em jump." Spanish mackerel were making quick silver arcs, cutting through a huge black cloud of minnows.

When the drag slowed, Joey tightened down and reeled. He had a fine sense of how much tension would snap the line. Close to the boat, the fish veered, and made another brief run, but Joey soon had it over the side, slapping the varnished floorboards. Hank grabbed it with a towel, removed the hook, and dropped it into the cooler, pausing to look at the bronze stipples on its flanks. In order not to drive them deep, Hank held the boat on the fringes of pocked water that was the school. Soon they had five more, one a four-pounder for sure. Joey was all teeth and laugh lines.

On the next pass, he had another strike, but the rod tip really dove this time, almost touching one of the aft cones, and the drag whirred at a higher pitch. "God, this guy's still running. I'm not kidding. This is something big."

"Take your time. No hurry."

Whatever it was, it took a hundred yards of line before Joey could apply more drag. Slowly he won back line, more than half; then the fish took off on another run, stripping most of the spool.

Hank killed the motor. Waveslap echoed in the vinyl air tanks. It was very quiet. In the cooler, one of the dying Spanish fluttered, scaring them both into laughter. Joey kept his eyes on a spot where the fish should be. Half an hour measured itself in drag clicks and return windings. Joey said, "I wish he'd jump so we can see what we got." With the motor off, the boat turned, and the fish seemed to be towing them out to sea. A light, steady wind had swung around to the northwest, but how fast they were moving from land was hard to tell. Hank squinted. Land disappeared at fifteen miles—they might be half that. Distance over water was impossible to judge. He was angry with himself for not having bought a hand-held radio in case of trouble. The swells were becoming chop, and the sun was a red ball balanced on the cottage roofs. Not another boat in sight. Hank suddenly realized the Zodiac amounted to no more than a speck out here. He saw the face of an old black guy at the fish market, recalled his comment about a recent boating death: "You caint mess wid Mother Nature—she always got the las' word."

Hank was all for cutting the line and being content with six Spanish, but the kid would be upset. "I don't know, Joey, they've got teeth like razors."

"We can keep him away from the air tanks."

He laughed and said, "Oh really?"

"Absolutely. We hit him with an oar while he's still in the net."

The sun, low in the sky, sank deep shafts of light into the jade-colored water, and thirty feet off the port bow, well below the surface, in a brilliant light shaft, Hank saw it turn slowly, roll its long silver-white length.

Joey pointed. "There it is!"

"I see it." Then he could only see green again as the fish went deep and below the boat. Joey reeled and line rubbed along the gunwale.

"He's going for the prop!"

Hank quickly tilted the lower unit out of the water. The drag sang out again, and the bow of the boat turned toward shore. It was a short run, and minutes later the fish circled the boat at fifteen feet, slowly, maybe a dozen times, line taut, the sun striking flanks that were a silver brown, the fins tipped a brilliant yellow. "Check those eyes," Hank said. "He's looking right at us."

"A king mackerel," said Joey. "He's a beauty." His rod was nearly bent into a circle.

Hank had never caught anything this big, or even been close to anyone who did. "We've got to make our move."

"Take the rod," said Joey. "I'll grab him."

Leaning overboard, Joey grabbed for the trolling lead, missed, then got it, wrapping the line around his fist. With no rodflex or drag, the thing pulled wickedly. The floorboards banged—Joey was on his knees with the net. The fish, ten feet down, flashed and shot under the boat. Suddenly the line went horribly slack.

Joey slumped against the gunwale. The two read each other's faces for a long moment. Hank shook his head and looked at the floorboards that were bloody from the Spanish. "I'm sorry," he said. "Those first Spanish must have frayed the leader."

For a while the boy said nothing, then: "Hell, wasn't nobody's fault."

Hank repinned the oar.

"Besides," said Joey, "the fight is the best part anyway."

Hank had been too absorbed to notice how far the current and the offshore wind had carried them. The coast was just a smudge, and the houses, backlit, were tiny game pieces. Hank said, "We've gotta haul ass." He tilted the lower unit back into the water and yanked the cord. The motor didn't start, and goose bumps stood quickly on his arm. But the third pull had them under way, shouting to each other over the motor and waveslap about what could have been done differently. "Do you think," Hank yelled, "this could ever get old, you know, like bottom fishing?"

Once past the end of the long fishing pier, the cottage bobbed into view. Seas were pitching higher now, and Hank knew that landing could be as treacherous as launching out. You had to keep the following sea well astern without riding up the back of a breaker and pitchpoling. Joey said, "Look, they already spotted us." Ellen waved. Everyone was filing down the boardwalk to the beach, the kids running ahead. It could have been a scene from years ago at the lake, Hank and his uncle returning with a stringer of big calico bass—a quiet moment, oar knocks and echoes. Not like the hiss and boom of this surf. Hank held the boat between breakers, gunned the motor after the last big banger fell forward, then hopped into the shallows. Joey grabbed the gunwale ropes, and they hauled the boat half onto the sand. One of the kids looked at the bloody floorboards and said, "Oh, gross."

"All the brothers were valiant," said Jim.

Connie followed suit, "Home is the sailor," and winked.

"You were gone so long," said Ellen, "I was going to call the Coast Guard."

Jim said, "After a while, we couldn't even see you with the old binocs."

Everyone helped, and they dragged the boat up past a line of tidewrack. Joey had the cooler open. Neighbors and strollers gathered around the boat. Hank watched Joey dangle the biggest Spanish by its red gills from a hooked finger and bask.

Jim focused his Nikon and snapped. "Perfect. Now, let's get a group shot. C'mon, everyone at the bow of the Zodiac." And he snapped again.

A small boy with sun-boosted freckles said, "Look at them teeth," testing their sharpness with his finger.

"What kinda bait did you use?"

Joey said, "Clark spoons."

A jogger stopped to ask if they could be caught from the beach.

Joey was enjoying the moment. "Nah, you gotta go *way* out, troll for 'em."

Hank looked up toward the *Times* guy's porch—empty.

"Quite large," said a wrinkled woman with bleached hair.

The story of the king came out in fragments. Hank let Joey tell it, then added details. Remembering how his uncle used to praise him, Hank said to Jim, "It was more than a fair fight, what with only twelve-pound test. We never expected a king. Joey really knows how to use drag, played that fish like a pro."

"How big was it?" asked Jim. "No fish stories now."

Joey looked at Hank. "Fifteen or twenty pounds."

Hank nodded. He could still see it slowly circle the boat, trying to pull free of the diamond-shaped spoon in the side of its jaw.

Even at the dinner table, he still felt himself rising and settling on the ocean swells, saw the king flash in and out of those deep shafts of light. At the end of the great room, on the TV screen, the president, color boosted with cosmetics, wagged his head from behind a podium. This was followed by aftermath images of a terrorist bomb in Beirut, then something about the anniversary of Japan's surrender. In spite of everything, Hank felt alive all over.

After dinner, after Hank and Jim had filleted the mackerel and thrown the gurry to the crabs, the boys came pounding down the wooden walkway. "Can we play Trivial Pursuit?"

"Sure," said Hank, "but without me."

"Dad, we want *you* to play *too.*"

Hank said, "Let me think about it."

Jim said, "Hey, guys, take a break," and followed them inside.

The ocean was going dark. Hank took the binoculars and trained them on a trawler; its nets were hauled, and he could make out two men at the fantail under dim lights. Only a few gulls hovered and plunged, and after a few minutes even these left the boat and headed for night roosts. He thought of his parents, of their time.

Jim yelled from the doorway and hoisted a beer can.

Hank nodded yes.

Jim came down the stilted walkway. Delight crinkled his eyes, creased his cheeks. He put his hands on the rail, the skipper of something outward bound. He cleared his throat. "Well, Mr. Gump, it looks like we're in for a nor'easter. Best see that the hatches are battened down." His face was pure pleasure. He squinted and scratched his oily forehead.

Hank knew he was supposed to play along. "Aye, aye."

"Mr. Gump?"

"Yes, Tuan Jeem."

"Is there something wrong?"

"Not exactly, sah. Why do you ask?"

"You're—well, you're all gumped up!"

"I can't help it, sah, it is my nature."

Jim clapped him on the back. "Very well, Gump, carry on." They laughed and clanked beer cans. They stood looking out, lights now brighter on the trawler. The offshore breeze came in freshened gusts, its briny scent perfection. A great wave detonated on the beach. He remembered the offshore quiet, the water's glassy green, the distant white line of sand. Hank felt lucky. It was luck that hooked the fish and luck that let it go. He was glad the king was gone.

Jim said, "You ready?"

"I am," said Hank, opening the door.

In the corner of Ellen's eyes, Hank could see a fan of white lines from squinting in the sun.

"He's on our team," smiled Joey.

"Yeah, Dad."

"Prepare to lose," Connie said.

"Just roll the dice," Hank said. He grinned and deepened his voice, "Just roll the dice."

Booger's Gift

GREG STOOD AT THE WINDOW, phone to his ear. He was watching a raccoon atop the bird feeder and talking to the same guy who called yesterday, a well-oiled baritone named Booger Siems. Booger lived about forty miles away and wondered if Greg could meet him just west of the city: *Greg, I think we kin make us a deal. If it's in the condition you say. The speed limit don't hit fifty-five 'til you git out past the Walmart, and I need to put her up to sixty at least, without us gittin' stopped by the po-lice. . . .* The squirrel-proof feeder was like a birdcage, seed tube in the center, but the raccoon figured out how to get his black paw in there for those sunflower seeds. Greg didn't feel like driving twelve miles to accommodate this guy, but the ad had been running for more than a month, at a cost of seventy bucks. Only two or three inquiries, and not one of the callers ever showed up. Twice he had the newspaper drop the price, three hundred bucks each time. Having detailed the car himself, he was tired of keeping it clean, not to mention paying the insurance, especially since he was now driving a new Ford pickup. Booger Siems proposed a meeting place. "Okay," said Greg, "two o'clock, Walgreens parking lot."

After hanging up, he watched the raccoon. Probably had little ones to feed. He tapped the window. The masked bandit looked right at him, slid headfirst down the pole, then wobbled across the yard, his thick ringed tail disappearing into the woods.

Greg ground up some beans, started a pot of coffee, and stood by the window half listening to an FM classical music station that

Linda used to play on Sundays while reading the newspaper. Waiting for the coffee, he sat down and started reading a piece from the Arts & Living section entitled "March Madness." There was a series of interviews with fans from Duke, NC State, and Carolina about why they needed their fix. One fifty-year-old fan so loved his team he had a ram's head tattooed on his shoulder. Another said he wanted to be buried in his Blue Devils sweatshirt. Another said Cameron Stadium was the only church he cared to attend. A Wolfpack fan confessed he had family members who were Carolina alums, and his relationship with them over the years had dissolved.

Greg imagined Linda laughing, saying something like, *I've heard of religion and politics getting in the way, but a bunch of guys tossing around a hunk of inflated rubber? More important than family? Please!* Then that squint and the way she jacked up the side of her mouth always made him laugh. They laughed together, but they argued too. Greg didn't want to think about the arguments.

The electric coffeemaker let go with a final huff and sigh. He put down the paper and went to the kitchen. Titmice, chickadees, and cardinals were back at the feeder. No sign of the bandit. The lawn was empty. Pretty soon it would be green—he'd be mowing again. As a kid in a family where money was tight, he mowed lawns, delivered newspapers, shoveled snow. These jobs produced stories he probably told once too often to Billy and Marianne by way of letting them know their childhoods were soft compared to his. Billy would laugh, roll his eyes, and then start to bow an imaginary violin.

When he opened the closet and grabbed his jacket, dozens of wire hangers clinked against each other. *Coat hangers multiply faster than rabbits,* his father used to say. Growing up, Greg enjoyed his father's stories about the farm, about the Great Depression when he made and set snares to catch rabbits for the table. Dad could build or repair just about anything. Greg loved the smells of freshly cut wood in his shop where he learned about miter boxes, beveled edges, and dowels.

Once in the car, he felt himself slowly becoming another person. He hated playing games about money, hated it when people dickered with him about job estimates. Booger on the phone sounded charming but already had the upper hand—Greg driving twelve miles out of his way to show the car. Booger's voice and accent made him think of his boss at the Home Improvement Center. W. K. Marrow. An empty suit from Kinston. Family connections made him a manager. One spring day, he called Greg into his office. To the right of his desk were surveillance screens showing customers browsing the aisles from an overhead angle. On the wall hung two college degrees with unreadable calligraphy, deckle-edged gold seals, and a couple of red and green ribbons. Marrow was obese and often tipped his head toward the ceiling, gaping his mouth like a carp trying for air in a stagnant pond. After some fake genteel politeness, he shoved across the desk a yellow sheet. It read: "How to Put a Smile on Your Toughest Customer's Face by W. K. Marrow." Greg had seen a copy tacked to the corkboard in the break room. His workmates laughed at the thing, joked that it was the whole of his master's thesis. Second of the five points was "Compliment the Customer on Anything." So the guys would laugh and say, *What lovely tits you've got!* Or, *That bulge—I wish I was hung like you!* Barely a year on the job, Marrow not only managed, but also managed to make himself despised. He told workers how to dress, timed their coffee breaks, and would phone your desk to say you hadn't smiled enough while waiting on that last customer. Once he told Greg that his shoes needed polish. Greg shoved the yellow sheet back across the desk, said he'd already read it in the break room, and shrugged.

Marrow gaped his mouth several times, then said, "I'm very sorry, but we've had 'nuther customer complaint 'bout you."

Greg said he knew the customer, no surprise. A blonde woman, yesterday afternoon. High heels, dressed as if for a swanky nightclub date. He had dragged the trundle stairs from another section of the floor, closed the aisle at both ends according to regs, climbed twenty feet up, and muscled down three different vanities. With four other customers waiting. She was full of tsks and smelled of booze. She said the product was junk, and when he tried to defend its features, she looked at him as if he were a lavatory attendant and called him a flunky. "Really, W. K., I'd like to know how you would have handled this woman."

"To you, I am '*Mister* Marrow.'"

"Well, you're a year, maybe two, older than my son, and I don't call him 'Mister.'"

His eyes goggled upward, looking for that surface air, before he said, "It seems you need a course in angah management."

Greg said, "Tell you what. I'll take that course if you take a course in diet and weight loss, you spoiled, fat walking sack of shit!"

Linda couldn't believe it. Was Johnny Paycheck's "Take This Job and Shove It" Greg's favorite tune? Was he crazy? After ten years, giving up benefits? Who was he performing for? *Proud, hard-headed know-it-all*—her final judgment stung and echoed still. But Greg dusted off his tools and began painting houses, refinishing floors, the kind of work he learned from his father. At first, his son, Billy, worked with him. Billy was good with his hands, a quick study when it came to repairing or replacing chair rails, crown molding, wainscoting, and baseboard, good at setting up scaffolding, taping, spackling cracks, using disc and belt sanders, applying varnish and poly. But unlike his older sister, Marianne, Billy hung out with a crew that specialized in smoking weed and playing video games. He grew less and less reliable. They argued and Billy quit, followed one of his girlfriends to Florida, where she at least had the good sense to attend college. Linda always made excuses for Billy's behavior, this time saying he was just like his father, a major-league hardhead. The only time he heard from the kid was when he needed money. Now not for months, probably siding with Linda.

Greg missed him but adjusted to being alone. Unlike other painters, he didn't listen to a radio or tapes while working. Once he was on a job with a guy who had preachers ranting from a boom box all day long. It came close to a fistfight before Greg packed up and left. The guy was older. It would have been like punching his father. Now it was solo. The quiet agreed with him. After finishing a room, he liked to stand in the middle of all that blank white, smell the freshness, feel the peace of it, like snowfalls from his New England childhood. Heavy canvas drop cloths he had inherited from his father covered the floors, spattered like phony abstract paintings. He almost believed that his father, only a few months dead, watched from some extra dimension, shaking his head in disapproval over his split with Linda, but Greg had to do things his own way. Once, after listening to Sinatra's "My Way," Linda said the lyrics made her want to puke.

Crossing the bridge, he looked down on water that was still a cobalt blue against which the white clapboards of dockside houses were dazzlingly chalky in the sunlight, every chimney brick a bright red. A lone trawler was headed seaward, leaving a thin white seam of a wake. Greg wondered what this Booger would look like. He invented a face for him, gave him a potato nose and ruddy cheeks.

In the Walgreens parking lot he immediately spotted the beige Crown Victoria he was told to look for and memorized the license plate: PMZ 1223. The guy had on a dark suit, white shirt, and green paisley tie. He was the same height and build as Greg. Aside from a red beaky nose, he was very pale, one eye covered with a black patch, the other robin's egg blue. They shook hands. "Booger Siems, vera nice to meet you," he said, putting a fist to his mouth to cover a cough. Greg remembered his coughing on the phone, guessed the guy had at least fifteen years on him. "Car looks good," said Siems.

In the Crown Vic's driver seat was a kid in a camouflage jacket and light-blue Carolina baseball cap, the bill tubed. He growled, shook his head, and pounded the wheel with this fist. Siems said, "That's Jordan, mah nephew. Listen, can I ask a favor?"

Greg said yes.

"Could we give him about ten minutes? I'm gittin' the car for him, but he's listenin' to a game in overtime. An' Duke is winnin'. No way I can git 'im out that car. Say, how about I buy you a drink across the road?"

Greg said okay. Siems tapped the car window and pointed to the bar/grill with a sign on the roof that said: "G. T.'s Alibi." The kid nodded and waved him off.

Bottles doubled and glittered in the mirror behind the bar. At either end were large plasma TV screens, flickering away in bright high-definition color. On the other side of the hall-like room were four pool tables and two more moving screens. Balls crashed, then softly clacked to the tune of country music. Blue smoke churned in the half dark above the pool tables.

"What a you drinking?"

"Really, there's no need to buy me a drink."

"Well, it's the least I can do for holdin' you up. Or my nephew holdin' *us* up. But he's basically a good boy, and I sometimes indulge his behavior."

A willowy blonde was tending bar. "What's it gone be, shug?"

Greg said, "You first, Mr. Siems."

"Booger, please. Everybody calls me Booger. Jack Daniels on the rocks."

Greg said, "Same for me."

Booger looked into the distance toward the pool tables. He took a deep, wheezy breath. There was an upswell to his lower lip. The face and voice reminded Greg of an elderly Albert Finney except that his hair had fallen, not so much in a pattern of onset baldness, but in patches, as if from some kind of an attack. The big screens flickered with basketball, soccer, hockey, and kickboxing.

The blonde put down their drinks. Booger's one eye watched her move away down the bar. "Lord have mercy."

"I'll drink to that," said Greg.

They touched glasses. "You married?" asked Booger.

"Well, sort of split up at the moment."

"Lawyers involved?"

"No, not yet."

"That's good. You might could work things out. Any kids?"

Greg said, "Two, boy and girl, grown and out of the house."

"What they do?"

"Well, the older one, the girl, she just got her degree in pharmacy. Works in Charlotte."

"The boy?"

Greg hesitated. He forced a smile, "Best not go there."

"Well, Jordan out in the car's my grandnephew. His daddy got kilt in Eye-rack. Hates his momma's new husband. Real bad blood. So I'm kind of a father, you might say. Boy's got no sense whatsoever how to save a penny." He sipped his drink. "But I contribute that to his whole generation." He shook his head and sighed. "We best not embark down that road."

"Does he work?"

"He works for me. I manage some rental properties, and he takes care of a lot of it, a good fixer."

It was quiet for a moment. Someone yelled. There were cheers by the pool tables.

"Why's he so ramped up about this game?"

"Well, he's a big Carolina fan, was a student there 'til he dropped out."

"Why did he do that?"

"Wish I knew."

"At his age, I only got revved about games I had money on."

Siems shook his head. "Didn't you ever love just one team?"

"Sure, when I was a kid we lived an almost equal distance between Fenway Park and Yankee Stadium, and I was a Yankee fan, loved Mickey Mantle, Yogi Berra, Roger Maris, all those guys."

Booger laughed, "Well, that makes sense. You a Yankee!" He slid off his stool. "I got to drain mah dragon, but with this here prostrate, it takes me about a hour to pee. If I'm lucky."

Greg watched him limp down the bar. One of the screens showed a European soccer riot in full swing. Greg remembered his last time home, having a drink at the Half Keg. There were TVs at either end of the bar, one for Boston fans, the other for New York. Sonny Morgan got into a fistfight because of a remark made about

Billy Martin. Greg could still see Lump Cone kicking the hell out of Sonny, who was trying to escape under a car in the parking lot, but his big belly wouldn't allow it.

Greg finished his drink. The bar was beginning to rearrange itself slightly. Sound was turned off on all the TVs, the commentator's words appearing in closed-caption crawls. This way the most god-awful country lyrics ever to escape though a pair of nostrils were able to fill the room without competition. He tried to think what was worse, the cigarette smoke or the music. Then he thought about the raccoon with its paw in the bird feeder, slid from his stool, and went to the front door, whispering the plate number to himself: PMZ 1223. Across the street the two cars still sat side by side, unmoved. The kid's fidgeting shadow made him think of a caged animal.

"I know what you thinking," said Booger. "You wondering why I'm wearing this here coat and tie."

"Not really."

"Well, it's Sunday. You might say these are my church clothes. You go to church?"

"I used to."

"What happened?"

"Our pastor was arrogant and ignorant. Couldn't take it anymore."

"A shame. They was a fine homily this morning on Luke 12. 'Be on your guard against all kinds of greed; for one's life doth not consist in the abundance of possessions.'"

"I've got no quarrel with that. I paint houses, refinish floors. That doesn't exactly lead to an abundance of possessions."

Booger pointed to their empty glasses. "Ready for another one?" He signaled the barmaid. "What say we do doubles this time?"

Greg smiled. "You're not trying to get me drunk, make me lower my price, are you?"

The fine lines on Booger's face seemed to harden. There was a frown in his voice. "You got to open up, son, trust people. 'Love covereth all sins.' Proverbs 10:12."

Greg laughed. "Doesn't it also say that, ah, let's see if I can remember, 'He that is surety for a stranger shall smart for it'? Well, I just don't want to smart for it."

"You know the Bible!"

"I know it can be used to justify just about anything."

The barmaid clicked down the two drinks.

"But it's beautiful, isn't it? Words console me, like a drink sometimes, or a woman. 'A virtuous woman is a crown to her husband.' But I never did find no virtuous woman. I know they out there, but I didn't find one. What does your wife do?"

"Well, she's living in Raleigh now, managing a bookstore."

"Enough people buyin' books?"

"Well, you've got three big universities and a bunch of colleges in the Raleigh area. You'd be surprised."

"That's why sports fans up there hate each other so much. All them schools. Once upon a time it was worse, with Wake Forest right there too. All of them within twenty-something miles of each other. Buddy a mine tells me when he goes to church, first thing he does is get on his knees and ask the good Lord to forgive him for hatin' Duke so much."

Greg laughed. Booger took a sip of his drink and massaged the pale skin on his jaw.

A few moments slurred by. There was a cheer from a group at the end of the bar.

"You smoke?"

"It's the only thing I didn't try when I was a teenager."

"You was smart."

"Not really. One night, with two friends, we boosted a car for a joy ride, a new Impala with the keys left in it. We're speeding down some back road, and my buddy Jerry offers me a cigarette. I told him to forget it. Told him he was crazy. I mean, here we are driving around in a stolen car, and I'm telling him *he's* crazy!"

Booger shook his head and smiled. "I had a feeling you was a bit wild."

God, why was he telling Booger all this? *Only a fool uttereth all his mind.* He needed to keep up his guard. And where the hell was that kid, Jordan? Keep this on a business level.

"I did," said Booger. "I knew you was wild. And I knew before I met you that you was somebody goes his own way. Pretty much had a picture of what you looked like too. I got a gift. Most often, I kind of know things about people."

Greg sipped his drink and smiled. "You a magician?"

"No, sir. But tell me if I'm right. That son you mentioned"—he closed his eye and tilted his head back—"I'm getting that he's down in Flower-da, and you ain't happy about it. I'm getting that your parents are passed away, your daddy just months ago."

Greg couldn't believe it. How could he possibly know?

"Close?" said Booger.

"Very. My son's in Fort Lauderdale." He was astonished, and curious about this gift, tempted to ask questions, but he was uncomfortable too. What else did the guy know? If Greg wasn't careful, he'd end up going to church with him, probably some snake-handling fellowship. To change direction, he said, "Booger, let me tell you a few things about this 4Runner. I've got an office folder full of maintenance records to show you, 122,000 miles worth. Closest thing to a warranty you can get. Brand-new tires, timing belt, and oxygen sensor. New inspection sticker. You won't have to worry about inspection for a whole year. No fender benders—the car's in perfect shape."

"But the price is a mite high according to the blue book."

"I don't give a damn about the blue book. I know what the car is worth."

Just then Jordan, the kid, came in, all scowl. Booger introduced him to Greg and they shook hands: "Hey."

The wind had picked up. In the parking lot an empty Coke can clinked one way, then another across the asphalt. Greg opened the passenger door and gave Booger the folder of receipts. Jordan walked around the 4Runner, looking closely for nicks in the paint. He kept making stripping sounds in his throat and had a lot of blond hair curling out from under the sides of his blue Carolina cap. Booger asked Greg how long he had lived on the river. He seemed more interested in Greg than the 4Runner. There was something gentle about him.

"About ten years."

"Sure is a pretty place to be. Except during the harrykin season, I reckon."

"You reckon right. The river's tidal. I got flooded once." Greg opened all the doors, lifted the tailgate and hood. He took out the ball insert for the trailer hitch and slid it into place with a clank. "You probably know these are easily stolen," he told them. "When I finish towing my equipment trailer, I always put the ball connector under the backseat."

Jordan got on his knees to look under the rear end. "Heavy rust on that differential," he said.

"I'm sure that Crown Vic has it too," said Greg.

Getting to his feet, the kid looked at Greg, leaned to the side, and honked out a pellet of yellow snot. "Let's take her for a spin," he said.

Greg gave him the keys and sat in the backseat. They headed up the highway past the Pagoda restaurant and the Chevy dealership. Jordan asked about the four-wheel drive, asked if he could try it. They pulled onto a country road and rolled by an old tobacco barn chinked with concrete and smothered with kudzu vines. Jordan engaged the four-wheel, then tried the radio and CD player. Credence Clearwater came on, John Fogarty singing "Who'll Stop the Rain?" Greg remembered seeing the film with Linda, Nick Nolte playing the loyal dog soldier.

"Nice," the kid said. "But I wish it had sixteen-inch wheels and the chrome-pipe running boards." He had a nose-clogged voice, slightly elevated.

"You're talking about the Limited model," said Greg. "I told your uncle this was an SR5."

The kid cleared his throat. "Standard fifteen-inch wheels are wimpy. Big wells make 'em look like roller-skate wheels. No muscle."

Booger, leafing through the maintenance records, said, "Why you selling it?"

There were two reasons. It got poor gas mileage, but Greg decided to go with the main reason. "Well, the dealership I bought this car from screwed me, and I had a blowup with the service manager. I told myself I'd never go back."

"What was the blowup about?"

Greg hesitated, but the three shots of Jack had loosened him up. He told them about the dashboard check light going on. Talking about it made him angry all over again. They charged him a flat rate of two hundred bucks to hook his motor up to their diagnostic computer—something he told them not to do. A friend at AutoZone had already done that and determined the check-light problem: broken oxygen sensor. Greg almost bought the sensor and put it on himself, but he needed to have oil service, tires rotated, and a few other things. Presented with the bill, he told the service manager that two hundred bucks was a rip-off *and* he had instructed them *not* to use the computer. Just replace the oxygen sensor. The service manager explained that for reasons of liability they couldn't simply take his word. Greg said, *You mean for reasons of highway robbery*, but the manager went on as if Greg had said nothing. Their computer, he said, was state of the art, a very expensive piece of equipment that had to be paid for. Greg started yelling: *Then why the fuck not charge me another two hundred bucks for the computer you used to calculate and print out my bill. That's a sophisticated piece of equipment too, you goddam crooks!* But he didn't tell Booger that part, or the part about being pushed out the door and threatened by some Hulk Hogan at the desk. But maybe Booger, with his gift, knew it anyway.

Nobody said anything. Booger leaned back. He stared, as if into another world, and then said, "Let her go, Greg. Life's too short to dance with a ugly woman. I got one foot in the grave, and it makes you see everything different."

The boy sighed loudly and shook his head. He looked over his shoulder at Greg and said, "Uncle B here's gonna outlive you, me, and everybody." His voice seemed to hold more fear than irritation. Then he floored it. The passing gear kicked in, and they flew past a guy in an old Dodge pickup. He held to sixty-five until his uncle told him to slow down. "Very smooth-riding machine," said Booger, then began to cough. "Jordan, we can turn around any time now, but before we get back, I've gotta tell Greg a little story he might find—well, interesting at the very least."

The boy turned around at a convenience store with a bright Shell sign. As they passed tall stands of Carolina pines fringing trophy houses on the country club road, Booger told about a neighbor he had some years ago. The man and his wife were going away for about a month. They asked if he would take care of their parakeet, a blue little thing less than a year old. Booger agreed. His momma loved parakeets, and he grew up with several in the house flying from room to room, sometimes landing on your head or shoulder. When he got the neighbors' bird in his kitchen, he felt like a boy again, enjoyed watching the little thing take a bath in a cereal bowl with a leaf or two of lettuce in it. He explained that they were afraid of clear water and felt safer with lettuce. Bird splashed all over the kitchen counter. One day he started saying "Tar Heels" to the bird. He'd stand by the cage and repeat the words for a long time, no other sound distractions. Well, in a few weeks, the bird was saying it, and very clearly. When the owners reclaimed their bird, he realized he might have made a mistake, but it hadn't been deliberate. A few days later, when he met his neighbor at the mailbox, the guy refused to talk to him. Simply walked away. "See, these neighbors was Duke fans," Booger said.

Greg said, "What, no sense of humor?"

"Well," said Booger, "not about Duke. And that ain't all. These neighbors burned trash in a big barrel in the backyard. One day, Bud Fardle—that was his name. Bud come out the back door toward his burning barrel. He knew I'd be watching a game in the living room, sitting in the lounger by the glass patio door. They was big flames leaping out the barrel. Next thing I knew, Fardle was there with the cage and the little blue parakeet in it. He looked at me for a couple seconds 'til he knowed I was looking, then threw it, bird and all, right in the flames."

"My God!"

"That's exactly what I said," said Booger. "'Bout broke my heart." There was a long silence. Greg didn't know what to say, then asked if Booger had any regrets about teaching the bird that phrase.

"Not me. I wouldn't," the kid said. "Them Duke fans are a bunch a nut jobs!"

Booger said, "Jordan, pull in here, please."

The kid pulled into a McDonald's.

"I swear, this prostrate's running what's left of my life."

Greg watched Booger limp and disappear into the side door. Shaking his head, the kid said, "He can be embarrassing."

"He doesn't look in the best of health," said Greg.

"That's because he drinks and smokes."

"Is he married?"

"Divorced years ago."

"Children?"

Jordan shook his head no.

Greg said, "That's a shocker. I mean, that story about the parakeet."

Jordan looked into the backseat. The bill of his Carolina cap masked his eyes. "My uncle B loves to talk, magnify everything. Drive me nuts."

"Does his wanting to buy you a car drive you nuts?"

For a moment, he was silent. Then he said, "No, sir, but he probably got his reasons."

Greg watched a huge fat man with thinning blond hair waddle toward his Yukon XL. He couldn't get the parakeet out of his mind; he had had one too as a kid, a green and yellow bird with clipped wings named Mickey. His mother accidentally stepped on him. She wept for days.

The kid turned around again. "He quote you some scripture and tell you he was in church this morning?"

"He did," said Greg.

The kid turned around and snorted.

When they got back to the Walgreens parking lot, the kid lifted the hood again and leaned inside. He motioned for Booger to look at something. Between grayish clouds headed south the sky was a vivid blue. Booger said, "Could you give us a few minutes?"

"Sure." Before walking into Walgreens to buy a roll of breath mints, Greg looked at the Crown Vic plate again: PMZ 1223. When he got back, the kid was animated, shaking his head no, no, no. Booger just stood there, hands at his sides, calmly nodding his head. Greg was getting annoyed. He had already wasted too much time, but what else would he do? Watch a ball game? Fix the float in the bathroom toilet?

Booger said, "Greg, I'm gone write you a check for seven, right now. Make this burden disappear."

Greg tried not to imagine Booger telling friends later over a drink: *Yessir, real nice car. Definitely got the best of that Yankee.* "Nice of you to tell me what you're going to pay me, but I told you on the phone that my price is firm."

Booger said, "You not afraid of losing this sale? I seen your ad in the paper for more in a month now. Twice lowered the price, didn't you?"

"I did. But I'm not lowering it a single penny more. The question should be—aren't *you* afraid of losing a car in such excellent shape? That folder of receipts shows you just how well I took care of it."

Booger laughed. "Maybe we should have us another drink."

"No thanks. That's all I need is to get flagged for DUI."

"Seven," said Booger. "Right now."

"I wouldn't take anything but a cashier's check, and it's Sunday. Banks are closed. And the transfer of title needs to be notarized. Nothing can happen today even if I decided to lower my price, which I haven't. Booger, it's been nice meeting you. You've got my phone number in case you change your mind."

When Greg drove off, his rearview showed the kid in his tan boots and camouflage jacket. He threw up his arms, then ran to the Coke can that had been rolling about and kicked it flying. Greg turned on the radio to coverage of another suicide bombing in Baghdad; he turned it off. There was little traffic. The sun was at his back as he eased up the bridge. A heavy black tug with a red pilothouse was plowing against the current.

The sound of the front door closing amplified the silence. Sometimes Greg still half expected Kootney, the orange cat, to appear meowing, rubbing against his ankles, but she went with Linda to Raleigh. His jacket reeked of cigarette smoke. He reopened the front door and draped it on a porch post to air out. He could almost hear Linda say, *You smell like you've been in a fire.* She would probably also tell him to meet Booger's offer, that it was only money, and dickering just another male ego game.

"But let's not forget principle," he said aloud. You sell a car yourself to avoid getting screwed by a dealer on a trade-in, and you end up getting screwed anyway. And if he lowered his price, he'd be an accomplice to the spoiling of that kid. Buying new wheels and tires for a car that already had brand-new tires. "How stupid can you get?" he said to the empty living room. Then he felt the emptiness. "Christ, what's wrong with me?" He thought about Booger. Under it all, there was something likable about the guy. And he was trying to help the kid, no matter whether the kid appreciated it or not.

Greg was hungry. He also needed a drink. After putting a frozen pizza into the oven, he popped a can of beer. Wind made the joists creak and tick. While he was tossing a salad, the phone rang. It was Booger. He was sorry about this afternoon. If Greg could drop the price, say, just two hundred dollars, not five, Booger would have a bank check ready tomorrow at noon. He was really worried about Jordan. The boy had been talking about joining the Marines, and Booger couldn't bear to think of his ending up in Iraq where his daddy got killed. Maybe if the boy had the 4Runner and worked toward getting those new wheels and that chrome running board, he'd forget all about the Marines. And Jordan's two-year-old son . . .

Jordan's *what?* Greg was astounded. That spoiled kid was a father? Hard to believe. The kid had said Booger magnified things, but . . . When Greg felt the first stirrings of anger, he again saw that blue parakeet in its cage sailing into the flames. If nothing else, the story of the bird was a worthy parable. Booger was going on about the kid moving toward divorce, being angry and depressed—

"Booger?"

"Beg pardon?"

"We'll do it. Just tell me where and when."

Even when asked if he could drive all the way up to Kinston to the First Citizens Bank, Greg said, "Fine."

Booger then said, "Maybe we could eat some barbecue before I drive you back home. On me. I need to talk to you about a few things. One of my properties got a natural wood floor needs redone. I could show it to you, and you might could give me a price."

"But if I give you a price, there's not going to be any of this dickering, okay?"

Booger had a coughing fit before he crooned, "Son, I trust you. And I know the work you do is first-rate."

After hanging up, Greg stared out the window. No sign of the bandit. Wind swayed the tree limbs. Joists and rafters clicked and moaned. The bird feeder held one last caller, a bright-red cardinal. The sky was losing its powder blue to the dark. He thought about the parakeet again and wondered how Booger could possibly have known about his father, or that Billy was in Florida. What might he say about Linda? He had already suggested they compromise. Greg should probably phone her, reopen the door, admit a few mistakes. Lord. If nothing else, one thing that Booger said was true, uncomfortably true: he had been dancing with an ugly woman, for too long, and her name wasn't Linda.

Diving the Wreck

WENDELL DIDN'T WANT to be thinking bitter thoughts. Be thinking, period. That's why he sat at the open-sided bar on the Reef's back deck. A low sun left copper streaks on the water. Red and white oleanders swayed along the walkway to the finger piers where the charter boats moored. P. J. asked if he needed another beer.

Wendell checked his watch. Another might put him late, but he was uneasy about the arrival of these old friends. "Yeah, let's do it."

P. J. loved to talk, but Wendell wasn't in the mood. He wasn't quite ready for Kevin and Yvonne and their teenage son to arrive from Pennsylvania. In graduate school, Wendell had been with Yvonne, but when he couldn't make up his mind or commit, she began seeing Kevin. And having ranted about how bourgeois it was to be possessive, he was hard put to say anything once Yvonne and Kevin became serious. The three of them continued to play cutthroat tennis, go to films together, and have midnight beers at the Ron-Day-Voo. Good friends, better than family, they were regularly in touch with each other until a year ago when Wendell moved down to the coast and cut himself off.

P. J. was in a good mood, steering his belly back and forth behind the bar. He pulled the Killian's tap and nodded toward Wendell's boat. "What's with all them tanks in the skiff?"

"Some friends want to go wreck diving tomorrow."

He plunked down the mug. "You? You got friends?"

"Well, it depends on definition, I guess."

P. J. snorted. "Definitions. Man, you bad as Bill Clinton. 'It depends on what "is" is.'" They laughed. P. J. looked out at the water. "Marine Weather's calling for light and variable."

"So I hear."

"Be nice out there tomorrow. Flat as bird shit on a Beamer."

"Hey," said Jocko. "I read this book, and it shows how those weather guys don't know dick." Jocko had long, curly hair and arm tattoos and wore a silver stud in his ear. An African gray parrot called the Admiral rode on his shoulder and often left a white streak down the back of his Hawaiian shirts.

"Oh, he read a book," said P. J., and stirred the air with his forefinger. "He's always got to tell us about these books he's reading so we won't think he's a loser."

Loser. Wendell winced at the word. Kevin never called Wendell a loser but, after a few beers, enjoyed reminding him of his impracticality, his off-the-wall decisions, some related to booze or weed. That was the past. This time Wendell had a list, had seen to details, checked things off. Yvonne and Kevin would be impressed. He was ready for anything, Kevin's condescending smirk included.

Jocko said, "I don't have no college degree, but if I did, I wouldn't be tending bar."

"Wouldn't be tending bar," squawked the Admiral, then began preening his wing.

The drinkers hooted. One of them said to P. J., "The Admiral nailed you, man."

Wendell watched a fifty-foot Viking with outriggers and a tuna tower idle along the waterfront. Five sunburned clients stood in the cockpit laughing and drinking beer. The skipper reversed its screws. The big diesels gargled. He watched the mate in the bow grab the mooring lines from a piling. The boat was probably some rich guy's tax write-off. Wendell knew he needed to start thinking about money, a better job, but it was more pleasant just to watch the tall oleander bushes along the dock sway their red and white blossoms. Yvonne—she was lovely beyond words, really cared about people, especially her students.

Jocko was saying that this sorry state needed a lottery. "I'd get me a ticket every day, change my luck."

P. J. stirred the air with his forefinger again and began to sing "Beautiful Dreamer."

"Hey, don't knock luck. You never know."

The Reef attracted color. Jocko repaired outboards for cash, was divorced and hiding out. An excellent scuba diver, he dove with Wendell and taught him a few things. P. J. had been a cop—dirty, some said. Lenny, on the other side of the bar, detailed boats, was a fiberglass pro, an ace at repairing gelcoat dings and gouges. Fat Ernie, the chef, had a habit and sold what Jocko called "devil's lettuce" from the kitchen door. And Wendell didn't see himself as any better, played cards and gambled with them, but the Reef often had the feel of a bad movie he was trapped in.

As Wendell was freeing the bowline, a girl with long brown legs walked down the dock looking at boats and drinking a strawberry daiquiri through a straw. She gave him a big smile. It would have been easy to chat, ask if she thought her daiquiri might like to go for a ride. Her face was familiar, reminded him of Jenelle Winters, a former student he'd rather forget, lovely though she was. He'd also rather forget one of Kevin's digs: *You're only as old as the women you feel.*

He eased the skiff through the no-wake zone, picked up speed at the end of the channel, and swung west under the bridge. Water was a dark mirror streaked with red and orange. A brown pelican atop a channel marker gave him a long, disapproving look.

Before Kevin and Yvonne moved out of the state, they had helped him get a job in the county school system where he last taught. This was after Wendell's divorce from Betty. Betty was a police dispatcher. Toward the end, she hit him in the face with a cup of hot coffee. She could lose her job, she screamed, if he ever got busted for possession. But their problems were more basic than weed. Betty was ambitious and wanted what Wendell's country club parents already had. He wanted none of it, wanted to tell her the trip wasn't worth the effort, but he never did. They weren't on the same page, the whole foggy thing a mistake.

He throttled back and idled up the canal. The house had a lot of plate glass to show off the vaulted ceiling and was set back in a grove of live oak and palmetto. A wall of yucca stood on the lawn's edge in front of the screened-in porch, its blossoms like phosphorus in the long shadows. Kevin was standing on the seawall.

"Wendell P. Bennett III. Right on time, *as usual*."

"Sorry," said Wendell. "Got hung up. You have any trouble finding the place?"

"No. Good directions," said Kevin.

He tied the boat, fixed the fenders, and climbed up.

They shook hands. Grinning, Kevin said, "You asshole." He had a buzz cut and small gray eyes that crowded his nose. He was trim and muscular. He used to try to get Wendell to jog with him, but Wendell had a few strong opinions about health clowns and sports junkies, had bad memories of tennis camps, country club tournaments, his competitive parents and ugly scenes.

"Look at you," said Kevin, touching Wendell's ear. "Gold hoop, and the Fu Manchu ponytail. I like it. And a tattoo for good measure. What's the character?"

"The *Tao*."

"Ahhh!" Kevin nodded and gave him that patented smirk. "Puts me in mind of the Turn family. Remember the Turns?"

"I do. Wasn't the punch line, 'Never leave a Turn unstoned'?" Irony and jest seemed wired into Kevin's DNA. But that tired punch line was really a question: *Are you still smoking dope?* Wendell wasn't, but the reference annoyed him nonetheless, and he said, "I read this novel. One of the characters says, 'There is no such thing as a grown-up.'"

Kevin tilted his head to look at the earring again and said, "Hey, from where *I* stand, the author's got *that* right. But it's not perpetual adolescence that's so terrible. It's apathy. Everybody's drowning in apathy nowadays . . . but I don't care."

Wendell took a deep breath and shook his head: "Man, that was muy stinko."

"Yeah, and worse—we're facing a terrible shortage of dwarves."

Yvonne and Sean came across the lawn. She gave Wendell a big hug. "It's beautiful down here," she said. "Is that the boat we're going diving on?" She was trim too, tanned, and wore her blonde hair much shorter now. Touch, scent, the way she looked at him—Lord, everything came back.

Wendell said, "Hey, Sean, give me five."

The boy gave him a loud smack on the palm. "Hey."

"How old are you now?"

"I'll be twelve next week."

Wendell laughed. "I forget sometimes how long you guys have been married."

Sean said, "Cool boat."

Kevin said, "You've done okay for yourself. That beautiful house and, wow." He pointed to the thirty-foot Grady-White that read *Floating Options* in fancy cursive below the starboard gunwale.

Wendell explained that the owner of the house and boat, though wealthy, was a regular guy.

"The rich are different," said Kevin. "They have more money."

"That's not exactly it," said Wendell, "but I'll let it pass. Hey, before I show you where you're going to sleep, help me transfer these tanks from the skiff to the big boat."

Leaving Sean in the house to channel surf the satellite TV, they took gin and tonics and walked through the maritime forest to a deck that overlooked the ocean. They sat on the railings and watched their faces become indistinct in the lowering light. Waves crashed over and over, and the great blue distance redefined everything. They reshuffled scenes from graduate school; they talked about movies, books, mutual friends, and one of their professors who had recently died. Wendell asked about their new jobs. They were both working at a private school. Yvonne taught French and wrote speeches and correspondence for the principal. Kevin coached the soccer team and taught English. Sean got free tuition.

Kevin said, "So how did you meet this *Floating Options* guy?"

"His name's Bob," said Wendell. "Bob Moody."

"Now I get the connection—you're both moody."

"Kevin, please," said Yvonne.

"Right, we're getting too old for that shit," said Wendell.

Kevin said, "Well?"

"I clean his house. That's what I do now. I clean houses, do repair work, maintenance."

Yvonne said, "When did this happen?"

"Little more than a year ago. I got sacked. Political hassle."

A wave thundered on the sand below, retreated with a hiss. After a moment, Kevin said, "Buying from a student isn't a very bright move."

Wendell wasn't really surprised. The news had to have come from a mutual friend. Kevin had a lot of friends, was a fanatic about keeping in touch. In fact, he was surprised Kevin hadn't yet told him what a lousy correspondent he was. "The deal was that I—"

"Not a very bright move," Kevin repeated. "Man, you need to get it together. You need to—"

"Join a country club? Build a portfolio? Buy into some piss-elegant community with gates and guards? Drive a Beamer? Become a slave to appearances—"

There was a loud whistle. It was Yvonne. Wendell had forgotten how she could whistle like a guy. "Time out!" she yelled, then slowly: "We've had a long drive and—"

"We're getting too old for this shit," said Kevin.

"Riiight!"

They laughed and watched the surf ignite, then darken. Nobody spoke. Waves broke and hissed around the pilings of the deck.

Kevin said, "You want your life back?"

Wendell said he had a life.

"But not the one you ought to have."

"What, did you guys come down here to gloat?"

Kevin said, "You know us better than that."

Yvonne shook her head. "Dell, no need to cop an attitude. Look, if you want back into teaching, you've got it. Our school's looking for a history teacher. We recommended you."

"Thanks, but—"

"Jesus," said Kevin. "Just think about it for a while."

"I'd need recommendations, and when the story about me buying weed from a student comes out, end of story."

"Not a factor," said Yvonne. "Besides, this is a private school. No hiring committee. The principal does all the hiring himself. He's a friend, and we've told him about you, the whole thing, and what a damned good teacher you are. He's interested."

"Whoa. You act like I don't have a life. I've got friends here. And there's Jen. You'll meet her tomorrow. In case you haven't noticed, the island's beautiful. Some people would say *I'm the one* who's got it made."

"*Got.* You got health insurance?" asked Kevin.

"Ahh . . . Mr. Practical."

Kevin went into his Rod Steiger routine. "That's great when you're a kid. But you're pushin' on, Slugger. It's time to think about gettin' some ambition."

"Yeah, I know, I cudda been a contendah."

"Will you guys please stop it!" said Yvonne, shaking her head. "And men wonder why women . . . *Jesus!*" Her voice seemed suddenly drained. She stood up. "I'm really tired."

Back at the house, they agreed to leave the dock at nine. Wendell turned on his running lights and took off in the skiff. There was a big moon, and the channel markers stood up in silhouette from the silver-blue surface. It was easy running. He watched the wake move outward, breaking in a long white line to the north where the channel rose to the low-tide flats. Yvonne . . .

Tying the skiff to a mooring buoy in the shallows, he waded ashore, and walked up the single street in Marina Mobile Park. Dogs barked. A yellow Camaro rumbled to a stop. A shirtless guy with tattoos and a bandito mustache got out and limped toward a Confederate flag snapping from a rail pole.

"Rusty, how's it going?"

"Dell, you need anything?"

"Nah, I'm good."

The bedroom light was on, Jen probably leafing through *Monet*, the book of paintings he got for her birthday. A skilled rehab nurse, she was addicted to trash novels, but she loved painters and had done a few seascapes that showed promise. Wendell stopped to look up at the sky. A lot of stars. High pressure holding. On a line between porch posts, his blue wet suit fluttered its arms and legs in the onshore breeze like some restless ghost.

When he eased into the narrow room, Jen was facedown on the bed in her bathrobe, her long cinnamon hair fanned out on the pillow like the algae swirls you saw when diving on a wreck. She didn't move, and for a second he shivered, then took a few steps. The aluminum skin of the trailer creaked. When he sat down on the side of the bed and touched her elbow, she pulled her arm under her body; it was a sulky kid reaction and made him smile. "C'mon, don't be like that."

"How do you expect me to be?"

"How about . . . more flexible?"

"I don't even know these people. They're from your past."

Wendell said, "Your pals, Karen and Dana, are from *your* past. Did I act like this when they were here? Did I once complain about Dana's total lack of interest in anybody but himself?"

"That was different."

"How different?"

"I discussed it with you before they came. We talked it over."

Wendell sighed. "Okay, I'm sorry. I should have talked it over with you before I told Kevin to come down."

"This trailer is so small, you can—"

"Hear a mosquito fart in the next room. I know."

"Well, you *can*." She rolled over and looked up at him. "Dell, we got to get off this island."

"We're going to talk about that."

"When?"

"Pretty soon. But let's focus on one thing for now. It's important to me. I've made arrangements for them to stay in one of the houses I take care of."

"Are they here *already?*"

"Yes."

"God, you never tell me *anything.* Where are they?"

"Bob Moody's place."

"Did you ask him?"

"We're going diving tomorrow morning. I was hoping you would come along."

Jen remained silent, then said, "You're using his boat too?"

"He told me I could use it whenever I wanted. Look, sweetheart, you don't have to cook, don't have to do anything."

"I'm going to feel awkward. These people are going to be thinking trash about our age difference and what all."

"Hey, they can think what they want. We know what we have going, right?"

She smiled.

"Fine," he said. "Listen, all you have to do is stay in the boat while we dive."

"I can barely swim."

"You're not *going* to swim. You just have to keep the deck clear, help people get back on board after the dive. We'll fly a dive flag, but you might have to wave boats off if they get too close. A lot of boaters don't know the rules."

"I guess." After a moment, she smiled again. He leaned down to kiss her. She opened her arms.

They eased out of the canal into the main channel and headed east toward the inlet, passing a boat on the flats, a guy on the bow with a throw net. Kevin asked what he was after. Over the engine and wind noise, Wendell yelled, "Menhaden. Good live bait."

"What for?"

"King mackerel, cobia . . ."

When they crossed the bar, Wendell keyed in the GPS coordinates for the wreck.

Kevin asked how the electronics worked.

"Mini computer, measures signals from different satellites and tells you your position."

"Sufferin' succotash," Kevin lisped.

Wendell looked to the stern. Jen and Yvonne sat in the deck chairs, talking and laughing. He called Sean to the wheel. With something to do, the kid might not think about getting queasy. Wendell put his arm on the boy's shoulder and showed him the bearing number on the screen, then told him to keep the compass needle on the same heading. Sean hopped into the captain's chair with a big smile. His eyes were green like his mother's.

Kevin looked back toward the women, then leaned closer to Wendell. "It appears you've taken a turn for the nurse."

"Jesus, don't you ever get tired of that shit?"

"She's real nice," Kevin yelled. "Hey, how fast can this thing go?"

"Depends. With five people and all these tanks, maybe forty knots, under millpond conditions."

He had to hand it to Kevin. The guy had a curiosity that wouldn't quit. But Wendell was curious too. Who hatched the academy idea, and why? Yvonne or Kevin? Maybe Wendell had inherited some of his mother's paranoia after all. Maybe not. But gratitude got old, could be heavy, like a ball and chain.

There were no other boats on the horizon, which was good. Some sites were overvisited. Dive boats could arrive at a wreck site like tour buses at the Grand Canyon. Wendell deliberately chose a small wreck instead of one of the huge freighters or the German sub, and one that wasn't too deep. But there was a trade-off—currents were sometimes strong.

Kevin gave him an elbow. "Hey, how about them Red Sox?" It was an old chain-pull routine. Kevin knew he hated team sports, obscene salaries, and all the sports-builds-character crap.

"Hey, how about O. J. Simpson?"

"Lance Armstrong," Kevin said.

"Bobby Knight. There's a shitty character for you."

"Great coach."

"Sure! Hey, how about these kids?"

"What?"

"Here come the kids!" Wendell pointed. Four dolphin came leaping toward the boat, veered off, and shot to the bow where, two on each side, they lifted their flukes and rode the wake. Wendell said, "Teenagers. They get bored quick, then range off looking for some other oceanic mall to hang out at."

Kevin laughed.

"Cool," said Sean. "They can really jump. Mom! Check it out."

When they got to the wreck, acres of surface were pocked with baitfish. P. J. was right. Water was flat, and so clear the wheelhouse of the wreck, a 140-foot trawler, was visible. On signal, Kevin heaved the big danforth overboard. Wendell had told him how to figure-eight the line and snug the cleat, but Kevin was having trouble, so he made his way to the bow. "Like this," he said.

Kevin apologized. "I couldn't remember if you said the rope went over or under."

Wendell said nothing, pleased with the mistake. Kevin was now in Wendell's world. Then later: "No, like this," he said, when Kevin had attached Sean's second-stage regulator upside down. He cautioned them to make sure the O-rings were in place before they tightened down regulators to the tanks. He felt good; it was like teaching again, being in control.

When they were half in their wet suits, the safety lines set at bow and stern, he said, "Listen up. Refresher course. You've probably heard this before, but we plan the dive, then dive the plan." Then he outlined what they were going to do. Kevin insisted on buddying up with Sean, who had only just been scuba certified. Wendell would be with Yvonne, an excellent swimmer. "I know you've had experience, but remember, you come back onboard with 500 psi. Standard procedure. When we first hit the wreck, look around so that you can find the anchor line again. Stay together. But the water's so clear, all you really have to do is look up, and you'll see the boat. Oh, don't be freaked by the barracuda. Sometimes they come right at your mask and veer off, just to let you know whose territory you're in. Everybody cool?"

"Cool," they said.

The boat rocked easily on the swells. "What do I do?" asked Jen.

"Nothing," said Wendell. "Wave the dive flag if another boat comes along and gets too close. Relax. We won't be down more than forty minutes."

When Kevin, Sean, and Yvonne had eased off the swim platform into the water and were holding the safety line, Wendell did a back roll off the portside gunwale to take the lead.

Holding the anchor line with one hand, he tugged the air release on his vest and began to go under. Taking two or three deep breaths to calm himself, down he went, hand over hand. Below the flat tips of his swaying fins he could see the outline of the trawler with three dark squares where hatch covers had been. A school of silversides billowed, and then the rusty deck reappeared. Yvonne's blonde hair swirled around her face. Wendell pointed to his nose, then squeezed to remind her to equalize. Even with features distorted by mask and mouthpiece, she was lovely. Exhaust air became silver discs that grew into plates and platters and wobbled toward the surface. Long, slim barracuda were the first to appear, nasty-looking choppers exposed, grinning caricatures of evil. Yvonne pointed. Wendell nodded and gave the okay, thumb-and-forefinger circle.

The anchor had barely hooked onto a rail thickened with barnacles and urchins. Wendell gave it an extra turn and then wedged both flukes into a gap in the bulkhead. Along the bottom flew a large diamond-shaped shadow, its wing tips churning up brief whorls of sand. Yvonne pointed, and opened her hand: *What?* Wendell wrote "Manta" on a slate tethered to his vest. She nodded, widened her eyes, and began to drift upward. Wendell pulled her back. He pointed to her dump valve: *Release more air.*

Kevin and Sean were suddenly there. All signaled okay, and together they eased off along the deck umber with rust. Yvonne pointed to a small growth of staghorn coral, yellow and thin as a wire coat hanger. They floated over beds of polyps, strands of kelp, anemone, bright, rosy fronds. Everything swaying. Motes of plankton slanted across the wreck, like falling snow. He saw Kevin and Sean on the far side of the deck near the wheelhouse where the spadefish were. He had told them how, on a wreck, fish establish territory and defend it, and now they would see just what he had explained they would see. Good, except they shouldn't be off on their own . . .

He touched Yvonne's arm, then forked his fingers to his eyes: *Watch.* He pulled his dive knife from its ankle sheath, pried loose two purple urchins, and chopped them open. In a few seconds, they were surrounded by a slow-motion cloud of spot-tail pinfish feeding on the chopped urchin. Back and forth they looped, their large ventral fins a violet bright as neon. It was a trick he had learned from diving with Jocko. Yvonne shook her head, eyes wide and fiery green.

He checked his air gauge, then hers. Plenty of time. Down over the side into the sand. On the bottom, he spotted what he was looking for. He pointed right at it, but Yvonne didn't see. Then he touched it with his forefinger. From a small exploding cloud, the flounder shot away with undulant strokes, hugging the bottom, leaving a trail of sand smoke. Being underwater was a bit like smoking dope—you focused on small intriguing particulars and lost track of time. An insight he'd have to think about later. When he turned for Yvonne's reaction, she was gone.

At first he thought she was playing a game. Maybe she slipped into that great gash in the hull. He peered inside and saw only shadows and the bulldog face of an amberjack. Kevin might do something foolish, but not Yvonne. He turned on his back. On the great shifting field of silver overhead, only the black shape of the boat's hull. Nothing else. He could hear the frightened thump of his heart. Maybe she went to Sean and Kevin. He shouldn't have let them go off on their own.

When he reached the deck, Sean was at the wheelhouse corner. He was motioning to Wendell, looking at something out of sight.

It was Kevin, caught in a tangle of fishing line. The line was snagged between Kevin's tank and vest. Wendell pulled out his knife and cut. Though he wasn't sure, he wrote on his slate: "Yvonne topside." Then he beckoned them to follow.

When he surfaced at the transom, Jen's face was right there, blurry with tears. She was yelling, "I . . . away."

"Where is she?"

Jen was sobbing. "I threw a rope, but it wouldn't reach."

Wendell yelled, "Hey, stop! That's not helping! Where is she?"

"The current pulled her away."

He removed his fins and threw them into the cockpit. Then his mask and snorkel. Jen held onto the floating vest and tank until he was topside, then Wendell hauled them up. His weight belt clunked on the deck. God, it was taking forever. And Kevin was screaming questions, instead of getting onboard. Sean was slumped forward in the deck chair. Wendell yanked off the boy's vest and tank, then helped Jen pull Kevin onboard.

Wendell murmured, "Dear God . . ." To the north, the ocean was huge blue distance, horribly empty. To the south, a tugboat, and a barge at the end of an invisible towline.

Kevin yelled, "Radio the Coast Guard!"

Wendell said, "No, that will waste time. We're closer."

Kevin grabbed his arm, "Listen, I—"

"No, *you* listen! I *know* what I'm doing!"

He reminded Kevin she was an excellent swimmer. Her vest would keep her afloat. He only hoped she wouldn't panic, ditch vest and tank, and try to make it to the beach. He started the engines, the cockpit a mess of loose gear. His mouth was dry. *Dear God, please.*

Jen said, "What about the anchor?"

"Shit! Cut the line!"

Jen took the knife and went to the bow. She stooped and began sawing.

Kevin turned to Sean, put his arm around the boy. "We'll get her."

Jen jumped into the cockpit and yelled, "Go!"

Wendell hit the throttles and cranked up the rpm's to 4700, the twin Yamahas roaring. The surface current was running from southwest to northeast. The boat jumped quickly on plane, and he brought it to a heading of 50 degrees. He felt light-headed. Everything wore a black halo. He visualized a coil of white line slowly ballet its way down to the anchor wedged into the bulkhead. It felt as if he were still on the wreck, but without a tank. His breath came hard, mouth so dry he couldn't swallow. To the north was an empty sweep of water, a thin white band of beach, and a jumble of cubist beachfront houses, tiny under a towering billow of bruised cumulus. He was trying to keep himself from thinking about what a new anchor would cost when a dot of bright yellow popped into distant view. Kevin saw it at the same time. "There!" he yelled.

"Got her," said Wendell.

Yvonne was laughing when she came on board. "I've got faith," she smiled. "I knew you'd find me." But she had the shivers. It was a good act. Wendell knew she was a pro at appearances.

"You weren't afraid?" said Jen, still sniffing, but trying to lighten up. "I'd of peed my pants."

"I guess my belt was underweighted. Couldn't stay down."

Wendell said, "And the suit made you lighter."

"Right. Last dive was in the Caymans—I didn't need a wet suit."

For a while, they just drifted on the swells. Wendell asked if they wanted to go back to the wreck. The boat had plenty of line in its anchor locker. He could swim it down and tie on to the rail again. Kevin was against the idea. His face wore a look that Wendell had never seen. Incredibly, Yvonne said she was up for what everybody else wanted. Jen was with Kevin. "Never mind *that* wreck," she said. "Look at *this* one." She pointed to herself. "Enough for today."

They ran toward the inlet at half speed, saying little to each other. The billowy clouds over the land had darkened and lowered into a black wall. The wind picked up and shoved the water into white ridges. Then it began to rain. They crowded under the canvas top. Wendell stood at the helm. Yvonne stood next to him and once put her arm around his waist when the ocean surged. She gave him one of those old smiles and quietly said thanks.

It got rough. Wendell pulled back on the throttles. Kevin went into the rain, threw open his arms, and laughed when lightning crackled. Then he worked to separate regulators from vests, vests from tanks. Ever the neat freak, he bungeed the tanks into their racks and packed all loose equipment into dive bags until the cockpit was uncluttered and spacious again. Finally he came out of the weather, and they watched the beachfront houses get larger. Jen called Yvonne and Sean to sit in the cabin.

After a while, Kevin said, "I should have had a knife. What an asshole I am!"

Wendell remembered how angry Kevin got after losing at tennis, how much he enjoyed telling Wendell that he needed to get his shit together, become a detail person. And Wendell thought he had. So much for those details and plans. Something had to be salvaged. The boat plunged ahead into the deep swells, spray sizzling against the windshield, visibility barely twenty feet beyond the bow. When they were finally leeward of the long stone jetty that protected the inlet from southwesterlies, the water flattened, and the rain began to relent. Wendell said to the boy, "You going to be hungry pretty soon?"

Sean nodded.

"Well, I know where we can get some good nachos."

"Cool. My dad says you're a great tennis player."

"He lies."

A sky-blue shrimp boat moving seaward passed them in the channel. The skipper waved from the wheelhouse.

Sean said, "Think you can check out my backhand later on?"

Winking, Wendell said, "We might be able to arrange something." From the helm, he could see Jen and Yvonne facing each other from opposite bunks in the cabin below. Jen was telling her the kind of nursing she did, but how she wanted to get into the management part of it, and how she would need an MBA.

They were passing the giant red gantry cranes of the port. A Russian freighter was being loaded with cargo containers. Kevin leaned toward Wendell, his voice full of shadows. "Man, I thought I was going to die down there. I should have had a knife. Then not seeing Yvonne, I was thinking all kinds of bad shit. And the worst is I don't even know how I can thank you—"

"Kev, whoa. I didn't do anything. Relax."

They were moving parallel to a line of eelgrass islands, white sand and clear water. Yvonne and Jen came up from the cabin laughing. They seemed like sisters who had never soured on each other, never soured on anything.

Jen said, "Look." She pointed.

Water turned a radiant green where a single spoke of bright light moved over a sand spit in the distance. Behind thinning clouds, the sun was a ghostly circle; then it dazzled, sparks spreading quickly on the water. Holding up his hand to shade his eyes, Wendell said, "Oh, wow."

Kevin laughed, then said, "I haven't heard 'Oh, wow' since the Age of Aquarius."

The motors hummed softly. Sean began talking about what he had seen on the dive, those purple spiky things that were on the deck and rails.

"Urchins," said Yvonne.

"Those things that looked like a bouquet—what were they?"

"Either tube worms or anemones," said Wendell.

"And those bright, rosy fronds," said Yvonne. "Just beautiful."

"Yeah," said Sean. "They were cool."

Kevin cleared his throat, as if making an announcement. "Anemones are nice, but with fronds like these, who needs anemones?"

Sean said, "Dad, that was *so* bad."

They all booed, then laughed. Later, thought Wendell, he'd hit some tennis balls with the kid. He tried not to think about the academy and the possibility of teaching again. Expectation was too risky, a bad habit. Bob Moody would be coming to the coast next week. The house would have to be cleaned, the sheets and towels washed. The biggest problem would be the anchor. He'd have to revisit the wreck with a tank. He'd free the anchor in less than a minute, swim up with the line, then haul. Maybe get Jocko to go along, just in case. About luck, Jocko had been right. But it was more than luck. He needed to say something to Kevin and Yvonne. He told himself to stop thinking. He watched his hands on the wheel. The boat turned into the back channel that led to the Reef.

Family

MY COUSIN CASH phoned me late one night. Though my contact with her is minimal, I knew the voice immediately, a sharp, nasal monotone. At Christmas, she sends out cards with a generic letter detailing her political and church activities. Last year her card included a printed leaflet with a color photo of an aborted fetus in a surgical basin. Merry Christmas. Not one for polite preambles, she got right to the point—our aunt Sophie had developed critical heart and lung problems. It had been too long since the family had last gotten together. Cash was organizing a gathering at the farm and hoped I could make it.

Aunt Sophie was a teacher who never married. She was the aunt who visited, the only one I recall staying the night in my boyhood home. Visits often meant some small gift for me. When I outgrew toys, she gave me books, then pocket money on the sly. Her colorful talk was always a treat, but this summer trip up to Connecticut seemed a great effort: long check-in lines, delayed flights, airport crowds, risky food, no-leg-room seats, the usual irritations.

My wife, Nicole, phoned from Bordeaux, and I told her about Cash's gathering of the clan, and why. She urged me to make the effort. Suddenly I felt guilty about not being in France with her. But she sounded buoyant. It gave her great pleasure, she said, to see our sons getting reacquainted with their cousins and improving their French. They actually seemed to be enjoying the visit. Before saying good-bye, she told me not to take my family *trop au sérieux* on certain subjects, and not to drink too much.

I arranged to see an old college friend in Connecticut, caught a plane from Atlanta to Hartford, and rented a car. I drove southeast toward the farm where my father and his three brothers and five sisters had been born and raised. Stone walls that ran through pastures and woods, white wooden churches, picket fences—the perfect postcard of New England, so familiar, had become strange to me. So had lilac and white birch, which didn't grow in Georgia.

I turned off the Boston Post Road, a slight detour from the farm still thirty miles distant, and drove down a country lane past the white clapboard house that used to belong to my parents; it sat on a grassy rise surrounded by trees on three sides. At the old Wallace place, I reversed direction, approached it again, and parked with the engine running. Once I knew that house completely—from the underscent of mildew in the crawl space to the odd sourceless light that sometimes wavered in a corner of the attic. On hot nights, the white curtains in my room ghosted back and forth in the screened windows, as if the earth were breathing.

The sign still read The Olde Flower Shoppe.

The Dereloos, a Dutch family, used to own the place. I had worked one summer in their nursery, digging, planting, and watering. The gum-chewing teenager with green hair and a gold nose stud said she had never heard of the— "Dereloos," I offered, pushing a pot of daisies toward the cash register. "Whatever," she said. Her father owned the place now. I asked if she liked the flower business. Her brown eyes rolled up as if to check out the underside of her brain. "Yuh, right," she said. "I'm, like, outta here first chance I get."

I drove into the cemetery, turning left and right along avenues lined with tall, dark cedars. Ragamuffin sparrows splashed in a puddle under a spigot. On the twin-bedded plot, under the outstretched arms of a tall Sacred Heart of Jesus made of bronze, I was surprised to see a rectangular box of bright geraniums. Odd. All Mom's and Dad's friends were dead. Who could have brought the flowers? Probably some mistake. I knelt and looked at their birth and death dates. I tried to say a prayer, but no words came.

On Gilead Road, in front of St. Paul's, a banner proclaimed the good tidings of bingo every Friday night. This was where my parents had gone to nine o'clock mass every Sunday morning without fail. Lest I be tempted to run him over, I hoped not to see Father O'Brian, the pastor, following his huge belly from the rectory.

Connecticut woodland, pale green, flowed past, and I was jolted to find myself so quickly at the closed piano factory with its gaping black windows and fangs of broken glass. Then up the hill to the pond where I used to swim with Cash, Anne, Frankie, and my other cousins. The old brick pump house had a catwalk a few feet above the water, a good place to dive from. Huge granite stairs rose from the water and took you back to the catwalk.

Aunt Sophie's house with its wide porch was one of three built on what remained of the hundred acres my grandfather once owned. It was the first place you came to after an entrance framed by stone pillars at the bottom of the hill. Eight or ten cars and a few pickup trucks were helter-skelter on the lawn. A keg of beer sat in a shiny galvanized tub in the shade. The Petroski and Vodek families from downstate were there. I looked for Stan but didn't see him. Stan, four years older, organized our games when we were kids. First in the family to go to college, he was now an investment banker in San Diego.

Other cousins, replacements for my uncles, stood around the keg with cups of beer. Frankie was there with his chef's hat on. Aunt Sophie, thin and pale, was in a lounger shaded by a huge maple. Several women sat in aluminum lawn chairs on either side. My aunt Stella, Cash and Anne's mother, was coming down from her house on the hill. She poked along with her cane, scanning the grass for chipmunk holes. Her husband, my uncle Zag, died years ago in a car wreck. Somebody whistled. It was Jerzy, waving at me. A few other hands went up. Instead of parking on the lawn, I drove up the hill to the farmhouse, barn, and sheds.

A huge millstone served as the back-door step. I stood for a few moments in the shade of the porch. How long had the well with its rope and bucket been gone? Joe, our last remaining uncle, had lived here and was painting the house when a massive heart attack killed him, about six years ago. Frankie finished the painting. The house was empty now. I wondered why the family didn't rent it. But the place was small, all kitchen really, with a great wood-burning stove. How my grandparents ever managed here with all those children was a mystery.

Sweat was dripping from my nose. Had Connecticut summers always been this hot? I walked toward the falling-down barn. Tata had once taken me there to feed the cows during a snowstorm. He said some words in Polish, trying to teach me. *Krowa:* cow; *stodola:* barn. That's about all I remembered. My cousins lived on the farm and could speak Polish. They used to tease me, saying things I couldn't understand, keeping secrets. My parents wanted me to spend part of the summer there to learn the language, but I rebelled.

"Hey, Doc."

It was Frankie, my uncle Vlad and Stephanie's son. I liked him a lot. Frankie and his wife, Hinch, were always helping Aunt Sophie out, mowing grass and doing repairs. He was short and stocky. I poked his paunch. He said, "Hey, man, dat's always a problem for a cook." I had forgotten the Connecticut *dis* and *dat*. The accent, too. Nicole, when we first met, told me I had a strong accent. Having lived away for the past twenty-five years, I could finally hear it.

"When'd you get in?"

"A few hours ago."

"Go by the old house?"

I nodded.

"How's Nicole and the boys?"

"They're in France."

"Doze boys must talk pretty good French by now."

"Well, they'll speak it a lot better by the end of the summer—put it that way." I asked about his children.

"They're okay. One's in New York; the other two are in Boston and Maine. I'll tell ya later." Then laughing, he said, "You've got to check out our cousin Jerzy."

"What's he up to?"

"Well, he's up to beer as usual, but he got dis tattoo he's showin' everybody."

"Midlife crisis?"

"Well, I don't want to spoil things. He's been pulling off his shirt every time somebody new gets out of a car."

We walked down the hill past the house where Aunt Stella lived, where Cash and Anne grew up. When we entered the side yard, Jerzy yelled, "Hey, it's Doc, the professah!"

Jerzy had been in Vietnam with the Marines. His tanned legs showed jagged shrapnel scars. He was a house painter and worked when his mood swings allowed.

"Jerz. How's it going?"

"Going fine, but you seem a little stiff. We got to loosen you up, man." He reached into the ice chest and pulled out a bottle of Zubrówka vodka. From the picnic table, he took two shot glasses and handed me one. "You drinking with me?"

"Looks like I have to." I didn't feel like getting started. The sun by itself was strong enough to make my head spin. The sky was a taut blue sheet where a hawk made teetering circles.

"We're celebrating being together," Jerzy said. "Poles get together, they celebrate."

"Or polkabrate," I said.

"Yeah, too bad we ain't got a band."

"You can count on Jerz to celebrate." It was Johnny, Frankie's younger brother, tall and thin, with a gaunt face and large dark eyes. He reached out and we shook. "Doc, you ever think Jerz would still have a liver?"

Everyone laughed.

Jerzy tipped the bottle and filled my shot glass. Then he filled his own. "This is good stuff," he said. "I brought it back from Kraków. Blood of Poland." We clinked glasses and said, "Nazdrowie."

When I tipped my head back, I saw the hawk buckle its wings and plummet behind the trees. The vodka was icy and had what seemed like an almond tang. I caught Cash out of the corner of my eye. She would probably have something sarcastic for starters.

"Let me talk to Aunt Sophie before—"

"Yeah, go," Jerzy said, clapping me on the shoulder. "She's—well, you'll see."

Cicadas were screaming. I talked to Billy Petroski for a few minutes. Then I hugged Frankie's wife, Hinch, and said hello to several of the Vodek women from my grandmother's side of the family. I barely knew them. Hinch spared me the embarrassment by saying, "You remember Natalie Vodek, don't you?" She did the same with the others. I had almost reached Aunt Sophie when Jerzy Jr. grabbed my arm. "Uncle Mark, come on, let me try to get the ball by you. I'm better than last time."

"You're bigger, too. How old are you now?"

"Twelve."

Kicking a soccer ball was not what I wanted to do, but I noticed that some neighbors had surrounded Aunt Sophie and showed no sign of soon leaving. I also remembered how our uncles always made time to play with us, so I said, "Okay, let's do it." I followed him beyond the cars to the open lawn where other kids were kicking a black-and-white ball at a white tubular goal with a yellow net. I watched the goal and tried to break up their passes until my shirt was soaked. Jerzy Jr. and one of the Vodek girls were good dribblers, had very quick feet.

"Mark, there you are!" Cousin Anne gave me a hug. She looked nothing like her sister, Cash. No gray had yet threaded her short blonde hair. Her cheekbones were high, and her face always seemed to be smiling. She asked about Nicole and the boys and then told me about her new job in New Orleans where she worked for an import company. Lowering her voice and looking about, she said,

"Aren't you *glad* you got out of Connecticut? My sister, Cash, thinks I betrayed the family or something."

I thought about my parents, especially at the end.

Still speaking softly, she said, "They don't give each other any breathing space. Every day they take each other's pulse."

I said, "On the other hand, I wonder if it's good to be so far from family? I mean, I'm in Georgia, you're in New Orleans, Stan is out in California. Is he coming, by the way?"

"Couldn't make it," Anne said.

"Anyway, we're painfully far from the people who know us best, who—"

"That's what friends are for," she said. "Come on! Do you think Jerzy knows who you really are, or Frankie? Do they know who I am?"

I thought about families flying apart, people living alone. I looked toward the trees. A cloud moved, and the sun touched strands of a spiderweb, making it visible.

"Remember how our parents, every summer, rented that big cottage on the lake?"

Anne laughed, "You mean where I almost drowned?"

"Is that all you remember?" I asked.

"Okay, how about being eaten to death by mosquitoes, about not being able to sleep at night because it was so hot."

"Funny," I said, "I remember catching pickerel and perch, and at night listening to Uncle Joe's great ghost stories."

Anne shook her head, then smiled. "I think you're making more of it than it was."

"I guess what I'm thinking," I said, "is that our kids barely know each other. Look around. There's a whole missing generation."

"Well, that's geography. You go where the opportunities are. Shoot, here comes my sister."

In blue shorts, Cash, a few years older than us, was trim and had a golf tan, a pouting lower lip, and a squint in one eye. Her hair was mostly dark, but starting to gray. She taught high school PE in the next town. I opened my arms for a hug, but she leaned away and shook my hand instead. "Look what the cat dragged in," she announced.

The old comeback was automatic: "You look good too. Vic, who's her mortician?"

Her husband, Vic, had the build of a fullback. He sold insurance and spent a lot of time in the gym. "Doc, I couldn't tell you," he said, crushing my right hand. "Good to see ya."

Cash said, "What kind of bull did my sister just feed you?"

"None, but you could ask me about Nicole, or about our kids, or about how I'm doing."

"Now, now, I was just getting to that."

I patted Cash on the shoulder and said, "Sure, I know you were." I wasn't anxious to talk to her, so I pointed to Aunt Sophie and said, "I'll catch you in a few minutes."

Sophie was attached to an oxygen tank on a silver frame with wheels. The tube that passed under her nose looked like a greenish mustache. She had lost weight and was very pale, her hair white and wispy, making her more otherworldly than ever. She remembered everyone's birthday and, incredibly, still sent me a card with a few dollars in it, telling me to buy some candy to keep my disposition sweet. Sometimes she answered my letters with news about the family, always saying she remembered me in her prayers. She went to mass daily until she could no longer drive the ten miles of twisty back roads to church. Her letters often quoted something she thought worthwhile: Hildegard of Bingen, Andrew Greeley, or Meister Eckhart. I didn't know if she read their books or if what she put in her letters came from an anthology of spiritual quotations. It didn't matter.

She held up her arms and smiled. I knelt down. She leaned forward and put her arms around me, giving me a dry peck of a kiss on the cheek. "Oh Mark, Mark, Mark. I'm so glad you could come."

"Tell me how you are," I said, sitting on the grass.

Still holding my hand, she leaned back and lowered her voice: "I am eighty-five years old." She inhaled. "And we are not going to talk about my medical condition." She put a thin, knobby finger to her lips, then patted the back of my hand. "Are we?"

"I guess not." Never one for theatrics, she meant it.

"Good. Last week I read something that has stayed with me. Saint Catherine of Siena. It's wonderfully true. She says, 'All the way to heaven is heaven.'" She closed her eyes. "Isn't that lovely?"

I said it was.

"I knew you would like it. I've been thinking of you and your father lately. You look just like him. But tell me about Nicole and the boys."

I told her about the boys, both on college break and in France with Nicole. "I have a picture."

After fumbling with her reading glasses, she looked at the photo and then smiled. "Well," she said. "Handsome, but there would be no mistaking either of these faces for the map of Poland, as your father used to say."

We both laughed.

"They favor Nicole," she continued, "but my good luck is that *you* favor your father. Looking at you, I'm looking at him. It's uncanny. Oh Mark, I've been thinking about him a lot lately. Your father was so good-natured. Us being the youngest, I followed him around like a puppy dog." She bit her lips and shook her head with some memory. "Did you know your father was a daredevil?"

"Sort of. I mean, I knew from his scrapbook he was crazy about motorcycles. And a couple of times he drove right into the school yard on his Harley to pick me up. The nuns didn't like it and phoned my mother."

"The nuns," she said, shaking her head. "Poor, ignorant creatures. Most of them at that time anyway. But did you ever see the photo of your father standing up on the seat of his Harley, riding with no hands?"

"It's in the scrapbook."

"Yes, it is. Do you know the story behind it?"

I told her I didn't.

"I took that photo. One of the Bingiorni brothers bet him he couldn't ride standing up, not touching the handlebars, from the railroad tracks in the middle of town to the piano factory. You should check the mileage when you leave. You'll find it's over six miles. The bet was twenty dollars, a lot of money in those days. I was hoping he wouldn't do it. But I got in the backseat of your uncle Vlad's Ford convertible with one of those old Brownie box cameras." She stopped, shaking her head. She seemed to be looking into the sky beyond my shoulder. "I can almost smell the car wax. My brothers were crazy about their cars. Well, your father got the Harley moving, set the throttle, and lifted himself to stand on the seat, letting go of the handlebars. He even made it look easy leaning into the curves. Your father's smile could be—resplendent."

"Yes, he had all his teeth, right to the end, and no fillings," I said.

"You're teasing me, just as he did," she said.

"I guess I am."

"But, I've never seen that smile wider—except the day you were born—than when Charlie Bingiorni counted the bills into your father's open palm."

"He told me a lot of job stories, adventures moving houses, bartending, working in a fruit market, but never that one."

"Well, your mother—God bless her—didn't really approve of his motorcycles. She was probably afraid you'd follow suit." She wheezed and seemed to sniff hard at the oxygen. I waited, still holding her fragile hand, alarmingly dry, even with the humidity. The skin was thin and bloodless, the fingers spatulate, a swollen knob at each joint and knuckle. Then she resumed. "Can you guess the best part of this story?"

I shook my head.

She inhaled deeply again. "When everybody cleared out, he gave half the money to me. Just like that. Your father didn't care a jot for money. Never argued or got into fights, like his brothers. He simply loved to see people happy."

The rumble of distant thunder startled her. I looked up. The sky was black and came down almost to the tops of trees far across the valley. I said, "Rain might put a damper on things."

"We're together. A little rain can't hurt a thing."

Cash said, "Want a beer?"

I asked her what she was selling.

"Bud," she said. "Don't tell me you're a beer snob."

"Bud will do."

"Excusez-moi!"

"That's not what the French would actually say, but I get the insult." I took the bottle. "Thanks. What have you been up to? Golf?"

"Not that much. I've gotten involved with an antipornography group in our church."

"In addition to your pro-life work?"

She nodded. "But that's not something you'd be sympathetic to, I'm sure."

"That's your problem, Cash."

"What?"

"That you're sure, certain of everything."

"Tell me you're not First Amendment to the death."

I remembered Nicole's caution. "I'm not telling you anything."

Cash said, "Last time I saw you, you were still pouting because of that priest. So the whole church, I suppose, is worthless because of one little incident?"

When my mother died, the young pastor at St. Paul's wouldn't lead a rosary at the wake. Over the phone, he told me he was meeting with priests from another parish, a "group therapy" session. He was "stressed out." Things had been "heavy" lately: he needed to get in touch with his "inner feelings." I thought of Father Loftus and Father Shea—priests I had served as an altar boy, their solid likenesses never to be seen again. Dad had always been a generous giver to the church and was hurt. When he died two years later, toward the end of a long letter to that priest and his bishop, I wrote, "Reacting to somebody like me, Daniel Berrigan said, 'Yes, the Church is an old whore, but she's still our mother.' Well, so much for Jesuit wit. Whores don't make good mothers and intelligent children have recently begun to disown their parents, with good reason." On some level I had hoped to get a response, maybe an apology telling me not to give up on the church, or even a stern rebuke telling me to stop acting out. But the letter went unanswered. Nothing. I mattered to the church as much as I mattered to USAir, which had just lost my suitcase. Wayward suitcase. Wayward soul. There were so many. I might just as well have been angry at the universe. But I knew I had best not get into any of this, especially with Cash. I simply said there was a lot more to it than I cared to discuss.

"Enlighten me."

"I don't think so," I said.

"Please. I really want to know."

Frankie put a hand on my shoulder. "Hey, Mark, you wanna take a ride? We need some ice."

It was an out, heaven sent. I remembered a terrible argument my mother had with Uncle Joe, the only Republican in the family. Mom, as Aunt Sophie once said, could be "disputatious." If she thought she was right, nobody could make her back down. I was just a kid and couldn't recall what it was about, but the faces of arguing grown-ups got red and very ugly, and on the way home Mom said, "I don't think I can ever forgive Joe for that remark." And, typically, Dad had tried to smooth things over: "Mary, you take that political stuff too seriously."

As Frankie and I drove to the store for ice, we took the route of my father's no-hands motorcycle ride. Aunt Sophie was right; it was at least six miles. Frankie reminded me how Dad gave all of us rides on his motorcycles, a new one every other year. And we laughed about the time when we were nine or ten, the time Cash tricked us into taking off our clothes in the barn, promising to do the same so that we could check out the difference. Then she and Anne jumped out of the hay with all their clothes on. "Cash was always great for dat kinda stuff," said Frankie. "But her sense of humor's been gone for a long time."

For a while we just watched the trees slide by, and then he began telling me about a funeral. It was a second cousin I vaguely knew, a freak accident involving an electrical outlet. Frankie had never seen so many people turn out for a funeral. The whole town, it seemed. Everyone in the community knew him and loved him. "That's what I call success, real success," he said.

It was a remark I never expected from Frankie. His story put me in mind of a memorial service for one of my colleagues. Barely a dozen people turned up to stare at an urn of ashes in a room with blank white walls. Frankie hadn't finished. He was telling me about another relative. The relationship seemed more involved, but when I asked a question in order to seem interested, it turned out he was talking about a first cousin who lived in Moodus. I said it was impossible. I knew all our first cousins.

"You sure?" he said.

"Are we talking about Gaskas?"

"Yeah. You don't know about Tata's brother?"

I was astonished. "What?"

"Your father never told you about the Moodus clan?"

I remember my mother sometimes complaining about how the family closed her out, about how secretive the Gaskas could be. Frankie went on about how Tata sponsored his brother and family to come to the States from Kraków, helped set them up, then something happened. He wasn't sure what it was.

"What was the brother's name?" I asked.

"Stanislaw."

"So Uncle Stan was named for Tata's brother."

"Yeah." He laughed again.

"Did you ever see him?"

"Once. What I heard was dey was always invited over for Christmas and other holidays, but never came. I don't know. Looked just like Tata, the mustache and all. He was the older brother. Anyway, dey was out by da barn, yelling at each other in Polish about something."

I asked him what he thought the problem was. He shrugged and laughed, "Ask Aunt Sophie, or Aunt Stella."

"Maybe he was jealous of Tata's success." My grandfather did well for himself with a general store, two school buses, and a deal with the town.

"Hard to say."

"Aren't you curious?"

"Yeah, but it's kinda late to find out those things."

"Why'd you bring it up?"

He laughed again. "Probably 'cause I had too much to drink. How 'bout you drive on the way back, okay?"

The expected rain never made it, but by the time Frankie and I got back, everyone had moved to the screened-in porch to escape the thickening mosquitoes. I sat in the kitchen with its black and white tile floor. The remains of my second helping of kielbasa and potato salad sat before me. My head was turning with vodka and this story about the Gaskas of Moodus. My father *had* to know. Why had he never told me about the rest of our family? I sipped a beer and looked at the light-blue walls: a framed Sacred Heart, a Black Madonna, and the Infant of Prague. The place was like a shrine. Sweating, I sat next to Sophie, who was in a recliner we moved into the kitchen. Her head rested on a white pillow.

Jerzy came in from the porch where the keg now sat. "Okay, Doc," he said, "you've got to check it out." He pulled off his shirt, arms shiny with sweat, and brought his right shoulder close for inspection.

"Beautiful eagle," I said.

"Eagle?" he said. "Dat's da Polish Falcon, man."

"Well, I'm still impressed."

"Never too old for a tattoo," said Jerzy.

I said everybody was getting them now.

"Not the Falcon, man. After we came back from Poland, I got it. That country makes you really feel Polish. Something kicks in. Mark, you should go to Kraków and Warsaw. You'd love it, man."

Aunt Stella looked at me and said, "Never mind going to France all the time. Jerzy's right. You should visit Poland, see where our parents came from, get to know some of our cousins over there."

I remembered my aunts urging my parents to make the trip, but Dad didn't share their interest and, unlike his sisters, had no intention of making a pilgrimage to Czestochowa, Jasna Goro, or Kraków. And *he* knew the language. I didn't. Dad delighted in Polack jokes and over the years told me one almost every time I phoned home. But he cautioned me never to repeat them to his sisters because they were, as he put it, "professional Polacks," and would be offended.

Jerzy tipped the vodka bottle, filling my shot glass. "And vodka is cheap as water, and way better den Russian vodka. We was there a whole month." We clicked glasses. "Nazdrowie." The black and white tiles of the floor seemed to stretch and then square themselves against each other.

I was half thinking about the Gaska family in Moodus. Just as I was on the verge of asking Aunt Stella or Aunt Sophie about Tata's brother and that part of the family, Cash sat down on the other side of the table. "You have to go to a country like Poland," she said, "to find the old values. Nobody has any respect for life anymore." She lit a cigarette and drew our attention. She went on. "Nowadays people want to pick and choose what to believe. But you have to accept what the Bible says."

I tried to concentrate on my breathing. Deep and slow. I needed to stay quiet. She went on about the Bible for a few more minutes. Finally I said, "Sorry, the Bible is a complex and contradictory document. Which Bible are you going to live by?"

Cash said, "Do you accept the Bible as the Word of God?"

"Which Bible?" I asked. "Do you think the Bible floated down in a golden parachute with a flashing neon light that said: 'The definitive version and translation as dictated by God Herself'?"

Everyone laughed. Cash said, "Wait—"

"Cash, don't make me laugh. You sound just like Jerry Falwell. Is there any difference between Catholics and Baptists anymore?"

"What's wrong with Jerry Falwell?" she said. "He's against pornography at least."

I laughed. "He's apparently not against gluttony. Take a look at him. The guy's got at least three chins."

"Nobody's perfect," she said, squinting at me with one eye. Her smoke curled toward the light over the table where a moth was bumping against the bulb.

"Let's talk Christian then," I said. "Do you think it's Christian to crucify somebody because that person is gay? Remember the time Falwell smugly called Ellen DeGeneres 'Ellen Degenerate' on national television? Tell me, do you really think Christ would do something slimy like that?"

"Wait, do you accept that the Bible—"

"No, *you* wait. Which of these statements do *you* accept: 'Judge not lest ye be judged' or 'An eye for an eye, a tooth for a tooth'? They're both from the Bible. Which one do you buy into?"

She exhaled a cloud of smoke, shaking her head.

"You didn't answer my question," I said.

"You didn't answer mine."

"I know a couple of 'good Catholics'—and this is truly disgusting—who were happy when that gay kid was crucified on a fence out in Wyoming."

Cash shook her head, one eyelid at half-mast. "Are you defending the promiscuous gay lifestyle?"

"I wouldn't defend heterosexual promiscuity, so why gay? Being gay, though, isn't a matter of choice. Did you choose to be hetero?"

"That's ridiculous."

"Did you? Why would somebody deliberately choose to be scorned, ridiculed, and worse? It's a helluva lot easier being straight." I watched her drag on her cigarette, the smoke hanging between us like toxic angel hair. "By the way," I said, "you need to get a little consistency in your life." I reminded her she was smoking, and in a room where somebody was on oxygen.

She stubbed her cigarette into a saucer. "Everybody's entitled to some little vice."

I imagined that brittle smile of hers breaking into smithereens and raining to the floor. "Little?" I said. "Cigarettes kill. They took out my mother and two of our uncles. Why don't you people attack Philip Morris instead of—"

"Abortion clinics?" she snapped. "The Industry of Death?"

I took a sip of beer. Now there were two moths bumping against the light. "Ve-ry good," I said, trying to get as much sarcasm into my tone as possible. "I like that. 'The Industry of Death.' Nice little ring to it. Did you make up that bumper sticker all by your little self?"

Anne caught my eye from the doorway to the living room. She was laughing and gave me a fist-pump yes. Then Aunt Stella jumped in. "What's wrong with what Cash said?"

I thought I saw an opening. "Good. Indulge me. Did you ever hear of Peter John of Olivi?" I looked at Cash.

She said, "Duh, I have a feeling you're going to tell us."

Jerzy said, "Is dis gonna be on the final exam, Doc?"

Everyone laughed. Jerzy's timing was great. I said, "No, no exam. Peter John of Olivi was a thirteenth-century Franciscan, a brilliant scripturalist in Paris after Abelard and others had done their best thinking for the church. Well, Olivi came close to being excommunicated, or worse, because he didn't go along with the crowd. He said, 'There is no blessedness in universals.' He believed that Christ's life was too rich and complex to be reduced to a neat set of theological abstractions designed, of course, to beat people into submission. Pray, pay, and obey."

"What are you talking about?" said Cash.

I had thought I had a point, even felt inspired when I began, but it was probably a trick of the booze. I sat there completely blank for a moment. The opposing black and white floor tiles made me dizzy. Then I said, "I'm talking about working out belief on your own, away from the church."

"Gówno," she snorted. Everyone laughed. "Pardon my Polish, but that smells like intellectual *crap* to me."

Her comment was a head slap. I was center stage, slapped. I was in a freeze frame. Everyone had stopped talking and was listening. Jerzy leaned against the refrigerator, a cup of beer in his right hand. I looked down at my hands, bulged blue veins on the backs. I turned my palms up and made my fingers slowly flex. I looked to my right. Aunt Sophie was dozing, her head on the white pillow of the recliner. When I heard my voice, it didn't sound like mine: "My fault, my fault, my most grievous fault. I guess I made the mistake of trying to discuss theology and church history with a PE major. How silly of me! Cash, your mind isn't up to it. Your time would be better spent smoking and watching sitcom reruns—the laugh track will tell you when to cackle."

Vic yelled, "Hey!" He made a pistol with his forefinger and thumb and aimed it at me. "You're outta line, pal." Vic had a huge neck with a gold cross around it. He was a church deacon and put me in mind of the sweaty body builders you saw on the Christian channel—guys who were always tearing up phone books in the name of Jesus and breaking cinder blocks with their heads. I looked at Aunt Sophie. Vic's voice should have awakened her, but her eyes were closed, her mouth slightly ajar. She seemed already to have embarked on that long flight, her face a marble effigy. I was relieved when her rattling breath filled the sudden quiet. Nicole's favorite line echoed in my ears: *No fight, no blame.*

I looked up at Vic. "You're right," I said. "I was out of line, way out of line." I turned to Cash and told her I was sorry, that I had gotten carried away.

She wouldn't look at me and said nothing.

Jerzy said, "Hey, Cash, a horse walks into this bar. Bartender says, 'So why the long face?'"

Everyone laughed except Cash. She got up and left the room.

Frankie said, "Did you hear the Polish government bought two thousand septic tanks? True. Soonz the Poles learn how to drive 'em, they're gonna attack Russia!"

Aunt Stella turned to Frankie. "You should be ashamed," she said. "After what the Russians did to Poland!" She crossed herself. "Some things are sacred."

I told her I agreed. "In fact," I added, "everything is sacred."

Then the kitchen fell into a deep quiet again. It was unbearable. I no longer wanted to be at that table. Soaking wet, I looked at my watch and got to my feet. "Gotta go," I said.

"Hey, it's only six thirty."

I said I had to make it to Hartford. I was staying the night with an old friend and his wife. I also told them that the airline had lost my suitcase. I needed to stop at a mall to buy a few things. I bumbled my way through good-byes. I remember nothing but kissing Aunt Sophie. "I'll be up this way in the fall," I lied. "I'll see you again pretty soon." At the kitchen door, I turned once again to look at her in her blue housedress. She smiled, then blew me a kiss. *All the way to heaven is heaven.*

On the porch, Jerzy Jr., wearing a Yankee baseball cap, said, "Hey, Uncle Mark, is it true you're a doctor?"

"Yes, but not the kind that makes you better."

I climbed the hill. The brightness made me squint. Maples that flanked the drive were golden green, each leaf veined with light. I started the car, letting the air conditioner cool things down. I looked at what was left of the barn. When I was nine or ten, my father showed my cousins and me how to throw apples, but not in the usual way. With a jackknife, he whittled a point on a thin green stick pulled from a maple branch. It was about two feet long with good spring. Then we walked into Tata's orchard. Dad showed us what to do. You pushed the point of the stick into a windfall apple. That way you wouldn't get stung if a yellow jacket was burrowed inside. The skin popped, and white juice gathered in bubbles around the stick. Dad held up the impaled apple. Then he whipped it, and the apple soared over the barn roof far into the woods. It didn't take long for us to catch on, to have contests to see who could throw the farthest, to see who could hit a target chalked on the barn wall, apples exploding and leaving their wet circles on the paintless wood. After Tata came out and told us to stop because we were scaring the cows, it seemed inevitable we would start firing at each other. Frankie, Cash, and Anne ganged up on me. Apples thumped and really hurt when they hit. My back and legs were wet with apple juice. I began to cry. Cash called me a big baby. Still crying but furious, I chased her across the orchard toward the barn. She ran toward the sun that was going down at the corner of the barn, forty feet ahead of me. She was still running when I stopped, set, and fired. The stem of the apple made a wicked sizzle in the air. I still see the flight of it in slow motion. Cash stopped to see where I was when the apple caught her square in the side of the head, haloed brightly by a tinsel of outward flying juice and chunks of exploding apple meat.

I put the car in gear, turned the circle in front of the barn, and headed down the hill to the house where Frankie and Aunt Stella waved good-bye. Cash and Vic stepped in front of the car.

I cringed. What now? Vic would haul me out of the car and snap my bones in the name of Jesus. Their faces were rigid and unsmiling. I was certain they would say, *Love us, or you're dead!*

But it was worse than that. I rolled down the window. Cash leaned down and said, "I don't know if you've had time to go to the cemetery, but don't worry. Vic and I drove over on Memorial Day and put some geraniums on Uncle Ted's and Aunt Mary's graves."

I could barely breathe. I told her that I had seen the geraniums. They were beautiful. I thanked them. "Listen, I'm sorry, I'm really—"

"Forget it. We're family. We argue." She kissed me on the cheek. "Don't be a stranger. You don't have to be, you know?"

"I know."

I drove away into a tunnel of trees that were shot through with light and shadow. It was the first time she had ever kissed me, and as I drove through the altering colors of sunset, her kiss burned like a brand on my cheek.

Distance

"POLITICIANS ARE *NOT* PEOPLE," I said.

"You weren't talking about politicians," said Nicole. "You were talking about Jim."

"Jim was just an aside."

It was sunny, hot, late afternoon. We had been on the road since early morning. Even after New York City, traffic was heavy, stop-and-go, far into Connecticut. I lowered my sun visor.

"But he's not what you say he is," Nicole insisted.

"What's that?"

"A complete swine."

"But he *is* a politician," I said. "He schmoozed himself upstairs into administration, then forgot us. That's what politicians do when they get to Washington. Jim could easily have made a case for our department, but now he's top tier, got the big bucks, and a new set of pals. I have no use for somebody who puts money before friendship."

"Maybe money's turned his head, but he's not a complete swine. Lately you've been saying that about a lot of people."

"Look, I'm wiped out. I don't want to argue."

"Because you're wrong," she said. "Nobody is a complete swine."

"Can I quote you for the record?"

"Not even the politicians you hate."

"Well, Jim's just begun his fourth marriage. I'll bet those ex-wives would agree with *me*, not *you*." What burned me most is that I'd misread the guy, never saw through his winsome veneer.

We'd just come off a high bridge doing seventy when a black BMW swerved in front of me. In the years since I'd last driven it, I-95 had become the Highway to Hell, once-courteous drivers now cutting back and forth across three or four lanes. "That idiot's probably on a cell phone," I said.

"Relax," said Nicole. "I wish you could hear yourself."

"Once upon a time you could bet that guy was a drunk. Now it's just some asshole on a cell phone."

"Or a complete swine," she said.

I let the words eddy. Traffic began to slow again. All day long we had been moving in and out of areas of summer road repair: flag men, dump trucks, rollers, backhoes, barricades, swirling dust, and the smell of hot asphalt. Here was another. Creeping around a downhill curve, I could see in the distance black smoke billowing up, the flashing blue lights of police cruisers. Two lanes were merging into one. For several minutes, we inched ahead. Then a cop in a blaze-orange vest waved his arms and stepped in front of the BMW.

"Shit, why couldn't he let a few more cars get by?"

"Must be a complete swine," said Nicole.

"Okaaay, okaaay!"

I took deep yoga breaths. My rearview showed a line of sun-glinted cars disappearing around the uphill curve. The guy who got out of the BMW wore long black pants and a lavender shirt. I watched him talk to the cops with a lot of hand gestures. Trees rose up on both sides of us, tops riddled with sun. Cars swished past in the opposite direction, southbound toward New York City, a few faces laughing at our logjam. Now at a dead stop, I was suddenly exhausted. All these cars—where in hell were they going? I shut off the motor, got out, stretched, and stood there yawning. The BMW guy walked my way. He had a friendly smile. "We have a twenty-minute wait," he said.

"What's up?"

"There's a tractor trailer with hay bales caught fire."

A siren wailed and whooped. A fire truck edged past us blaring. We held our ears. When the noise level lowered, he extended his hand, "Stefan. Steve, they call me." His eyes were bright blue. Lean and narrow shouldered, he wore a small gold earring, and his hair, touched with gray, was gelled and spiked slightly in the front.

"Mark." We shook hands. "Your accent is familiar."

"I was born in Poland," he said.

I smiled. "I thought I detected abnormally high intelligence."

His eyes got big, and he pointed at me. "Polski?"

I grinned and nodded. "Tak. Jak panu idzie?"

We laughed. Then he was off and running in Polish. "Whoa, whoa," I said, and explained I knew only a few phrases from my grandparents and cousins, most not suitable for polite company. He asked where my family came from. When I said Kraków, his eyes again got big.

"I thought you look pretty intelligent too," he said.

I told him that my grandparents actually met here in this country, at St. Stanislaus, a Polish church twenty miles from where we stood.

"So you live close?" he asked.

"Used to. I grew up here, but live in Virginia now."

"People in this country move all over the place."

"Not in Poland?"

"Well, once the Wall come down, people start moving, looking for better jobs."

"Is that when you came to the States?"

He said it was. I put my hand to my mouth to hide another yawn. Nicole got out of the car. I introduced her to Stefan and told him she was French, unfortunately not blessed with superior intelligence like us. She slugged me and we laughed. More people got out of their cars, then back in, engines idling to keep the A/C going.

A bulky woman in a light-blue granny dress and wearing new black-and-white sneakers approached us. Head covered with a red bandanna, she carried a big silver thermos with some Styrofoam cups and a brown paper bag. We told her about the delay.

"I saw you yawning," she said to me. "You need some java." She had big front teeth and kept drawing down her lips to cover them. Her eyes were puffy, the whites threaded with red.

Nicole doesn't drink coffee, but Stefan and I each took a cup. "Thanks, just what I need," I said.

"If you want milk and sugar, I've got it in the car."

"Black is fine," said Stefan. "Thanks."

"For me too, thanks."

Then she offered us homemade brownies from the bag.

"How awfully nice of you," said Stefan.

Nicole said no to the woman's offer, but she insisted, "Please, I have plenty."

Nicole looked at me and asked if I'd share one.

"Okay," I said, "but usually I only eat brownies spiked with ganja."

The coffee woman jiggled with laughter. She said she was a semiretired hippie and knew where I was coming from. She wished the state would okay medical marijuana because she recently had surgery for breast cancer and was going through chemo. Marijuana was the only thing that settled her nausea. She told us she had a lot of coffee and sweets in her car because she was headed to a support-group meeting. Stefan said he would say a prayer for her. He believed in the power of prayer.

"I do too," she said. "It got me through a very bad time."

Stefan said, "The church saved us in Poland and brought down the Wall. Poles have great faith, but they're very stubborn too." He looked at me and asked if I went to church. I lied and said I did. Nicole is a churchgoer, and I half expected her to expose me, but she didn't. I wondered if it was true that church attendance in Poland dropped drastically once the Wall came down. We were all sweaty. Stefan dabbed at his brow with a handkerchief. A spiral cloud of dust lifted from an embankment on the right and darkened; slowly it came toward us, drawing bits of straw, a plastic bag, and a long, thin strand of tarpaper. We turned our backs as it passed, raining small bits of dirt and dust.

"What was that all about?" I said.

Stefan said something in Polish. Then: "I don't know the word in English."

"Dust devil," said the coffee woman.

"Dust devil," I said. "That's right. That's what it is."

Nicole and the coffee woman began to talk about mammograms. Stefan asked me if I had ever been to Poland. Three years ago, after being prodded for years by cousins and aunts, Nicole and I made the trip to meet relatives for the first time. I remembered the old walled city in Kraków, the Florian Gate, and the cobbles of Ulica Florianska that led to the wide church square, flea markets, and art stalls. I told him about our climb to Wavel Castle, about the Jewish section of the city, and the square with oversize iron chairs, eerily empty, that Roman Polanski paid for to memorialize the murderous deportation of the city's Jews.

"Did any of these tourist places give you emotions?"

I said that the concentration camp at Oswiecim did, even though I had seen movies and read books about it. Words couldn't touch it. Then I told him about sitting at the dinner table with my extended family and hearing a story in piecemeal translation through my cousin Mika, the only English speaker in the family. My great-uncle, whom I'd just met, told about being sent at age fourteen into forced labor at a munitions factory in Germany. After more than a year, he and two friends couldn't stand it any longer. One night, they went over the fence, got away from the compound, only to be chased down by guards with dogs. They were shot and left for dead. His two Polish friends were in fact dead, and he was barely alive. When Mika finished translating a segment, my great-uncle placed his hand on the dinner table and made a slight movement with his fingers. A German nurse that night happened along, and what she saw were his twitching fingers. At great risk to herself, she and some friends carried him to a doctor and nursed him back to health, all the while moving him from one hiding place to another. Through an underground network, he slowly made his way toward Poland, returning home just at the war's end. Some of the story's details were as scorching as the heat on I-95. I hadn't thought about that evening in Kraków for a long time. When my great-uncle stopped speaking, silence had a different quality. He looked at me and mumbled something in Polish. Mika said, "He wants to know if you have any questions."

I told her to ask him what he thinks now when he hears German or Russian tourists in the streets of Kraków. The old man nodded, rubbed his gray wrinkled cheek, then looked at me. "With what they have done to the Polish people, I have no love for Germans or Russians, but our lives are short, too short to waste on hating people. And I wouldn't even be here if not for that German nurse and the others."

"He is a wise man," said Stefan, nodding seriously. We watched a helicopter come in low over the trees, bank toward the smoke, hover, and slowly rotate in the distance. "Do you know about the Katyn Forest?"

"A little bit," I said.

"It's near Smolensk. Four thousand Polish military officers were shot in the back of the head and thrown into huge pits." His mouth disappeared into a hard line. "My grandfather was one of them."

I didn't know what to say.

"Then for decades we had to live under those commie bastards. So when your great-uncle says that hating is a waste of time—well, I admire him, really, but I am still a pretty good hater."

"When I was in Kraków," I said, "I bought one of those McLenin Golden Arch T-shirts that are on sale everywhere. That's pretty good revenge."

He laughed and said he had one too.

The sun got lower, burning the tops of trees. Between the idling cars came toward us a dark-skinned Indian man. Stefan wondered if Nicole had her purse in a safe place. The Indian introduced himself as Patel. He was tall and very thin with deep-set eyes.

"It is only Dursday, vhy all dee traffic?" he asked.

We told him about the fire. He showed us his handheld GPS and told us that it indicated no alternate routes, as it was supposed to. A programming problem. Computers were his field. The coffee woman offered him coffee. He thanked her but said he was a tea drinker. She had hot water and tea bags in her car and would be happy to make him tea. He told her she was entirely too kind, but declined. We asked each other's destinations. Patel was heading to MIT, where he had just taken a position in computer network security.

"What does that involve?" I asked.

With a smile, he said, "I vill be keeping the world safe from hackers."

"Is your family here in the States?" asked Stefan.

"No, in Delhi."

"Ah, distance," said Stefan. "That's a big problem." He told us he was also going to Boston, but to visit his mother in an assisted living home. He wanted her to move to New York where he had taken a new job, but she had made friends at the home and didn't want to leave. He wished his brothers were in the States because he needed help looking out for her. His brothers were happy enough to take the money he sent them but in no hurry to leave Poland.

Patel said, "Aging parents need much care indeed. My brothers and sisters in Delhi have all the responsibility. I feel very bad."

"Well, I could use a little care myself," said the coffee lady, "but I'm divorced, and my children . . . Never mind. I'd better not go there."

On the verge of a few confidences, I was saved when one of the cops blew a whistle and waved us on.

"Oops, we've got to go," said the coffee woman. She gave Nicole and me a hug and said how wonderful it was talking to us. Nicole thanked her again for the brownie.

Patel shook hands with everyone and said good-bye.

Stefan hugged the coffee woman, Nicole, then me.

Opening my car door, I called to Stefan, "Powodzenia."

He turned and gave that great smile of his. "Dziêkujê. Dowidzenia."

I followed the BMW until traffic backed up again. Then I flashed my lights, beeped my horn, and saw Stefan one last time wave to us as I took the exit. Nicole asked where I was going. The old Boston

Post Road was only two-lane, but my hunch paid off. Very little traffic, and in thirty-five minutes we would be at my cousin's house.

Nicole said, "Was that amazing, or what? Such friendly people."

I agreed. "You almost feel you've known them for a long time."

"We're lucky," she said. "Emily, the woman with the bandanna, has quite a load to carry. Not only cancer, but she told me her oldest son just went to prison for armed robbery."

"Nice guy," I said. "Interesting way to help out his mom."

"Probably a complete swine," she said.

I let that float for a while, then asked if she knew about the Katyn Forest. I told her how the Soviets rounded up Polish officers, plus teachers, priests, anyone who might be a problem for the postwar regime, executed them systematically, and shoved them into mass graves. "Let's go back to complete swine for a minute," I said. "Lavrenti Beria and Uncle Joe Stalin were behind those executions. And how about Hitler, Mao? And the list goes on. Are we not talking complete swine?"

Nicole looked at me. "You have a point, but don't you think your comparison is a bit unfair to swine?"

We both laughed. For a minute the strings of a Haydn quartet filled the car. Finally she said, "I'd still like you to bury that phrase."

At last a smile came easily. "Okay," I said. "I'll give it serious consideration."

The western sky was turning the color of blood. The road, flanked by tall trees, was a tunnel of shadows until we came to Rogers Lake, a wide expanse of water. Just above a line of trees on the other side, the sun was a red eye looking right at me. Every summer as a kid, I spent two happy weeks here with my cousins in a cottage our parents rented: fishing, swimming, rowing a boat, roasting marshmallows at night, and listening to my uncle's ghost stories. Then I thought of my great-uncle in Kraków, his twitching finger, the German nurse. I rolled down the window and let the lake air cool my face. Somehow I was no longer tired, and had no thoughts of arrival. I was just glad to be driving through this changing light.